The Cottage on Sunshine Beach

ALSO BY HOLLY MARTIN

SANDCASTLE BAY SERIES
The Holiday Cottage by the Sea

HOPE ISLAND SERIES
Spring at Blueberry Bay
Summer at Buttercup Beach
Christmas at Mistletoe Cove

JUNIPER ISLAND SERIES
Christmas Under a Cranberry Sky
A Town Called Christmas

WHITE CLIFF BAY SERIES
Christmas at Lilac Cottage
Snowflakes on Silver Cove
Summer at Rose Island

The Guestbook
One Hundred Proposals
One Hundred Christmas Proposals
Fairytale Beginnings

HOLLY WRITING AS AMELIA THORNE
Tied Up with Love
Beneath the Moon and the Stars

FOR YOUNG ADULTS
The Sentinel
The Prophecies
The Revenge

The Cottage on Sunshine Beach

HOLLY MARTIN

bookouture

Published by Bookouture in 2018

An imprint of StoryFire Ltd.

Carmelite House
50 Victoria Embankment
London EC4Y 0DZ

www.bookouture.com

ISBN: 978-1-78681-523-1
eBook ISBN: 978-1-78681-522-4

To my best friend. You sit there, by my side, every day and every night as I bang away on my keyboard. You're the first to hear a new chapter and though sometimes, OK, every time, you fall asleep while I read it to you, I know secretly you are cheering me on. You listen to my plot holes and character problems with unending patience and though the postman arriving is far more exciting than anything I've ever written, I know that's just to keep me humble and keep my feet on the ground. I tell you the exciting news of chart positions, paperbacks in shops, audio books and foreign deals and although it seems you'd rather lick your bum, chew on your paw or chase a fly across the lounge, I know secretly you're pleased, how else will I pay for your sausages? I know life with me is hard, long walks on the beach every day, chicken for dinner, and me disturbing your beauty sleep when I dance around the lounge like a loon, but you will never know the joy you bring me. Thanks for being there, Skip.

CHAPTER 1

Melody was late. She had big plans today, she couldn't be late.

She peered into the mirror and noted that the black mascara, the only bit of make-up she had attempted to put on that morning, was already smudged under one eye, making her look like she was attempting a new Goth look. She quickly wiped it off with a facial wipe, which left her looking a bit wonky with her pale blonde eyelashes on one eye and black ones on the other. She grabbed the mascara and tried again, stabbing the wand into her eye in her hurry. She cried out and blinked, causing spider-leg prints underneath her eye. She sighed and grabbed the facial wipe once more, wiping it across both eyes as she quickly left the bathroom.

Plans to do something wonderful and cute with her hair had gone out the window too, and she pulled her blonde curls haphazardly up into a ponytail.

Rocky, her two-month-old black curly-haired puppy, eyed her from his basket. The cause of her lateness looking all sweet and innocent.

'It's OK for you, you don't have to do anything to look cute in the morning, you just wag your tail, and everyone is putty in your hands. Some of us have to put in a little bit of effort.'

She ran into the kitchen, threw her rucksack onto the breakfast bar and knocked over the remains of a glass of orange juice in the process. Cursing under her breath, she grabbed some kitchen towel and mopped it up. She was the clumsiest person she knew. She got frustrated with herself sometimes for being so accident-prone; it was little wonder other people got frustrated with her too. If she made it through the day without knocking something over, spilling something or breaking something, it was a miracle. She tossed the wet kitchen towel in the bin and then threw some of the latest jewellery pieces she'd made into her bag. Thankfully she had carefully wrapped them up the night before and hadn't left them to sort out that morning.

She clamped her slice of jam on toast between her teeth and hopped on one foot as she tried to pull on her sparkly blue Converse. She smiled as she looked down at what she was wearing for work that day, a bright turquoise strapless sun dress with sea shells and starfish printed along the bottom. Just over a year ago, when she was working in her own exclusive jewellery boutique in London, she would have been wearing a smart suit. She earned a lot more money back then, selling expensive pieces she'd made or sourced to London's rich. Now she was making jewellery out of cheap gemstones, silver clay, shells and sea glass and selling them to the tourists. But it made her happy.

She wolfed down the rest of the toast as she snapped on Rocky's lead and he bounced up around her, excited about just leaving the house. Since her early morning walks to work had started to include meeting Jamie Jackson on the way, she was excited too.

She left Apple Tree Cottage, closing the bright yellow wooden door behind her as Rocky yapped at a bird as it flew into a rose bush.

'Sit,' Melody urged as the puppy strained on the lead while she tried to lock the door. His waggy bottom plopped down on the grass and she smiled. She had raised him almost from birth when his mum, Beauty, had too many puppies to feed by herself, so training had started a bit earlier than it normally would. Toilet training was almost perfect now but recall and other commands would take a while longer yet.

Melody opened the front gate and paused for a moment as she looked out on Sunshine Beach, just a few yards away. The sea was a glorious turquoise today with gold-crested waves sparkling in a straight path towards the horizon where the sun burned bright in a denim blue sky. The pineapple yellow houses that tumbled down the hillside and touched the seashore still looked half asleep, with their brightly coloured blinds and curtains drawn as if their eyes were still closed. Some early birds were awake – she could see them out on their balconies eating their breakfasts – but apart from a few stragglers the beach itself was almost deserted. The view changed every day, but it didn't matter whether it was rainy, misty, windy or blazing sunshine, it made her smile so much. God, she could look out on it forever.

Her commute was another thing that had changed in the last year; fifty minutes and three trains to get to her jewellery shop in London compared to a ten-minute walk along the beach now.

Her brother Matthew's death had affected her life so much and not just because of the gaping hole he had left behind. After relocating to Sandcastle Bay the year before to help her sister Isla with raising Matthew's son, her life had changed beyond recognition. She was happier here than she had been for a long time. Life was slower here, quieter, giving her a peace she never knew she needed growing up in London. And she got to look at this magnificent view every day. Everyone looked out for each other here and maybe, at times, they came across as nosy and interfering, but she wouldn't change them for the world.

Suddenly remembering that she was already running late, she hurried along the shore with Rocky yapping at the gentle waves lapping onto the sand. Of course, running her own jewellery shop, she didn't have a boss to answer to; opening and closing hours were very relaxed in Sandcastle Bay, with various shops opening whenever they saw fit. But even though she knew he wouldn't care – he was very laid-back – she didn't want to be late for Jamie.

Melody smiled as she spotted Jamie waiting for her on the beach just ahead, her heart leaping into her chest. He was definitely a reason to make her smile.

She saw Sirius, the puppy Jamie had rescued from the same litter as Rocky, tail wagging furiously, straining at the lead as he spotted his brother. All the puppies had found homes in the village of Sandcastle Bay after two strays, Beauty and Beast, had eleven puppies a few months before. There was a definite theme with Jamie's animals; he had three other dogs, Harry Potter, Ron Weasley and Hermione Granger – although he only ever used their full names when they were in trouble – and not forgetting his pet turkey called Dobby, all named after the characters in Jamie's favourite book.

Rocky yelped with excitement at seeing his brother and pulled her hard towards Jamie and Sirius. Despite his age, Rocky was a lot bigger than the average puppy and already really strong.

'Hi,' Melody said.

Jamie opened his mouth to speak but the puppies went into a wild frenzy, as if it hadn't been just a few days since the last time they'd met.

Sirius darted round the back of Jamie and Rocky chased him round the other side, so Melody was yanked hard against Jamie's chest.

His hand went to her waist to steady her, his touch making her pulse race.

'Hello,' Jamie laughed, his grey eyes gentle.

Her breath caught in her throat at being this close to him, reminding her of that night over a year before. The night of her brother's funeral, she'd gotten drunk in her grief for Matthew and Jamie had looked after her. When he'd escorted her back to the hotel she had been staying at, she had kissed him and, for a glorious, perfect few seconds, he had kissed her back. Well it had felt like he had; she had been drunk and upset and maybe she'd imagined it. Maybe he had actually been politely trying to extricate himself from her arms. There had never been any mention of it since. His lack of response to the kiss felt like a rejection, making her think that any feelings between them had been completely one-sided. When she had first moved to Sandcastle Bay a few weeks later, it had been embarrassing and awkward between them.

But over the last few months they had grown close as they had raised the puppies together. She felt so comfortable and at ease with him now. Recently, he had grown increasingly tactile too, hugging her, touching her when he was talking – she'd even had a kiss on the cheek from him on Saturday when they had parted ways for the remainder of the weekend. This affection and their closeness had given her hope that there *was* something between them that might be more than just friendship.

That was the big plan for this morning. She was going to ask him out.

She had come to a decision over the weekend that she wasn't going to pine after him any more. She had rehearsed what she was going to say in her head and out loud to Rocky, who had seemed quite receptive to it. She had thought about all the possible scenarios and come up with different responses. This was it. Today was going to be the day.

Elsie West from the chemist walked past with Mary Nightingale from the post office and they both looked at her in Jamie's arms, waggling their eyebrows, nudging each other and giggling. No doubt the whole village would hear about this by lunch time, and certainly in the next few seconds they would be on the phone to Jamie's crazy aunt Agatha, who liked to be kept apprised of all village gossip. But knowing this did nothing to make Melody want to step back, to move away from him.

She turned her attention back to him. He had such kind eyes, grey with sparks of silver and blue.

His gaze cast over her face and his eyes clouded with concern. 'Have you been crying?'

'What? No. What makes you think that?'

'You have mascara smeared under your eyes.'

Oh crap.

She quickly wiped under her eyes, cursing that she hadn't bothered to check her reflection after she had wiped off the mascara.

'Oh, I'm just rubbish at putting on my make-up.'

'And you, um… have jam on your chin,' Jamie said, his lips quirking up into a smirk.

So much for making a good impression. She reached up to wipe it off and Jamie slid his hand up to the other side of her face, using his thumb to gently wipe away the jam. Oh lord, maybe getting jam on her face was actually a good thing.

Rocky suddenly yanked on the lead again, pulling her from Jamie's touch as Rocky chased Sirius across the sand.

Jamie laughed. 'I think it's time we took these pups to dog training classes, teach them a few manners. Here, let me take your rucksack for you.'

He slid it from her shoulder before she could protest and started walking towards Starfish Court as if nothing had happened, as if something hadn't just passed between them. Maybe it hadn't.

She searched for a topic of conversation while she tried to calm her heart and pluck up the courage to finally ask him out.

'How are you doing with your idea for the Great Sculptures in the Sand Festival?' Melody asked, finally finding a nice safe topic. She had missed the festival last year as she had gone away on a two-week holiday with her sister Isla and her nephew Elliot, but this year she was really looking forward to it. The festival kicked off on Saturday with the Great Sandcastle Building Competition, which was only a bit of fun but apparently the villagers got very competitive about it. And come Sunday night there would be hundreds of sculptures filling the length of Sunshine Beach, all of various shapes, sizes and materials. There were going to be lots of different foods and crafts stalls on the beach throughout the day and then the official unveiling of the sculptures was going to happen at sunset, when there would be fireworks, music, dancing and a barbeque with a hog roast after. Everyone in the village was expected to contribute and people from the nearby towns and villages were making sculptures too.

He paused before he answered, then seemed to change his mind. 'What are you making?'

'I have no idea, I'm not the least bit practical or creative when it comes to something like this. Give me a necklace, bracelet, ring or brooch to work on and I could do something beautiful. But something big like this, I've got no idea. How big does it have to be?'

'Minimum of two feet.'

'God, that's huge. I don't even know what I'm going to make it out of.'

'What about using sea glass? Then it captures a little bit of you and your style too. I've seen some of your sea glass jewellery and it's stunning. The sculpture doesn't have to be anything 3D. It could be flat. A mosaic of your most loved thing in Sandcastle Bay. I would think it's easier for you to find what your favourite thing is, you haven't been here that long, so everything is still new and fresh for you. I imagine many of the locals look at it through jaded eyes. What do you love most about Sandcastle Bay?'

This, thought Melody, walking along Sunshine Beach every day with the man she loved.

'Oh god, probably the sea,' she said instead.

'Well, that's easy, you could just do a mosaic of some waves.' He drew the pattern of some pointy, curly waves in the air with his finger, evidently able to visualise how it would look in his head already, while what Melody was imagining was no doubt something far less amazing. Jamie probably had very high expectations for her waves.

'What are you making?' Melody said, changing the subject away from what would probably turn out to be very disappointing for him when he saw it.

'I started mine weeks ago. When I thought about the theme, there was only one thing I wanted to make, but I'm not sure it's really in keeping with the spirit of the festival. I'm not sure if I'm actually going to submit it to the competition.'

'What's it going to be?'

He grinned. 'That would spoil the surprise.'

She laughed, and their fingers innocently brushed together. She longed to slide her hand into his and she wondered what he would make of that if she did. She glanced down and wondered if his skin would be soft or rough from years of working with clay.

'The sculptures are meant to be things we love the most about Sandcastle Bay,' Melody said, forcing her eyes away from where their hands were nearly touching.

'Yes, the thing I'm making meets that criteria.'

'Then what's the problem?'

He looked down at her as they walked. 'Because I think people will do sculptures of the ice cream parlour or the famous heartberries or Sunshine Beach or something obvious like that, whereas my sculpture is going to be very… personal.'

'Everyone will interpret that theme in their own ways. Your sculpture is supposed to be the thing that *you* love the most, not anyone else. You need to listen to your heart.'

He nodded. 'You're right, but I worry what people will think of it.'

'When have you ever cared about what people will think?' Melody said. Jamie sometimes came across as quiet and sensitive but when it came down to his sculptures he always created the pieces he wanted to make, rather than bowing down to what was popular or fashionable. His sculptures were unique and special, and she loved that he felt free enough to do that.

'I care about what you think,' Jamie said, quietly and she looked up into his eyes. Her breath caught in her throat again. Why did he care what she thought?

'I love your sculptures, you're so talented. Why would you care what I think of this one?'

He pulled a face. 'Well, you'll see soon enough. I don't know if the plan was ever to submit this sculpture. I think it was always just for me. But maybe, if I'm brave enough, I'll let you see it and, if you like it, I'll submit it to the competition.'

He paused to take a photo of a happy-looking elderly lady, paddling barefoot in the sea, her long skirt held up to her knees. He fired off a few more shots from different angles. He was always taking pictures; people, scenery, nature, animals. They all helped to inspire his work. A few weeks before he had taken a photo of her dancing on the beach with her nephew Elliot. Though quite how that was going to inspire him, she didn't know.

Sirius leapt towards a seagull barking and yapping and Jamie stopped taking photos and knelt to reprimand the puppy.

'Sirius Black. That seagull has every right to be on this beach, in fact he probably has more right than you do. You can't bark at him for being in his own home.'

Sirius sat down and cocked his head as he stared at Jamie, as if he was really listening to him and taking on board everything he was saying. Melody suppressed a giggle as the lecture continued.

Jamie stood back up and sighed. 'There's puppy training classes starting on Saturday, in the town hall. Thought we could go together?'

Her heart leapt at what sounded like a date but then dropped again when she realised it wasn't a date at all. Having puppies that were brothers, it made sense to go with one another, especially as they had bonded over the last two months with nursing the puppies together.

'That sounds like a good idea.'

'I need to start leaving Sirius at home soon. As much as I love having him at work with me, Harry, Ron and Hermione are getting jealous that he gets to come to work with me every day and they don't,' Jamie said, talking about his three other dogs. 'And don't even get me started on Dobby.'

Dobby was Jamie's pet turkey who, having been raised with three dogs, was clearly convinced he was one too.

'Is Dobby jealous of Sirius too?' Melody said, trying not to laugh.

'He's not exactly happy about there being a new arrival at Meadow Cottage; he keeps stealing his dog food. Sirius loves him of course – well, loves to chase him – and Dobby isn't happy about that either.'

'Oh dear,' Melody said, trying and failing to keep the smirk from her face.

'It's carnage in my house right now; I barely get a moment's peace.'

They were approaching Starfish Court, a small cobbled courtyard just off the beach that held a collection of arty shops: her jewellery shop, Jamie's art studio, a shop that sold glass pieces, pottery, paintings, handmade chocolates, even a tattoo studio. It was a beautiful place and very inspiring. It was popular with tourists too; they always came here when they visited.

Melody and Jamie were just about to head inside their respective shops, after which they probably wouldn't see each other until the end of the day. And maybe not even then, as Jamie sometimes stayed late in the art studio to finish his work – he couldn't take his sculptures home the way she could take home her jewellery.

So here was the opening she so desperately needed.

Jamie handed her the rucksack and moved over to the door of his studio. She could see his business partner Klaus already wandering around inside.

She took a deep breath and, before she could change her mind, she asked him.

'Well, if you fancy a night off from the mayhem, you'd be welcome to come round my house for dinner tonight?'

That wasn't what she'd planned to say at all. Not even close. But it was out there now. She had asked him out on a date. She had done it. And it felt wonderful.

She watched his face for any sign of delight or, worse, shock or horror, but he didn't give any indication that this was something out of the norm for him.

'Oh, that would be great,' Jamie said, casually as he pushed open his door. 'Shall I come by around seven?'

Melody nodded, and he gave her a wave and stepped inside his art studio with barely a look back.

She stared after him for a moment and then quickly unlocked her door and let herself into her little shop, settling Rocky into his basket and moving to the tiny kitchenette out the back to make herself a cup of tea.

That hadn't sounded like he'd just agreed to go on a date with her. That sounded like he'd just agreed to spend some time with her as a friend. Just two mates hanging out together.

She thought back to what she'd said to him. Her offer had sounded very casual as well, it was no wonder he had taken it like that. Still, he was coming for dinner at her house. With no distractions, some nice food and wine, maybe she would be brave enough to tell him exactly how she felt for him that night. And, as she resolved to do just that, her head and her heart got carried away with imagining his reaction. She couldn't help the big smile from spreading on her face.

CHAPTER 2

'Hey Jamie,' Klaus called from the far side of the studio as he continued to build his driftwood sculpture. This one looked like it was going to be a wolf.

Sirius yapped his excitement at seeing Klaus and he turned and beamed, scooping the puppy up into his arms. Sirius licked his face as if they had been parted for months, not just a day. Jamie smiled. Klaus was so huge, and with his long biker beard and penchant for piercings and tattoos, he looked like someone you would cross over onto the other side of the street to avoid. Seeing him be all gooey over a puppy was such a contrast to his hard-man image, but Jamie knew that Klaus had a heart of gold and had never raised his voice to anyone, let alone his fists.

Klaus looked mischievously over the puppy's head at Jamie and Jamie quickly moved to the kitchenette, keen to avoid the topic of conversation they had every morning – well, every morning since he'd started walking with Melody to work.

'Shall I make a coffee?' Jamie said, noisily filling the kettle.

'I've already had one, just made one for you too, it's on your desk. Was that Melody I saw you walking with?'

Jamie sighed as he moved over to his desk. 'You know it was.'

'That's becoming quite the habit,' Klaus said, a big grin on his face, his driftwood sculpture completely forgotten.

'She lives near me, of course we're going to bump into each other on the way to work some days,' Jamie said, knowing that he always used to arrive at work a lot earlier than he had over the last few weeks. These days he timed his commute so he could walk with her instead and he knew Klaus knew this too.

'And now you have a date tonight,' Klaus said, and Jamie's head snapped up to look at him.

'It's not a date.' It wasn't a date, was it?

'It sure sounded like she was asking you out on a date,' Klaus said.

Jamie thought back to the very casual way Melody had invited him to dinner that night. It hadn't sounded particularly romantic.

'Hang on, you've totally misread this situation. She was just asking me if I wanted to hang out, as friends. There were no big declarations of love.'

'Men and women can't be friends,' Klaus said.

'Of course they can, that's ridiculous. I have lots of female friends.'

'That you hang out with like you do with your male friends?'

'Well, no.' He thought about Tori, his brother's girlfriend. He hung out with her sometimes but mostly when he was with Aidan, so he guessed that didn't really count. He wracked his brains for any other girls that he hung out with and came up blank. 'But why can't we be friends? She makes me laugh, we talk a lot, she's great company.'

'Because at least one person in the *friendship* always wants more. Case and point, she's just asked you out. Though she's probably regretting that right now.'

'What do you mean?' Jamie asked.

'"Oh, that would be great,"' Klaus said as he quoted Jamie's casual reply back to him, making Jamie sound a lot lamer than he thought he had. 'No girl wants to hear that when they've been brave enough to ask you out in the first place.'

He remembered Melody's face when he had replied. She hadn't looked particularly overjoyed by his response, but then she wouldn't be if it had just been a casual arrangement. He groaned – the very last thing he wanted to do was hurt Melody.

Maybe he should go over and say how much he was looking forward to tonight, to reassure her. But did he want to go on a date with Melody?

'Your face,' Klaus laughed. 'Anyone would think you've been asked to eat a jellied eel or clean out a septic tank. Why do you look so terrified at the prospect of going out on a date with Melody Rosewood? She's wonderful, funny, sweet, intelligent. And I thought you were insanely attracted to her.'

'I am, but…' Crap, he hadn't meant to give Klaus any encouragement, but truth be told, he'd had feelings for Melody for a long time, feelings that went way beyond friendship. 'I don't do relationships, you know that. I'm lousy at them. You know what happened with Suzie, I broke her heart.'

God, he still felt awful about that. She had told him she loved him, and he'd very kindly tried to explain he didn't see her like that. He remembered walking into the pub the night after they'd broken things off and finding her sobbing at a table. She was surrounded by all her friends who gave him death stares as he ordered his pint. Every time he'd seen her after that, she'd burst into tears and hurried away.

'You didn't do anything wrong with Suzie, you didn't string her along. You realised after a few weeks that you didn't feel that connection you were looking for and you ended it. It's not your fault she fell in love with you,' Klaus said.

'I know, but…'

'Is it really Suzie that's putting you off, or is it what happened with Polly?'

Jamie winced. Because he'd been in Suzie's shoes himself, falling completely head over heels in love with someone who just didn't return those feelings. He'd fallen hard for Polly Lucas. He'd thought that what they had was forever and when he'd told her he loved her, and she'd laughed and said it was nothing more than a bit of fun to her, he'd been absolutely heartbroken.

'You've known me for a long time,' Jamie said. 'Not one of my relationships have lasted. Polly was my longest and even that was only a few months. You know what she said about me, what quite a few women of the town say about me actually. I'm too nice. How can someone be too nice?' He thought about his other brother. 'Leo, who sleeps with women once and never calls them again, has girls falling over themselves to go out with him. As a teenager, he smoked, drank way too much and got all lairy. He skipped school, got into trouble with the teachers and police and the girls absolutely loved him, still do. Don't get me wrong, he's kind, fiercely loyal and I love him to bits. He has changed a lot since then but why is someone who has such a bad reputation when it comes to women so attractive to them? I can't treat women like that.'

He picked up his mug and blew on the steam that billowed from the top.

'Polly wasn't the first to finish with me, but I decided she was definitely going to be the last. I decided I wasn't interested in having any kind of serious relationship any more. I wonder if it's just easier not getting involved with anyone. Then no one gets hurt. I can't get involved with Melody because I know I could fall in love with her so easily and what if she thinks I'm just too nice for her, it would ruin our friendship. Equally, I never ever want to do anything to hurt her either – she's my friend and I like her too much to do that. She's had enough hurt to last her a lifetime, with Matthew dying in that horrible car accident, I certainly don't want to add to that. We really are better off staying just friends.'

Klaus placed Sirius down in his basket. 'Love is a crazy, wonderful thing, it's not something to run away from, it's something you run towards. Yes, it's painful if it doesn't turn out the way we want it to, but you can't shy away from it for the rest of your life because it might hurt. Love has a way of catching up with you anyway, and then to do nothing, to stand on the side-lines staring at the thing you want most in the world, that's got to hurt too. So surely it's better to be hurt over the things you did do rather than the things you didn't.'

'But this is Melody,' Jamie said, quietly. 'She's... special.'

'Then isn't she worth the risk?'

Jamie thought about this. He couldn't go out with Melody. She was one of his closest friends and he didn't want to lose that. He was rubbish at relationships and one or both of them would end up getting hurt.

'Well, if you really don't think you can go ahead with it, then you need to talk to her about your date tonight. Don't let her cook you a meal, go all out with candles and romance if you intend to treat the event as just two friends hanging out. You better go over and make clear the parameters,' Klaus said.

He sighed but he knew Klaus was right. This was why he shied away from relationships – because people got hurt. Going over to Melody's shop and telling her he didn't want a date would hurt her. And if it wasn't a date and it *was* just two friends hanging out then that would be a very awkward conversation.

Melody pushed open the door to The Cherry on Top, her favourite beachside café. It was owned by Emily, Jamie's sister, and in Melody's opinion she made the most amazing food in all of Sandcastle Bay. A view which was obviously shared by most of the residents because, even on a Monday lunch time, the place was almost full.

It had been a busy morning for Melody in her shop too. Although the schools didn't break up until later that day, Sandcastle Bay had seen a steady increase in tourists over the last few weeks. The hot weather had sent the holidaymakers to the beach in their droves and many of them wanted souvenirs of their stay.

She noticed her best friend Tori was already at a table waiting for her and she gave Rocky a little tug on the lead and made her way over. She noticed Agatha, Jamie's crazy aunt, sitting at a nearby table with her puppy, Summer, curled up in her lap. Agatha's hair was a bright turquoise today and it matched the sun hat Summer was wearing perfectly. She really liked Agatha, but interfering was almost certainly her middle name. She was desperate to see her and Jamie get together. Agatha would be over the moon if she knew they had a sort-of date that night, something she definitely didn't want to share with her.

Tori stood up to give her a hug and, as Melody moved to hug her, she knocked the mug on the table over, somehow catching it with her arm. She sighed with frustration. How could one person be so completely inept and ungainly? Tori quickly grabbed the mug and put it back down on the table; thankfully it was already empty, so there was no mess this time. To Tori's credit, she didn't even bat an eye as she moved to hug her again. Melody held her tight. She was so glad Tori was a permanent fixture of Sandcastle Bay now. They had been best friends all her life, even living together in London for several years, but after Matthew's death had brought Melody to Sandcastle Bay, she had left Tori behind in London and she had missed her so much. Now Tori was living here too, mainly because of Jamie's brother Aidan, and it meant she got to see her for lunch most days, although she hadn't seen her over the weekend as Tori had been so busy helping out at Heartberry Farm.

'How's it going?' Melody said, sitting down and settling Rocky at her feet. She noticed that Tori was already tucking into a big slice of red velvet cake.

'Good. The fruit-picking season is well underway, we're busy with the tourists picking raspberries, apples, blackberries, and even some of the strawberries are still ripe at this time,' Tori said.

Melody smiled. Life had changed for Tori as well and, to judge from the big smile on her face, it was for the better too.

'Who'd have thought you'd be working here on a fruit farm after living your whole life in London. Do you miss it at all?'

Tori thought about this for a moment. 'The coffee is better here than the chain stores, that's for sure. I never thought I'd say that but it is. I suppose I miss the variety, the different restaurants, the shows and the entertainment. But for me, London was always defined by the time I spent with you, Matthew and Isla. Once you all left, my life was pretty empty without you. This is my home now. I have this amazing view to enjoy every day, I get to spend time with you. I now have two dogs to look after, when I could barely look after myself back in London. It also helps that I get to share my bed with my sexy fruit farmer every night.' Tori grinned.

Melody couldn't help but smile. Tori had closed herself off from love and it had found a way into her heart anyway. She had never seen two people so in love as Aidan and Tori. Tori deserved someone lovely like Aidan and she couldn't be happier for her.

'I could say the same about you too,' Tori said, interrupting her thoughts. 'I never thought you'd call somewhere like this home. You used to love London. Do *you* miss your life there?'

Melody shook her head. 'Not any more. I did. When I first moved here I thought I would go crazy, life was so different. I couldn't get over how quiet it was. I missed the noise, the shops, the people. I missed the little bakery I'd pop into at lunch time and Mrs Gillespie who always gave me free cookies and told me about her life in America. I missed the next-door neighbour's dog, who always greeted me when I got home. I even missed Tom, the postman who I had a little crush on and was never brave enough to do anything about. Mostly, though, I just missed you. Over time, you were the only thing I missed. I've been here over a year now and I cannot imagine living anywhere else. Everyone important in my life is here. I guess my priorities changed.'

'I never knew you had a crush on Tom,' Tori said. 'Why didn't you do anything about it?'

'Oh god, you know I have zero confidence around men. I can never pluck up the courage to ask them out.'

'But you've been out with quite a few men over the years.'

'Yes, but they've always asked me out; I've never asked them.' Until today and that hadn't exactly been a huge success. 'And only two of those have been serious relationships. Well, semi-serious. The others all seemed to fizzle out before they'd even got started. Men want someone they can be proud to have on their arm, not someone who will throw their dinner down themselves every time they go out to a restaurant or knock their drink over.' Melody nodded pointedly at the mug she had knocked over minutes before.

'Don't say that,' Tori said. 'Any man would be lucky to go out with you. None of your dates or relationships fizzled out because you were clumsy. They fizzled out because you weren't right for each other.'

'Kevin dumped me because I dropped his laptop.'

'Kevin was a cock. Could you honestly see yourself spending the rest of your life with him?'

'No, definitely not. Even before that, cracks were starting to show.'

'You're the loveliest person I know. It's not a case of you not being good enough for them, but them not being good enough for you. You shouldn't define yourself by your clumsiness. Those who love you don't care about that.'

'My dad cared about it. So did my mum in the end,' Melody said quietly.

'Your dad had a short temper about most things, not specifically about you being a bit accident-prone. Don't bring that on yourself. And your mum was angry with the entire world once your dad left. Again, that wasn't to do with you.'

'I know. But it doesn't stop me being scared of men saying no if I was to ask them out.'

'You're such an amazing person, you just don't see that.'

'I'm not exactly beating off all the men with a stick,' Melody said.

'That's because you keep your head down when you're around new people, men especially. You withdraw. That makes it hard for a man to engage with you. Keep your chin up; show everyone how beautiful you are, inside and out.'

Melody smiled at this loyalty from her friend.

Rocky stirred below the table and both Melody and Tori looked underneath it to check on him. He yawned and went back to sleep.

'How are your dogs settling in?' Melody asked.

Tori and Aidan had adopted Beauty, the mum of the massive litter of puppies, after looking after her in the weeks after the birth. They'd also taken in Spike, one of the smallest puppies.

'Beauty is still scared of her own shadow, but she trusts us and she's slowly becoming more confident. Beast is still visiting her every day and Aidan hopes he might be able to persuade him to call Heartberry Farm his home eventually, instead of wandering the streets. Spike is the complete opposite of his mum, wants to investigate everything. He's brave and bold and hilarious to watch. I love having them around. It's like… we're a proper little family now. And maybe a few years down the line, we'll have our own children.'

Melody smiled at that thought. She and Aidan would make such wonderful parents.

'How's the advert going?' Melody asked.

'Good so far.' Tori's face lit up at talk of her other job.

Melody loved hearing her talk about her work. As an animator using plasticine models, Tori was in her element making little adverts for companies. She'd been involved in big animated films and TV programmes over the years, but her heart was in the little jobs she could see through from the very beginning to the end. She'd recently made an advert for Aidan's fruit farm, starring a cute little heartberry called Max.

'It went out on all social media about two weeks ago and already we've seen an uptake on sales,' Tori continued. 'I'm just about to finish one starring more of the fruit from the farm. We've seen some great merchandise sales too. It will take a while to build but I can see we could do a whole range of adverts, with each of the fruit taking a leading role. I have several other adverts for other companies I'm in the middle of making too, so the Heartberry Farm ones will have to wait a while. Plus, I'll do one for when Aidan is ready to release his range of fruit pies on the world. Emily is already stocking the pies he is making here, and people seem to love them. He's so excited about it all but it will be a while before we are ready to do it on a professional basis. We have to get all the certificates but I'm so happy he wants to go down this road. It's something he's wanted to do for a while.'

Emily came over then to take their order as Tori finished off her cake.

'Are you talking about my brother's pies? The customers love them. Aidan has always been good at cooking, so it's no surprise his pies have been such a big hit.'

Tori's smile lit her face. 'I can't tell you how proud I am of him for making this work.'

Emily nodded. 'You've definitely had a positive influence on him.' She rubbed her belly unconsciously and Melody smiled. At four months pregnant, she was already starting to show, but she knew that Emily would probably be working in the café right up to the very end.

'You're busy today,' Melody said, looking around the packed little café.

'Yes, and Marigold breaks up from school today so I will need to take a few days off here and there so I can do things with her. Although she's just happy playing with our puppy, Leia. Actually, I was going to come along to your jewellery course next week. Would it be suitable for Marigold too?'

Melody thought about the course she was running. This was the first time she had done anything like this and it was all a bit up in the air at the moment. She hadn't quite figured out what she would actually try to teach people in that hour.

'There might be a few things she'd find fiddly and we use a blow torch for some of it, but you could do that part for her. She'd definitely enjoy using the silver clay, anyone can do that.'

'That's fab, thanks,' Emily said. 'I need to find some things I can do with her this holiday. I'll bring her here too. She loves helping out, which means I can work in our busiest period and spend time with her. I have a few girls who are home from university for the summer who are helping out too, so we'll manage.'

'You don't want to take a few months off for maternity leave, put your feet up before the baby comes?' Tori asked.

Emily laughed. 'I haven't got time for that! Besides, there'll be lots of time for resting once the little one arrives.'

Melody doubted that, but she didn't say anything.

'Anyway, what can I get you both?' Emily asked.

'I'll have a sausage sandwich, please,' Tori said, licking the icing from her fingers.

Melody laughed. 'The red velvet cake was your starter, was it?'

'That was just a little snack, I'm starving.'

'I'll have a cheese and chicken toastie, please,' Melody said.

Emily scribbled it all down and hurried off back round the counter.

'So, enough about me and the farm,' Tori said. 'Tell me more of your news.'

Melody looked surreptitiously over at Agatha, who seemed to be engrossed in her book.

'I do have some news actually.' She glanced over at Agatha again. 'I did it.'

Tori, of course, knew of her plans to ask Jamie out, though hadn't known she was going to do it that morning. To be fair, they had been talking about how to do it for the last few weeks and Tori probably thought it was never going to happen. Tori looked confused for a few moments and Melody inclined her head towards Agatha to help her out.

Tori's face cleared, a huge smile spreading on her face.

'You did?'

'Yes,' Melody said. No need to mention that it had been far more casual than she had intended. She has asked Jamie to dinner and he had said yes. That was a tick in her book. 'And it was a positive result.'

'Ah that's great, I knew it would be,' Tori said, attempting to be vague for Agatha's benefit. 'I'm really happy for you.'

Melody sighed inwardly. She wished she could share her friend's optimism. Jamie was probably going to turn up at her house that night with no idea he was on a date.

'And, um… what will you wear to the… event?' Tori said.

'I have a silver dress I bought from the charity shop last week, thought that might suit the occasion.' She chanced a glance at Agatha only to find she was staring right back at her.

Giving up any pretence of not listening to their conversation, Agatha got up and came and joined them at their table.

'What's all this then?' Agatha asked.

Tori smirked. She knew what Agatha's interfering was like. She had stuck her oar in at every available opportunity when Tori was first dating Aidan. Now they were happily loved-up and living together, Agatha had turned her attention to getting her other two nephews married off. She had set her sights on getting Melody together with Jamie and she was desperate to see Melody's sister Isla together with Leo Jackson.

'Oh, nothing important,' Melody said.

'What's this event that you'll be wearing a silver dress to?'

'It's a jewellery thing,' Tori said, desperately. 'An exhibition, craft fair type thing where jewellers will showcase their wares. Melody didn't think she should go and I encouraged her to go for it.'

Agatha narrowed her eyes, obviously not believing this for one moment. But there was a jewellery fair over in Penzance. Melody had talked with Tori about how she might go the previous week. She quickly delved in her bag and luckily found the leaflet. She pulled it out and laid it on the table triumphantly. It was an exclusive event and she hadn't been sure whether her pieces that were popular with the tourists would fit in.

Agatha studied the leaflet and then sighed. 'I thought you might have finally plucked up the courage to ask Jamie out. I heard all about the two of you canoodling on the beach this morning.'

Melody couldn't resist rolling her eyes. 'We were not canoodling, I sort of fell and he caught me.'

Agatha shook her head. 'He adores you, you know that.'

'We're friends,' Melody said. 'Maybe that's all we'll ever be.'

'You are destined to be together,' Agatha said, her voice taking on a mystical tone.

Melody suppressed a smirk. Agatha was well known for predicting who was going to marry who, with not much success so far. She was so confident in her 'psychic' abilities, despite a large lack of results, that five minutes after Aidan had met Tori for the first time, Agatha had bet Aidan fifty pounds that he would be walking Tori down the aisle within a year of them meeting. She'd also predicted that Melody would be marrying Jamie, which she couldn't even begin to imagine.

'If you're so sure he has feelings for me, why hasn't he asked me out himself?' Melody asked.

Agatha shook his head. 'Jamie won't do that. He's been hurt and rejected badly in the past. He's not looking for a relationship.'

'Then what's the point in me asking him out?' Melody said.

'It's up to you to show him what he's missing, that being in love is a wonderful thing.'

Melody sighed. It seemed like a lot of hard work. Surely a relationship should be both parties going into it willingly rather than one more enthusiastically than the other? The heroines in the romance stories she loved so much never seemed to have this problem. The men seemed to go after their women with passion and determination.

'Have you seen your mum lately?' Agatha asked, seemingly changing subject so fast that Melody nearly got whiplash.

'Um, no, not really,' Melody said, feeling guilty that she hadn't.

Tori smiled at her sympathetically. She knew Melody had a difficult relationship with her mum. After her dad had an affair and walked out on them when Melody was only thirteen, her mum had been angry at everything and everyone, including her, Isla and Matthew. That anger with the world had never really gone away.

For several years, Melody had wondered if it had been her fault her dad had left. Had she not been clever enough, arty enough, sporty enough? Were her skills as a dancer not impressive enough to make him want to stay? Had she been too clumsy? He always got so frustrated with her whenever she knocked a drink over or dropped a glass or bowl. She'd wondered if that had been the final straw in the end? Her mum had never reassured her otherwise. She spent the next few years studying hard, working hard, trying to excel at every subject. No matter how hard she worked, she never came top of any class. She was distinctly average at everything. Looking back, Melody didn't know if she was trying to prove her worth to her dad, her mum or to herself, but she never got any praise from her parents. Her dad was absent for most of her teenage years and her mum was wrapped up in her own anger. That had driven a wedge between them that had never been repaired.

It was only later, when she was older, that she was able to see that her dad left because he fell out of love with her mum, that it had very little or nothing to do with her or her siblings. Maybe her mum's anger with her dad had always been there, which might have pushed him away.

After Matthew had been killed in that car accident, her mum's grief had manifested itself as anger too. When Melody and her mum had moved to Sandcastle Bay to help Isla with the task of raising Matthew's son, her mum made sure that anyone who listened knew what a sacrifice it had been coming here. Melody had spent a lot of time trying to build bridges when they'd first moved down here. Life was too short to hold a grudge. But she always came away from seeing her mum feeling so frustrated and hurt that eventually the visits had stopped. It was a small village and she bumped into her mum from time to time. Melody was always polite and civil, but she would never go out of her way to visit her.

'Carolyn's dating again,' Agatha said.

'What?' Melody said, in shock, her voice carrying over the whole café so everyone turned and looked at her.

'Are you sure?' Tori asked.

Agatha nodded, and Melody couldn't believe that Agatha knew before she did.

'Trevor Harris,' Agatha said, knowledgably.

'The policeman?' Melody asked. He was such a serious man and not someone she would have picked for her mum. But then she never thought her mum would ever find love with anyone again so this was definitely a step in the right direction, no matter who it was with.

'Yes. They're trying to keep it quiet, they don't want the whole village to know. But I saw them in here the other day, they were holding hands under the table. She seems… happy.'

Melody smiled. She liked the idea of her mum dating again. She didn't know whether they would ever get back the closeness they'd had when she had been growing up – too much anger and bitterness had tainted that for them – but she wanted her mum to be happy again.

'The point being that if someone like your mum, who has been so anti-love for so long, anti-everything by the sounds of it, can take a risk with her heart and find happiness again, then you can too.'

Melody sighed. She looked over at Tori. Neither she nor Aidan wanted to get involved in a relationship, but they had, and it had worked out pretty well for them both in the end. Maybe it would be worth the risk.

CHAPTER 3

Melody laid her new pieces in the display cabinet: two bracelets made from sea glass, a necklace with a pale-yellow amber heart, and a few silver clay earrings she had made the night before.

She looked around her shop. It was an eclectic mix. Her shop in London had sold very classic pieces. The kind you could get from any high-end jewellery store. There had been pieces that had a few tiny twists or something different, but nothing abstract or outlandish like she had here. She felt freer here to express her love of jewellery in any way she wanted. There were still some traditional items as some people liked that sort of thing, but the rest of the shop was taken up with bright colours, unusually cut gemstones, pieces that were inspired by different countries or cultures. Some of the jewellery wasn't hers. She loved scouring Etsy for something quirky, different, something that had never been seen before, and then she'd get in touch with the designers and offer to sell a selection in her shop for a small fee. It hardly made her any money, but people came in off the street because they saw something different or unique in her window and, once they were there, they would look at all the other pieces in the shop too.

The door opened and her five-year-old nephew, Elliot, came running in wearing a top hat.

She smiled. His dad, Matthew, would have been so proud of how Elliot was turning out. He was such a happy little boy and Melody knew that had a lot to do with how her sister Isla was now raising him.

'Good morning, Sir,' Melody said, formally. 'How can I help you today? Are you here to buy a diamond tiara for your wife perhaps, or maybe a sapphire brooch?'

Elliot laughed, taking his hat off. 'I'm not Sir, I'm Elliot.'

'Oh, it is you, I didn't recognise you under your very fine top hat,' Melody said, as she came round the counter and swept him up in her arms.

'I'm wearing a top hat because I'm a magician.'

'You are? How fabulous. Can you show me some magic tricks?'

'Yes. Leo bought me a magic set and it has over fifty different tricks inside. I'm still learning some of them and Leo is helping me, he said he's going to be my assistant and most of my tricks are at home, but I took one to school today to show the rest of the class and the teacher said I was a little Paul Daniels. I'm not sure who that is but I think he is a great magician too.'

'Yes, he was,' Melody said. 'Go on then, show me.'

She put him down just as Isla appeared in the doorway with Luke, their little black puppy.

'Are you going to show Melody your trick?' Isla said, closing the door behind her and letting Luke off the lead. Rocky greeted his brother with a bark from his basket at the back of the shop and Luke went careening off to play with him.

'I have to get ready first,' Elliot said as he moved to her desk at the far side of the room and unpacked a few things from his rucksack.

Melody turned her attention to Isla. 'Leo bought him a magic set?'

Isla smiled fondly. 'You know what Leo Jackson is like, he adores him.'

Melody checked on Elliot, who was still busy and most likely not in hearing distance. 'Just marry him, will you?' she said, quietly.

'You know it's not that simple.'

'Don't see why not, you're crazy about him,' Melody said, desperate to see her sister get the happy ending she deserved.

'Because not one of his silly marriage proposals have ever come with those three little words. Is that too much to ask for?'

Melody sighed. 'No, it isn't.'

'And we haven't even been on one date. Don't you think we should do that before I walk down the aisle with him? We're stuck in this weird friend zone and I don't think that will ever change.'

'He loves you, I know he does.'

'Then he needs to actually say it,' Isla said.

'I'm ready!' Elliot announced loudly.

Melody had turned to go and see her nephew perform when the shop door opened again and Aidan Jackson walked in. The eldest of the Jackson brothers, he was probably the tallest too. He had this easy, laid-back attitude that he shared with Jamie, but whereas Jamie was quiet and shy, Aidan had a confidence that Jamie just didn't have. She adored Aidan, especially as he had made her best friend Tori happier than Melody had ever seen her.

'Hey Aidan, you OK to browse for a bit? I have a very important magic show I need to watch.'

Aidan grinned. 'A magic show? Looks like I walked in at the right time.'

Melody smiled as they all walked over to see Elliot perform.

'Welcome to the greatest show in the world,' Elliot said, taking a little bow, and Melody's heart swelled with love for him. It hurt that her brother, Matthew, was not going to be around to watch Elliot grow up, to see his little personality grow and change.

'Here we have a coin, just a normal ten pence,' Elliot indicated a ten pence sitting on top of a red piece of card with a glass upside down next to it. 'I'm going to make it disappear before your very eyes.'

She had to smile. He was obviously reciting some practised lines that Leo had probably taught him.

He slid a tube over the glass and then moved the glass over the ten pence. He picked up his magic wand and swished it over the glass.

'Abracadabra.'

He lifted the tube away from the glass and, sure enough, the ten pence had vanished.

Melody, Isla and Aidan clapped.

'And now for the knotted rope trick,' Elliot said, unfazed by his adoring audience. 'Here is a knotted piece of rope.' He picked up a rope with a knot in the middle and tugged it on both ends. 'See that the knot won't come out.' They all nodded dutifully. 'Melody, hold the knot loosely inside your fist.'

Melody did as she was asked, the ends of the rope hanging down either side of her hand.

Elliot swished his magic wand over her hand and then tugged one of the ends of the rope so it slid from her hand completely knot-free.

'Elliot, that was fantastic.' Melody clapped as the others joined in with their applause and he took another little bow.

'I'll have more tricks soon.'

'I'll have to come back for that,' Aidan said.

Melody turned back to him. 'Did you come in to see me or is there anything in particular you wanted?'

'Well I'm glad you're both here, maybe you can help me,' Aidan said, his eyes falling on Elliot. It was clear he didn't want to say anything in front of him. 'I, erm… would like to buy a ring for Tori.'

Melody's heart leapt, and she let out a little involuntary squeak. 'A… special ring?'

'Yes, really special, the kind that I would get down on bended knee to find.'

She gasped, her hands going to her mouth. Tori and Aidan were completely in love with each other, anyone could see that, so it wasn't a total surprise that he would want to propose to her, but it was a little earlier in the relationship than Melody would have expected. They had only been going out for about two months. But they were so perfect together. Some couples, you just knew they were going to be together forever, and Tori and Aidan had so obviously found their happy ever after with each other.

She wanted to step forward and give Aidan a big hug, but she couldn't do that. In fact, she was too afraid to speak at all because whatever she wanted to say would be too obvious. Elliot was terrible at keeping secrets so they couldn't talk freely about this. She was so excited for Tori. Her best friend was going to get the happy ending Tori had never thought she'd have. Melody looked at Isla, who had a massive grin on her face too.

'I'm so happy for you,' Melody said, unable to contain her joy. She glanced at Elliot, who was looking at her in confusion and for good reason. Poor Aidan was trying to be subtle so that big secrets didn't get spread by loose lips and Melody was practically giving the secret away. 'I mean that I'm happy that you're going to buy one of my rings.'

Isla let out a giggle that turned into a snort. 'Melody is very attached to her rings, she always loves it when they go to a new home.'

'Yes, it makes me so happy when people buy… *special rings.*' Those last two words were delivered in no more than a squeak. Oh god, Tori was going to get married. She had to rein in her emotions otherwise she'd be a gibbering wreck within the next few minutes.

Elliot sighed and took Aidan's hand. 'There are some nice rings in this cabinet here.'

He led Aidan across the shop to a cabinet filled with rings made from large gemstones. They were beautiful statement rings that she was proud of but definitely not the kind of thing that Aidan was looking for to propose to Tori.

'I like this one,' Elliot said, opening the cabinet and sliding on one that was a large raw untreated cluster of iron pyrite or fool's gold. He flashed it around on his right middle finger. 'I think Tori would love this one.'

Aidan nodded. 'It is a beautiful ring, but I was thinking something a bit smaller.'

Melody smiled with the ease with which he could talk to Elliot, but then he'd had plenty of practice with his niece Marigold, Emily's daughter.

Elliot sighed and took the ring off and put it lovingly back into the cabinet.

'We have diamonds, some of them are very small.' Elliot pointed to what was traditionally the engagement ring section. 'And they're *very special*. I've seen lots of women get excited about those rings.'

Melody shook her head though Aidan didn't see.

'Not diamonds, I need something really special and unique,' Aidan said, and Melody gave a little sigh of relief.

'Well, what's her favourite colour?' Elliot said.

'Yellow,' Isla said.

'No, it's green,' Melody said.

Aidan shook his head. 'Blue, like the sea.'

Suddenly galvanised into action, Melody stepped forward. 'We have several blue rings that might suit your needs. We have this fluorite ring, which is a beautiful turquoise colour but has been cut so it has that polished look of a sapphire. It's set in a diamond circle and on a platinum band. Although if you prefer yellow gold or some other kind of metal I can easily change that for you.'

'That's very nice,' Aidan said as Elliot slipped it onto his finger and turned it around so it caught the light.

'Or we have this blue moonstone…' she trailed off as Aidan's face lit up as she passed him the ring. This was perfect for Tori, unique, rare, beautiful. It had so many different shades of blue all swirled together that glinted in the sun as Aidan held it in his hand. Three tiny marcasite beads sat either side of the moonstone, setting off the blue and the silver of the band perfectly.

'I could swap the marcasite for diamond if you wish.' She knew a lot of people liked there to be diamond somewhere in the engagement ring, even if it wasn't the main stone.

'No, this is perfect.'

Elliot peered at it. 'It's nice. Though are you sure you don't want the gold one I had on first?'

Aidan grinned. 'Quite sure. Now we need to keep this a secret OK, no telling anyone, especially not Tori. We want her to be surprised when I give it to her.'

Elliot nodded. 'I promise.'

'And no telling Marigold either,' Aidan said, referring to Elliot's best friend.

'OK.'

Melody took the ring back off Aidan and checked the size. Tori had bought several rings from her over the years so she knew her size and this was a perfect fit. She polished it on a cloth and popped it in a box.

'When are you going to… give it to her?' Isla said, coming over to admire the ring and nodding with approval.

'I'm not sure, I have a plan but I'm not sure when it will happen yet. It's a little bit weather dependent.'

'Well, if you need any help,' Melody said, keen to be there when he popped the question, though she knew that he might want to do it privately.

'I might take you up on that,' Aidan said.

'Bring Tori for dinner tomorrow night, around seven,' Isla said. 'Leo will be there too, so you won't be the only man. Jamie and Melody are coming as well.'

That was news to Melody, though she didn't have any other great plans and Isla probably knew that.

'Sounds great,' Aidan said.

'And if you wanted to, um… ask Tori any special questions during dinner, I could bring some champagne just in case,' Melody tried.

Aidan laughed. 'I think if I had any questions for Tori, I might ask her a bit more privately.'

'I don't think she'd like that,' Melody said. 'The more public the better.'

Aidan looked worried. 'Really?'

'Oh, don't listen to her,' Isla said. 'Melody just wants to see it. You do it how you want to do it, although if you can film it, we'd – well Melody especially – would be eternally grateful.'

'You spoil all my fun, but yes, I suppose Tori would prefer it to be done privately,' Melody said.

Aidan sighed with relief.

'Just you, her, some romantic music,' Melody smiled, dreamily, as she imagined the wonderful romantic proposal that Aidan had planned for her best friend. 'Maybe you'd ask her under the stars, dancing barefoot on the sand.'

'Will you leave the poor man alone to plan his own... question,' Isla said, glancing over at Elliot who was now trying on a tiara with a pearl necklace and posing in front of the mirror.

'Sorry, you're right. I'm sure you have something amazing planned,' Melody said.

'Well, I hope so,' Aidan said, fishing out his wallet as Melody rang up the sale on the till. He slipped the ring box into his coat pocket and waved goodbye to them. 'See you tomorrow night. Thanks for the help, Elliot.'

Elliot waved goodbye as he wrapped another beaded chain around his neck and Aidan left.

'Elliot Rosewood,' Melody teased, putting her hands on her hips. 'Are you intending to try on every item in the shop?'

Elliot grinned. 'Yup.'

'And why aren't you at school?' Melody suddenly realised the time; it was only just after lunch time.

'Today was the last day. I don't go back now until September. Last day of term always finishes at lunch time so all the teachers can go on holiday early.'

Melody laughed at that summary.

'And we had an appointment with Karie again, she gave me some chocolate buttons.'

'Did she? That's nice of her,' Melody said and turned back to Isla. 'How did it go with the social worker?'

'Oh fine,' Isla said. 'They're really happy with his progress.' She lowered her voice. 'Karie thinks we might be able to make the adoption legal soon as they still can't find his mum. Sadie seems to have completely disappeared off the face of the earth. Last time anyone heard from her she was in Australia but now they think she might be in Thailand. The powers that be in charge of our case would prefer to keep my guardianship as a residence order just in case Sadie comes back and suddenly wants to play at being mum of the year. Stripping her of her parental responsibility is a huge legal headache but I would prefer to make it all formal so Elliot stays with me permanently.'

Melody's heart dropped. 'They can't take him away from you.'

Isla shook her head. 'They have no intention of doing that. They want the best thing for Elliot and he is happy with me. Karie loves Leo too and can see how good he is for Elliot. As long as Sadie stays lost, there won't be an issue. I just don't want her to come back in a few years and try to take him. I doubt she ever would, she's never been the maternal type and I can't see that the courts would rule in her favour anyway, as she walked out on him four years ago, but I hate having all this hanging over our heads. Karie thinks, as it's been over a year and we still haven't been able to make contact with her, we might be able to push for a formal adoption soon so we'll have to see.'

'God, I hope you can get it sorted soon,' Melody said. 'It's crazy that she walked out on him, never made any contact with him since, and the law says she still has parental responsibility. Surely she gave all that up the day she abandoned him.'

'You'd think, wouldn't you. Apparently, we have to protect her human rights or some other such crap. I'm not too worried. She has no interest in Elliot, she made that perfectly clear when she walked out of his life. I just want it all sorted legally so it can't come back to bite us.'

'I get that.' Melody let out a heavy sigh. 'God, there are times when I wish Matthew had never met that woman. Apart from the fact that she gave us this wonderful little man.'

'I miss Daddy,' Elliot said, simply, as he tried on a sapphire choker.

Melody winced that he had overheard their conversation. His hearing was fine-tuned to any conversation he shouldn't be listening to. She wasn't concerned that he had heard them talk about Matthew, but she certainly didn't want him to worry about this legal nightmare that Sadie had left them with. She knew Isla talked to him often about Matthew so that he wouldn't forget him and to help him come to terms with his father's death. It was important that they were all open about how Matthew's death made them feel so Elliot would know it was normal to have these emotions.

'I miss him too,' Melody said, honestly. 'There is not a day that goes by that I don't think about him.'

She waited to see if Elliot wanted to talk about him some more. Sometimes he did, sometimes he didn't. She did miss Matthew; she used to talk to him most days when she was in London and he was living down here. Being a twin, they had shared this close bond all the way through their life and some days it was still hard to believe she would never see him again.

She wondered what he would make of this sort-of date she had with Jamie that night. He and Jamie had been good friends. Would he have been delighted for them or would he have played the protective brother card and told Jamie he wasn't allowed to kiss her until her wedding night? She smiled at that thought. He had always looked out for her. When their dad would tell her off for being clumsy, when their dad left and their mum fell apart, Matthew was always there for her. Now she had to pay him back through his son, be there for Elliot in any way that she could.

Elliot simply nodded and turned his attention back to the jewellery he was trying on. He so rarely cried for Matthew. He had been four when Matthew had died just over a year ago and although initially he'd had nightmares, still did sometimes, he had adjusted very quickly to living with Isla instead. The counsellor had said that children of his age didn't really have an understanding of death and were much more accepting of it. Melody bit her lip as he tried on a bracelet. It would be wonderful if she could just switch off from her grief like that too.

She decided to change the subject away from the adoption nightmare. She turned back to Isla.

'Hey, have you heard the gossip about Mum?'

'No, what's the news?' Isla said.

She looked at Elliot but as his attention was elsewhere she didn't think he would be listening.

'Apparently, according to the grapevine that is Agatha, she's dating Trevor Harris,' Melody whispered.

'Nooo! Really?'

'I know, that's what I thought. I never thought she would date anyone ever again. She always seems so angry at everyone; how did she mellow enough for Trevor to ask her out on a date?'

'She's not angry at me,' Elliot said as he pinned a large emerald brooch to his chest.

Melody cringed that Elliot had overheard that too. She had seen her mum get frustrated with Elliot on several occasions, but he never took her seriously, always finding her grumpiness something to giggle at. And when he laughed at her, Melody sometimes saw a glimpse of her old mum, the one who used to play, bake and laugh with her children growing up. She was obviously very fond of Elliot. He was the only one who could get under her skin, make her let her guard down. Melody was glad that Elliot saw that side of her and not the bitter woman Melody had come to know.

'It's true,' Isla says. 'Elliot seems to mellow her. I think things are starting to change with her. I came round to her house the other day to collect Elliot and they were making cakes together and actually laughing. Either Elliot is having a positive influence over her or *someone else* is.'

'If he makes her happy, then I'm happy,' Melody said, referring to Trevor. 'He seems very serious though. She doesn't need any more help taking life seriously.'

'Who knows what they get up to behind closed doors,' Isla said, which Melody hoped was suitably vague enough for Elliot. 'They could be learning the ukulele, belly dancing or have a whole host of… toys and, um, paraphernalia underneath the bed.'

'She has a toy in her drawers next to her bed,' Elliot said, simply, as he pinned a sapphire-studded fascinator to his head.

'Oh god, I don't want to know,' Isla muttered, quietly.

'It's bright pink with glittery bits and knobbly lumps down the side. It buzzes when you turn it on, but I think it's broken as it didn't seem to do much more than that, except for spinning around a bit. Not sure why it was in her bedroom though. I didn't ask her because I'm not allowed in her bedroom.'

Melody felt the laughter bubble up in her chest as Isla stared at him in shock.

'Then why were you in there?' Isla eventually said. 'If Nanny asks you not to go somewhere in her house, then I expect you not to go there.'

Elliot had the grace to look suitably embarrassed. 'Because I'd picked her some flowers and took them in there to leave by her bed as a surprise, but then I knocked the vase over and water went everywhere. I grabbed loads of toilet paper to clean it up and I opened the drawer to make sure no water had gone in there and saw the pink toy.'

Melody smiled and Isla visibly softened. 'That's a very sweet thing to do, but maybe next time, just leave the flowers in the lounge or kitchen, don't go somewhere you're not supposed to go.'

Elliot nodded, solemnly, and returned his attention to the jewellery.

Melody turned back to Isla. 'Oh my.'

'Well, there you have it. The secret to her happiness isn't Elliot or Trevor at all. It's something much more… exciting.'

'Unless Trevor is using it on her.'

Isla put her hands over her ears. 'I don't want to picture that. I mean, if she's having *S E X* again, that's great, but I don't want to picture it.'

'I'm having sex lessons in school,' Elliot said.

Isla's eyebrows shot up. 'Um, you are?'

'Yes, for a few weeks now.'

'That's very early, isn't it?' Melody said to Isla.

'What are you learning about it?' Isla asked, faintly.

'How to use your tongue mostly,' Elliot said. 'And which fingers to use.'

Isla sat down on a nearby stool.

Sex education had changed a lot from when Melody was at school. She had learned about putting a Tampax inside a milk bottle filled with water and then watched it expand, certainly nothing as graphic as this.

'And, um, which fingers do you use?' Isla asked.

'This one is B, this one is A, this one is G,' Elliot said, counting down from his index finger.

Isla stared at him for a moment. 'Oh, thank god. Saxophone lessons?'

'Yes, sax lessons, that's what I said.'

Melody sighed with relief.

'Is Trevor teaching Nanny how to use the saxophone too?' Elliot asked.

Melody giggled. 'Maybe he is?'

'I'll have to ask her about using her tongue,' Elliot said. 'I find that part the trickiest part of all.'

Melody looked away so Elliot wouldn't see her smile.

'Using the tongue is very tricky,' Isla agreed and Melody could feel her shoulders shaking with laughter. 'Maybe when you talk to Nanny, you should make it clear that you're talking about the saxophone.'

'What else would I be talking about?' Elliot said, innocently.

'Well, tongues can be used for lots of different things,' Isla said, lamely.

Melody snorted but turned it into a cough.

'Like what?' Elliot asked.

'Well…' Isla clearly tried to think of some child-friendly examples.

'I can touch my nose with my tongue,' Melody said, trying to rescue the situation and then demonstrated this feat.

Elliot tried and failed to do the same.

'And some people can lick their elbows, can you do that?' Melody said.

She watched Elliot try and fail to do that too. And then he set about trying to lick other body parts, his knees, his belly, his toes, giggling as he was doing it.

Since he was suitably distracted, Melody turned back to Isla.

'I didn't realise I was coming for dinner tomorrow?'

'Ah go on, what else are you going to be doing, sitting in your little cottage talking to Rocky?'

'Harsh. And you wouldn't be trying to set me up with Jamie, would you?'

'Of course not. I want dinner with my two favourite girls and Leo is always hanging around my house so of course he'll be there, so it makes sense to invite Aidan and Jamie too.'

'Subtlety is not your strong point,' Melody said. 'And who says I need your help? Maybe I'm brave enough to ask him out myself.'

Though she wasn't entirely sure she'd done that.

'And when are you going to do that?' Isla asked, watching Elliot fondly.

'I sort of did it this morning.'

Isla gave her all of her attention, staring at her in shock. Melody wasn't surprised by that reaction. Her feelings for Jamie had been ongoing for over a year now, probably a lot longer if she was honest with herself. It had started as a bit of a crush on one of her brother's friends. But every time she came down to Sandcastle Bay to visit Matthew she had fallen for Jamie that little bit more. Then, after Matthew died and Jamie had looked after her, and she'd moved down here to help Isla look after Elliot, her love for him had deepened even more. She had been promising Tori and Isla that she would ask him out for the last few months but had never plucked up the courage. And now she'd done it. Sort of.

'What exactly does *sort of* mean?' Isla asked.

'Well I asked him round to my house tonight for dinner and he said yes,' Melody said.

Isla broke into a huge smile. 'So that sounds promising.'

'I think he thought I meant, just as friends.'

'Ah, I see,' Isla said, pulling a face.

'I'm not sure what to do to rectify it,' Melody said. She looked over at Elliot and he had stopped trying to lick his knees now and was focussed on trying on every item of jewellery at the same time again. She moved closer to Isla anyway and decided to whisper the next part. 'Do I go over to the shop and say, "You know our dinner tonight, you do realise that what I actually want is for you to sweep our plates on the floor and take me on the dining table"?'

Isla laughed so loudly that Elliot looked over to see what they were talking about.

'I hope you're going to remember where each of those pieces of jewellery came from, Elliot Rosewood,' Isla said, trying to distract him. 'Because you will need to carefully put them all back before we leave.'

'I know exactly where they all go,' Elliot said, and Melody knew that he probably did. He was always good at remembering little facts and whenever she played Pairs with him, he had crazy skills at remembering where all the cards were and always beat her.

They waited until Elliot was immersed in the jewellery again before they carried on talking.

'I would love it if you did that,' Isla whispered.

Melody sighed, knowing she could never do that. It had taken her weeks to ask Jamie out and she hadn't even managed that properly.

'I guess you wait to see how he turns up tonight,' Isla said. 'If he makes some kind of effort with his clothes and not what he just normally wears, then I'd say he definitely considers it to be a date too. If he brings flowers, then that's also a positive sign. You don't bring flowers to a night where you just hang out with friends.'

'OK, take his cue, I can do that. And if he turns up in jeans and a stained t-shirt and brings a four-pack of beer, what do I do then?' The beer was probably unlikely, but the stained clothes were the norm. As an artist, he always seemed to have clay or paint on his jeans and t-shirts. It never bothered her, that was just Jamie's style, but she suddenly wanted him to turn up in a shirt or something semi-smart to show he wanted this to be a date as much as she did.

'You bring it up over dinner, you say something like, "We've been really good friends for a while now and I really, really like you. How would you feel if we were to take our friendship to the next level? Would you like to go out on a date with me?"'

'And then there can be no confusion,' Melody said.

'Exactly.'

'And if he says no?'

'Then the boy is an idiot and not worth your tears, but at least you'd know, once and for all.'

'But it would ruin our friendship.'

'It's not really a friendship if one of the friends is desperately hoping and waiting for the day that the other person will fall in love with them too. It's just a very painful, prolonged unrequited love and it really is better to put a stop to that now rather than letting it drag on and on for years.'

'That's true,' Melody said, sadly.

So tonight, she would know the truth. And it could end with her having hot sex on her dining table or losing her friend forever.

CHAPTER 4

Melody was just locking the shop door at the end of the day, when Jamie popped out of his art studio, his t-shirt and hands splattered in wet clay. He'd evidently just finished working on the potter's wheel.

'Hey,' Jamie said, stepping the short distance between their shops.

'Hey yourself,' Melody said as Rocky strained on the lead to see if Sirius was with Jamie.

They were silent for a moment and Jamie focussed his attention on wiping his hands on a damp cloth.

God, she didn't want this to be awkward between them. When she had first moved down here it had been awkward as hell every time they'd met, and she knew that was in part due to that one amazing kiss they'd shared and never spoken about since. It also wasn't helped by Jamie's aunt, Agatha, who was desperately trying to get them together every time she saw them. What would she make of this sort-of date they had tonight?

Above them, the sun was just starting its descent across the sky, painting the clouds a beautiful raspberry pink. The fairy lights strewn across the courtyard were twinkling already, casting little golden orbs of light on the cobbles. Any other time, this moment could be romantic – the sound of the waves on the shore nearby, just the two of them in this secluded little spot – but the silence had gone on too long for it to be anything but weird now.

'I, um… I'm…' Jamie tried. 'I'm looking forward to tonight.'

He glanced up, watching her closely as if searching her face for her emotions.

'I am too,' Melody said, not entirely sure where this was leading.

'It'll be fun,' Jamie said.

Her heart sank a little because, while she wanted the evening to be enjoyable, fun didn't sound like it was going to be the romantic evening she had planned. She noticed he had a splatter of clay on his cheek and without thinking she reached up to wipe it off. He blinked in surprise at her touch and then his grey eyes darkened slightly.

'We can have fun,' she said, softly, taking her time to gently remove the clay.

His eyebrows shot up.

Christ, had she just insinuated a completely different kind of fun? She was so rubbish at this dating malarkey.

'I mean, it will be fun to… hang out,' Melody said, but her voice was so breathy now with nerves that she even managed to make 'hanging out' sound sexy. She didn't want him to get the wrong idea of what the night held. As often as she had imagined what making love to Jamie would be like, she didn't know if she was brave enough to jump into bed with him on the first date. And, in reality, she didn't want the kind of relationship with him that was led by sex. She wanted love and happy ever afters.

She quickly stepped back away from him.

'Um, Melody.' He pushed his hand through his hair, leaving speckles of clay. 'About tonight…'

Oh god, he was going to cancel, she couldn't let him do that.

'We're not having sex,' she blurted out and then had to stop herself from running away and hiding from complete mortification. What the hell was wrong with her?

He stared at her and then his mouth twitched at the corners as he tried to suppress a smile.

She let out a laugh of relief and he laughed too. 'I'm sorry, I don't know why I said that. I was wiping the clay off your face and talking about having fun and I thought you might take that the wrong way and think I was offering a different kind of fun and I wasn't. That's not what tonight is about.'

Her hands were flapping around as she babbled nervously and then he reached forward and gently caught one of them in his, stilling her frantic movements.

'What is tonight about? Let's be clear so there is no misunderstanding between us. I don't want you thinking it's one thing and I turn up thinking it's something completely different. I don't want to do anything to hurt you.'

She swallowed because this was the moment to say those things that Isla had told her to say earlier. Except, right now, with his thumb ever so slightly stroking the back of her hand, she couldn't think of a single word of it.

'Well, I'll be there,' Melody said, lamely. 'And you will be too.'

He smiled. 'OK, that's a good start.'

'And I'm going to cook dinner for you.'

'OK. That's definitely cleared up what you meant by inviting me round for dinner tonight,' Jamie said.

'Has it?'

'It's as clear as mud.'

Melody laughed.

'Will there be candles?' Jamie asked.

Oh crap.

'I like candles,' Melody said, her voice strained. There was nothing casual about dinner with candles. 'So there'll probably be a few dotted around. If you're OK with that?'

He paused for the longest time before answering. 'I'm OK with candles.'

'OK,' Melody said.

'OK.'

Silence.

'So me, you, dinner, candles, no sex,' Jamie said.

'Yes, are you still looking forward to it?'

He watched her, his eyes intent on hers. He smiled, one corner of his mouth tugging up. 'Very much.'

Her heart filled with hope. 'OK then, I'll see you later.'

He stepped back and released her hand. 'Seven o'clock.'

She nodded and gave him a little wave as she left Starfish Court, but as she crossed the road and stepped out onto the beach, she knew that Jamie was watching her go.

Jamie walked back into his art studio and Klaus turned from his sculpture, eyebrow quirked.

'Well, was tonight supposed to be a date?'

'Oh yes, it was definitely a date.'

There was no doubt about that. Melody wouldn't have got that nervous about two friends hanging out together. When he'd held her hand, he'd felt her pulse skip. When she wiped the splash of clay from his cheeks, he'd seen her eyes darken. She liked him. But then he shouldn't be surprised by that.

That kiss. That one amazing kiss the year before. It hadn't been the kiss of someone seeking comfort from anyone in her grief. It had been the kiss of lust and desire and maybe even love. And he'd kissed her back. He rubbed his eyes, trying to dispel the image of her in his arms, her lips against his, his tongue in her mouth, tasting her, holding her against him. Because he should never have kissed her.

She had been a complete mess the day of her brother's funeral. She'd spent most of the night crying into her bottle of wine as he had tried to ply her with water and then made sure she got back to the hotel safely. When she had wrapped her arms around his neck and kissed him, for a few seconds he'd forgotten chivalry and taken advantage, kissing her back the way he'd wanted to do for so long. That was before he remembered that she was in no fit state to make any kind of rational decision about what she was doing. It had only lasted a few moments, but it had been seared on his brain ever since. He'd escorted her into the hotel, helped her into bed and then sat in a darkened corner of the room watching over her to make sure she wasn't sick in the night, creeping out only when the sunlight had dusted the room.

There had been no mention of it since and he had convinced himself that perhaps those feelings were never really there. Yet here they were, a year later, and he was going on a date with her.

'And did you put her straight, tell her you're not interested?'

'Nope, I have a date tonight,' Jamie said, throwing himself down at his desk.

'And you're not happy about this?' Klaus said.

Jamie thought about this. He adored Melody. The thought of dating her, of being with her in that way made his heart soar. He wanted to recreate that kiss. He wanted this.

'I'm happy.'

'Well try telling your face that.'

Jamie sighed. 'I really do want to go on this date with her but… I can't hurt her…'

'Is this really about her or is this still a self-preservation thing?'

Jamie guessed it was a bit of that too.

'Look, it doesn't have to be anything serious between you. Just have some fun.'

'It was never going to be anything but serious with Melody Rosewood,' Jamie said, not entirely sure he really could do serious again.

'Surely, it is better to give this thing a try between the two of you than pining after her for the next few years. Being friends, which means being close but never taking that next step, has got to be torture and so will watching her go off with someone else because you're not brave enough to take that risk with her.'

Jamie knew Klaus was right.

'Finding the one is hard. You fall in love and they don't love you back, they fall in love with you and you don't return those feelings. It's hard to find the perfect match but when you do, believe me, it's worth all that heartache. Go on this date tonight, give it a chance.'

'OK.'

'And for god's sake, try to enjoy it.'

Jamie knew he would enjoy his evening. Any time spent with Melody was always a good thing, even if they had suddenly taken their relationship to the next level.

Melody looked around at the candles that dotted the surface. Had she gone too far? Was it *too* romantic?

Gentle classical music was playing on the stereo and she screwed up her nose as she listened to the soft harp music. She had only downloaded that music half an hour ago to try to find something fitting for the evening, but it definitely wasn't this. This wasn't her at all. She picked up the remote and scanned through to her Westlife music, which was romantic without being clichéd. That would have to do.

The food was ready: three delicious courses were either warming or cooking in the oven, or in the fridge ready to be eaten.

Tonight was going to be perfect.

As long as they were on the same page and she wasn't entirely sure they were. He said he was OK with candles. Did that mean he was OK with the night being a romantic one or did it simply mean that he was OK with candles? God, why was she overthinking everything? This was Jamie, her friend. It was going to be fine, regardless what happened.

There was a knock on the door, sending a sleeping Rocky into a tizzy as he yapped and leapt around.

She quickly hurried to the door, took a deep breath and opened it.

There was Jamie and with the sun setting dramatically behind him he made for an impressive sight. His black curls were a little damp around his neck, like he'd not long got out of the shower. He was wearing a pale cream shirt, a black tie and a suit jacket and, though he looked incredibly sexy in it, it made her a little sad. This wasn't Jamie. He was the most relaxed, casual person she knew, and that was part of what she'd fallen in love with. As he tugged on his collar a little bit she could see that he was uncomfortable wearing it as well. She supposed she should be glad he'd made an effort. That was a good sign. Not that she cared what Jamie wore but if he cared enough to put on a clean shirt and jacket, then he cared about the importance of the evening as much as she did. She'd get him take the tie and jacket off later. Or maybe she'd take it off for him.

'Hi,' Melody said.

'You look…' Jamie paused as he looked at her. 'Lovely.'

He frowned slightly as he eyed the dress again.

She looked down at her dress, a new one she had bought the other day from a charity shop. It was a silvery pearl colour with tiny white and silver sequins sewed around the top. Why was he frowning? Had she spilt something down it? That was totally the norm for her.

'What's wrong?' Melody asked.

'Nothing, it's just… I'm pretty sure that's the dress Emily wore on her wedding day,' Jamie said, talking about his older sister.

Melody felt her eyes bulge out of her head.

Oh crap, was this really a wedding dress? No, it couldn't be. It was just on a rail with all the other dresses. She had fallen in love with the pretty sequins and she'd always loved clothes that were cream or silver or white.

'This is Emily's wedding dress?'

'Um… yeah.'

Oh god. What was he going to think of her?

'I mean, I don't think it's a proper wedding dress. It was a beach wedding. I think Emily just wanted something pretty and the right colour.'

'I didn't know. I can change.'

'Don't do that. You look lovely in it.' He smiled. 'All you need is some flowers and a veil and you'll be set.'

Melody laughed. 'I can't believe I'm standing here in a wedding dress on our first date.'

His smile faltered slightly. 'So this really is a date?'

This was going from bad to worse. He hadn't known it was a date. Well, he did now. She supposed it was better for it all to come out now rather than going through the motions of the evening and then being turned down at the end. Though what she was going to do with all the food she'd cooked and prepared, she didn't quite know. Should she invite him in for dinner anyway or was that completely redundant now?

'I thought you knew that,' Melody said, quietly.

'I sort of guessed it was and then talked myself out of it on my way over here. I wasn't entirely sure. The way you asked me this morning was very casual.'

'I… I've been meaning to ask you out for a while, had it all planned out in my head. It never came out the way I imagined.'

He smiled, sympathetically. 'It never does. You've really been wanting to ask me out for a while?'

Months, maybe even years. But she couldn't say that to him, that would make her look even sadder than she did now.

'Or hoping that you'd finally ask me out.'

He frowned. 'I'm sorry.'

'No, god, no, don't be sorry. It's not your fault if you don't have those feelings for me—'

He stepped up onto her doorstep, so he towered over her, standing so close his wonderful apple scent washed over her.

'It's not that. Believe me, it's not. I've had feelings for you for a long time. Even before Matthew died and you'd come down here to visit him. But you lived in London then, there didn't seem any point starting something with you. And then there was that kiss. I know you were drunk and probably don't even remember it—'

'I remember it. Vividly in fact.'

He stared down at her and she saw him swallow. 'I do too. I enjoyed it way too much considering I was taking advantage of your drunken state.'

'Taking advantage? I'm not some feeble little woman. I kissed you.'

'I know. That was sexy as hell. But you were so upset, and I should have been looking after you. God, Matthew would have beaten the crap out of me if he'd seen me kissing you when you were so upset and drunk. And then after, you never mentioned it.'

'You never mentioned it either,' Melody protested. This evening was definitely not going how she had planned it at all. And why was all this happening on her doorstep? It was not the backdrop she'd imagined when they declared their feelings for each other for the first time.

'I thought you might be embarrassed,' Jamie said.

'Of course I was, which was only made worse by the fact that you never mentioned it, like it was something you wanted to forget.'

'Believe me, I couldn't forget that kiss if I tried. It was… incredible.'

She stared up at him in confusion.

'So if you had feelings for me—'

'Have.'

'OK, have, and you enjoyed the kiss too, why didn't you ask me out?'

'Because I'm absolutely crap at relationships or reading women. I decided a while ago that I didn't want a relationship any more. Women get bored of me. I'm not edgy enough or mean enough. I'm too nice. I'm certainly not long-term relationship material. And I couldn't bear to date you and then see you walk away when you get bored too. And more importantly than that, the very last thing I wanted to do was hurt you. I've hurt women in the past and it's not a good feeling. I made Suzie McCallister cry. I don't want to do that to you, it would kill me. I figured it would be better for the both of us if we were to stay friends.'

'Avoiding relationships doesn't mean avoiding love; you can't stop yourself from feeling that.'

'Klaus said more or less the same thing.'

She wasn't sure what to say next. If he didn't want to take a risk with her then there really was no point continuing with the evening. But he was here. In a suit. He'd guessed it was a date and he'd come anyway.

A warm sea breeze swept in from the beach and surrounded them, catching her hair and blowing it around her. So much for taking the time to do her hair that evening. It probably looked like a bush right now.

She watched his eyes follow her hair as it blew like Medusa's snakes behind her.

'Siren,' he whispered. But then his eyes lit up as if he'd just had an idea.

'What does that mean?' She knew what a siren was, but she didn't like the implication.

His eyes refocussed on hers as if his idea had taken him somewhere else for a moment.

'It means that I think you're going to be trouble...'

She put her hands on her hips, opening her mouth to protest, but he interrupted her.

'You're standing here on our first date in a wedding dress, telling me off, and quite rightly so, because I never had the balls to ask you out. Being with you is definitely going to be trouble.' He took a step closer, pinning her against the doorframe with his weight. 'But like the sailors who follow the siren's call to their deaths, I just can't stay away from you any longer.'

He bent his head to hers and kissed her.

CHAPTER 5

Jamie gathered her against him as she trembled slightly in his arms. God, he'd never meant to kiss her tonight, that hadn't been his plan at all. He could tell Melody was as surprised as he was by the kiss but now he'd started he knew he couldn't stop. This kiss was so much better than the first one; he was no longer holding a fragile broken little bird in his arms but a fiery phoenix. The taste of her against his lips was sublime, her tongue in his mouth was the sexiest thing ever. She ran her hands round the back of his neck, touching his curls, and he lifted her so neither of them had to stretch to reach the other. Immediately, she wrapped her legs around his hips, moaning softly against his mouth. He quickly kicked the door closed and carried her to the sofa.

They fell against it, him on top of her, and he was suddenly aware of how much he must weigh against her tiny frame. Without taking his lips from hers, he tried to manoeuvre on her tiny sofa so she was on top, but she held him so tight to her, her arms and legs wrapped around him, he could barely move. Giving up, because she evidently wasn't bothered by his weight against her, he carried on enjoying the kiss. How could kissing her be so amazing? He'd kissed quite a few girls in his life, but this was something very different.

He reached up and stroked her face. Her skin was so soft. He needed her so much. Klaus was right. Denying his feelings for her was not going to make them go away; they had just intensified over the last year. And why the hell was he thinking about Klaus at a time like this?

He ran his hand up her thigh, realising as he touched her skin that her dress had a slit up the side. She was soft and warm and velvety smooth. His fingers touched the thin, wispy waistband of her knickers and she moaned against his lips. He wasn't sure if it was a moan of protest or a moan of desire, but it was enough to make him stop. There was no way he was sleeping with her tonight. He might have got carried away with this incredible kiss but if he was going to sleep with her, he was going to do it right.

He pulled away slightly and she looked up at him with those beautiful sea-blue-green eyes. He tried to steady his breathing and removed his hand from her hip so he could stroke her face again.

'Well, that was an unexpected start to our first date,' Melody said, her voice coarse with desire.

'It was the dress. It turned me on.'

She laughed. 'Someone who is scared of relationships getting turned on by a wedding dress, I don't think so somehow.'

'You looked so beautiful in it.'

'Well, it's now my new favourite, I may have to wear it every day.'

'Then I might have to kiss you like that every day.'

Her face broke into a huge grin. 'I'd like that.'

'We'd never get any work done. Your customers might be put off if I'm ravishing you like this against the wall of your shop or on the floor.'

'That's true. I'd have to take the dress off.'

Christ, he was supposed to be cooling his thoughts not igniting them.

'Definitely a bloody siren,' he said, kissing her again, just briefly this time before he sat up and disentangled himself from her arms. He slid his hands down to her waist and straightened her dress so she wasn't quite so exposed and then he offered out both hands to pull her up into a sitting position.

She took them and he hauled her up.

'Shall we continue with our date?' Jamie said.

'I don't know, I think we made some excellent headway already.'

Thankfully she got up from the sofa and headed towards the kitchen. He gave himself a few moments to catch his breath before he followed her. He took his jacket off and hung it over the back of the chair.

She started serving up mushrooms, bamboo shoots and water chestnuts onto slices of crostini. It looked and smelt delicious.

'There's wine in the fridge if you want to pour us some glasses,' Melody said.

He grabbed the bottle and poured out two glasses, bringing them to the little table, which was decorated with a solitary candle. Plenty of other candles dotted the surfaces around the kitchen and there was music playing softly in the background. He noticed something else was cooking in the oven and, judging by the number of dishes, pans and plates stacked up on the side of the sink, she had clearly been cooking and preparing the meal for many hours. She had made so much effort and it was clear she wanted the evening to go well. God, he wanted it to go well too. But he was crap at relationships, he never knew the right thing to do or say or even wear. He looked down at himself. He was sitting here in a shirt and tie for goodness sake. He never wore a tie; in fact he only owned one, which he dug out for weddings and funerals. Suddenly there was so much pressure to get everything right. It was much easier when they were just friends.

'So, that kiss...' Melody said as she brought the two small plates to the table for their starter.

She was silent for a moment as she tucked into her food, obviously hoping he would fill the gap and explain it. He occupied himself with taking a large mouthful of food. It tasted wonderful. He took another mouthful, letting the flavours seep into his taste buds. He couldn't say the kiss was a mistake, because something that amazing could never be wrong. But he knew his feelings for her went way beyond anything simple and he guessed she felt the same and so the potential for getting hurt and for hurting her was much greater. Could he really embark on a relationship? He didn't want to lose her. But he was already involved now, he'd kissed her. He couldn't walk away without hurting them both.

She was waiting for an answer.

'I really like you,' he said, though he knew that wasn't nearly enough to describe his feelings for her.

He took another few mouthfuls, making appreciative noises in the hope that that would be enough to fill the silence while he sorted out his thoughts. But after a few more minutes of him not saying anything, she moved in for the kill.

'It's just, when you arrived on my doorstep, it kind of sounded like you were trying to talk your way out of the date. And then you kissed me, grappled me to the sofa and only an incredible amount of restraint on your part stopped it from going any further.'

He cleared his throat. Not to stall for time, but because there was suddenly a tingly sensation at the back of his mouth.

'You clearly have feelings for me, but you're scared,' Melody went on.

He cleared his throat again as the tingly sensation seemed to spread, down his throat and up into his mouth. It wasn't unpleasant, but he'd had this feeling before. He took a huge swig of wine and then a large mouthful of water. He wiggled his finger in his ear, feeling like he had an itch somewhere inside he couldn't reach.

'So, are we really going to do this, are we going to date, see where it goes?' Melody asked.

The tingling was getting worse and it had now reached his lips. He could literally feel his lips swelling. He pulled at his collar, feeling suddenly hot.

'What were the mushrooms cooked in?' His voice was strangled.

'What?' Melody asked in confusion.

'What's the sauce?' Jamie said, taking another sip of water, but it made no difference.

She stared at him, obviously a bit miffed that he was changing the subject.

'It's just some Chinese stir-fry sauce. Jamie, are we...' she trailed off as her eyes widened. 'Your lips.'

He nodded. He knew they would be bigger.

'They're huge,' Melody said.

His eyes and nose were starting to water and he started scratching at his throat and face.

'Was the sauce oyster?'

'No, I know you're allergic to shellfish, I haven't got any fish in tonight's menu just in case.'

He made a humming noise with his throat, trying to stop it itching. 'Some of these Chinese sauces have oyster in the ingredients.'

She stood up and quickly moved to the side where there was an empty jar and she scanned the ingredients. Her cheeks losing all of their colour confirmed his suspicions.

'Oh god, no, I'm so sorry, I should have checked, I'm sorry,' Melody said. 'Do we need to get you to a hospital?'

He shook his head. 'No, it will pass. And I'm not being sick so it's probably only a small amount of oyster.'

His stomach gurgled and he felt suddenly very nauseous. He cursed that he had spoken too soon. Because if he was going to be sick, then there would be other bad stomach symptoms, and he definitely didn't want Melody to be near him then.

He stood up. 'I need to go.'

She looked at him in alarm. 'Go?'

'Home, I'm sorry.'

He was going to be sick and he needed to be out of there before that happened.

'No, please don't go. Just lie down on the sofa until it passes. What can I do to help, what can I get you, would Piriton or something like that help?'

He shook his head. 'I need to go, I'm really sorry.'

He didn't dare kiss her goodbye, in case he was sick all over her. He quickly opened the door and ran out onto the sand.

Melody scooped up a spoonful of the Eve's Pudding she had made and popped it into her mouth. This was her favourite dessert, it was also Tori's favourite and she had hoped that Jamie would be equally impressed, but he'd never gotten the chance to try it. Even this wasn't cheering her up right now.

Tonight had been a new low. She was used to spilling her dinner down herself or knocking a drink over and she had been a bit worried that she would probably do that during the course of the evening. She was always worried about that whenever she went out on dates with men but she had convinced herself that it didn't matter with Jamie, she felt comfortable with him, safe, and she felt sure he wouldn't care about stuff like that. But to poison the man she loved on their first date was a new level of clumsiness. He couldn't fail to be turned off by that.

She picked up her phone and dialled her sister's number.

It rang several times before it was answered and definitely not by Isla.

'This better be important,' a gruff man's voice said. 'I'm in the middle of watching the most spectacular magic show I've ever seen.'

She heard Elliot giggle in the background.

Despite everything, she smiled with love for Leo. He absolutely adored Elliot and the feeling was undeniably mutual. When she'd first met Leo on her weekend visits to see Matthew,

Leo had been a typical lad, going to the pub and getting drunk with his friends every weekend. By all accounts he'd been with a different woman every week. But all that had changed when Matthew died. Although Matthew had asked Isla to be Elliot's legal guardian if anything was to happen to him, he'd asked Leo to be Elliot's godfather and to look after him too. A job that Leo had taken very seriously. The drinking and the multiple girlfriends stopped and Melody was convinced that the latter was down to his feelings for Isla, though Isla didn't believe that. Melody wasn't surprised that Leo was at her sister's house. He'd been spending more and more time there over recent months. Isla insisted there was nothing going on between them, but Melody didn't think Leo was there just because of Elliot.

'Hi Leo,' Melody said, sadly. 'It's not really important, I just wanted a chat with Isla, but it can wait until tomorrow. I certainly wouldn't want to interrupt a spectacular magic show.'

'Melody, *you're* important,' Leo said, the gruffness gone. His voice held a softness that he normally only reserved for Isla. 'Whatever it is, Isla would want to talk to you. She's not here, she's just popped out to grab pizza for us all. Are you OK?'

'I'm fine.'

She certainly didn't feel fine. The date hadn't been anywhere near what she imagined or hoped it would be. Although that kiss was amazing. There was that.

'Didn't you have your hot date with Jamie tonight? If he's bailed on you I will personally go round and kick his ass.'

She shouldn't be surprised that Leo knew about the date. He'd probably heard from Isla or from Jamie himself, but she was always amazed that the people in the town knew more about her business than she did.

'It was the shortest date in the history of dates. I managed to poison him and he left after finishing only half of his starter.'

'Ah crap, was the starter shellfish?'

'There was oyster in the Chinese stir-fry sauce. I had no idea. I knew he was allergic to shellfish, so I made sure there was no fish in any of the food. I didn't think about the sauce. It certainly didn't mention oyster on the front of the jar.'

'Was he OK?'

'His lips swelled up, he was scratching a lot, his eyes were watering and then he bolted out of the house, though I'm not sure if that was anything to do with the allergy or the fact that I was pushing him to commit to some kind of relationship. I'm so stupid. He said he wasn't keen on getting involved with someone, but I pushed him anyway. I should have—'

'Melody, if he ran out of the house after eating oyster, I guarantee it was because he was going to be sick and didn't want you to see it, not because he wanted to get away from you.'

'You think he's being sick?' Melody asked with alarm.

'I think he'll spend most of the rest of the night in the bathroom either throwing up everything he's eaten in his entire life or sitting on the loo with his stomach being squeezed like a tube of toothpaste.'

Melody winced at that frank and gruesome image.

'Maybe I should go round, see if he's OK.'

'Hell, no. No man wants the woman they have the hots for to see them like that, it's enough to put them off for life. Give him some space tonight and I bet he will be making it up to you tomorrow.'

'What if he's really ill and needs to see a doctor? I hate to think of him alone and suffering.'

'His allergy isn't life-threatening. I'll give him a call and pop in and see him on the way home. He'll be fine tomorrow. Jamie really wouldn't want you there to see that.'

Melody sighed. What a disaster.

'Come round here, we have a ton of pizza coming,' Leo said. 'I have loads of food here that Jamie never got to eat.'

'Put it all in Tupperware containers and come round. Don't sit there alone feeling sorry for yourself.'

'I'm OK. I wouldn't want to intrude.'

'There is nothing to intrude on, believe me. Hang on, the master of illusion wants a word,' Leo said. There was a clatter as he evidently passed the phone to Elliot.

'Melody, you need to come round, we are having Hawaiian with extra pineapple and the extra-large hot gooey chocolate chip cookie for pudding. *And* I have a ton of new magic tricks to show you.'

She smiled; she never could say no to her nephew.

'OK, I'll be round in about fifteen minutes.'

'She says she's coming,' Elliot said, passing the phone back to Leo.

'Good job, buddy,' Leo said as he came back on the phone. 'Stay where you are, I'll get Isla to pick you up on the way back from the pizza place.'

Melody smiled. It would be good to not be alone tonight.

CHAPTER 6

Melody threw the last pizza crust down on her plate and sat back with her glass of wine and sighed, contentedly. There was something to be said for being around her friends and family when she was feeling down. A few slices of amazing pizza from Stefano's restaurant and a couple of glasses of wine and she was feeling all happy with the world. She glanced over at Isla who was looking slightly happier than Melody was.

'I can't believe you poisoned your date,' Isla giggled. 'I had such high hopes for the evening, you two are made for each other.'

Melody eyed Elliot and Leo as they sat in the adjoining dining room, finishing off their pizza and completely engrossed in learning how to do the next magic trick. Leo had bought Elliot a cuddly rabbit which they were going to learn how to pull out of Elliot's top hat. Isla's new puppy, Luke, was curled up at Elliot's feet.

Melody turned back to Isla. 'The evening wasn't a total loss.'

'It wasn't? It sounded like it was over before it started.'

'It was but... he kissed me.'

'Before he ran out the door to be sick? Nice,' Isla said, dryly.

'At the very beginning of our evening, before we ate.'

Isla looked at her and then put her plate down on the coffee table. 'I take it we're not talking about a peck on the cheek?'

Melody blushed as she remembered the intensely hot kiss. 'He pinned me to the wall, then carried me to the sofa where the kiss was so hot it very nearly progressed to... more,' she finished vaguely, for Elliot's benefit.

'Holy shit,' Isla whispered.

Elliot gasped and giggled. 'Isla swore.'

'Come on, buddy, let's go and practise this in your room,' Leo said, packing up the box of magic tricks. 'We don't want to give away any of our secrets of how the magic works, do we?'

'No we don't, a magician never reveals his secrets,' Elliot said.

'And it's nearly time for bed now, so we'll finish this trick and then you can brush your teeth and I'll read you a bedtime story.'

'The one with the dragons,' Elliot said, excitedly leaping onto Leo's back so he could give him a piggy-back.

'Yes definitely. I want to see how that one turns out myself,' Leo said as he carried him out the room, giving Isla a wink as they left them alone to talk. Luke yawned and sleepily followed them up the stairs.

'Leo's so good with him,' Melody said.

Isla stared after them fondly. 'I know. They spent the afternoon today on the beach practising for the sandcastle competition on Saturday. Elliot adores him.'

'And he's spending a lot of time here lately.'

'He practically lives here,' Isla said. 'He enjoys spending time with Elliot.'

'Not with you.'

'Well, yes, I suppose he does enjoy spending time with me too,' Isla said, vaguely, as she busied herself with the crumbs on her plate.

Melody narrowed her eyes. 'And nothing has ever happened between you?'

'I know you're desperate to see us married off, you're as bad as Agatha when it comes to that, but it's not going to happen.'

'That wasn't a no,' Melody said.

Isla smiled. 'Tell me more about this kiss.'

Melody stared at her sister. 'Something *has* happened between you, hasn't it?'

Isla laughed.

'Oh come on, after my terrible date tonight I need something to cheer me up, tell me some good news. Anything. I don't need details, just a tiny morsel of something happy.'

Isla took a swig of her wine and listened to the muted voices of Leo and Elliot in the room above them.

'OK, OK. God, I can't believe I'm saying this out loud, but we slept together, once, a long time ago. The night before Elliot's christening. It was just… a one-night stand with two people that were very attracted to each other.'

'Oh my god,' Melody squealed. 'I can't believe you never told me. You two had this thing—'

'It wasn't a thing. I went back to London and met Daniel who I dated for two and half years. Leo carried on sleeping with a different woman every week. There was no thing.'

Melody leaned forward. 'How was it?'

Isla laughed, awkwardly. 'It was the hottest sex I've ever had. We were at it all night, he couldn't keep his hands off me. It was wonderfully liberating.'

'And you didn't want to start anything with him?'

'Oh god, I think my heart did. My head was a little more sensible. The next day, at the christening, some woman came up to him and said she'd had an amazing night with him the night before I'd come down here. The night before he'd slept with me. I don't know why I was so disappointed by that. We weren't together in any way, so he hadn't been unfaithful. But I just thought I was obviously one of many. He was polite and friendly to the girl but after a few minutes he left her to come and sit with me. I looked over at her as he sat next to me and I could see how hurt she was by it. I felt so sad for her. Of course, I wouldn't want to hear him say how much he loved being with her and wanted to do it again, that would have killed me, but it was quite clear he had no intention of seeing her again. He was so casual with her. They'd clearly spent this amazing night together and she'd probably fallen a little bit in love with him because of it and it didn't mean anything to him. I figured if we were to continue what we had, if he even wanted to, I'd just end up like that girl, one of many that he slept with and then eventually rejected as he moved on to the next. It wasn't a great time work wise anyway. Being the head visual merchandiser in one of the biggest department stores in the world, I was about to spend the next three months travelling to different stores so I wouldn't have even been in the same country. The lead up to Christmas was always our busiest time so there didn't seem any point starting anything. He texted a few times once I'd gone back to London, but I didn't really know what to say to him, so it fizzled out pretty quickly. Every time I'd come up to visit Matthew there was this chemistry in the air between us, but nothing happened.'

'And now you live here, has anything happened since you moved down here?'

Isla shook her head.

'Except that he has asked you to marry him a hundred times.'

'That's just him wanting to keep a promise to Matthew that he would look after me and Elliot, that's not... anything serious. Leo doesn't do serious. Look, you know I'm crazy about him and I'm pretty sure he likes me and would like a round two but it's just not going to happen.'

'Why not?'

Isla sighed as she finished off her glass of wine and lay down on the sofa.

'I was with Daniel for two and half years, I thought he loved me. We'd talked about a future together, marriage, children, a little cottage somewhere. We'd even talked about maybe moving to the seaside in that way where you know it's a pipe dream but maybe, some day, one day. As soon as I told him that I would be having custody of Elliot a few days after Matthew's death, he finished with me. I know Elliot wasn't his, but we had talked about having children together. It wouldn't have been that different to having our own. In some ways it would be easier having Elliot than a baby. No sleepless nights, no dirty nappies, or late-night feeds. We had bypassed all of that. And moving here to Sandcastle Bay meant moving into a cottage by the sea, like we had always dreamed about. I know it meant I lost the job I love, but Daniel was an accountant, he could do that anywhere. I was heartbroken that he didn't want any part of my new life down here. Love is supposed to be for better or worse, no ifs and buts, and I need to know that whoever I end up with will give me that. Not just for Elliot's sake, God knows he's lost enough people in his short little life, but for my sake too.'

Melody's heart broke for her sister. If anyone needed a happy ever after it was her. Tori often teased Melody for being the eternal optimist, for wanting everyone to fall in love and have their happy ending. But Isla couldn't see what she could see. Leo was undoubtedly in love with Isla and, if she refused to see it, then a little nudge wouldn't hurt.

'You don't think Leo could give you that happy ending? He has changed, you know that. The drinking, the women. I haven't seen him with a single woman in the year since we moved here. He is here almost every day. And I doubt that's just because of honouring some promise to Matthew. Does he not deserve a chance?'

'I don't know,' she yawned, sleepily. 'I think my heart hopes for that and Elliot is completely besotted with him. I'm kind of scared of letting anything happen between us, because if he gets bored and moves on to the next woman, what would that mean for Elliot? Would Leo stop coming round here and seeing him?'

'You know Leo wouldn't do that.'

'I know.'

'Well then.'

'I just can't risk my heart on a "Marry me and I'll take care of you." I need more than that.'

Melody sighed. She was going to have to have serious words with Leo Jackson and his complete lack of romance.

'Tell me more about this kiss,' Isla said, rolling on her side to face Melody and effectively closing down the subject of her and Leo.

Melody smiled. 'It was everything a kiss should be.'

'It was hot?'

'I honestly thought he was going to make love to me right there on the sofa.'

Isla smiled. 'Well if it was as hot as you say it was, there's no way he is walking away from that.'

'I hope not. He didn't seem keen on the idea of dating or having a relationship. I think he would prefer it if we stayed friends.'

'You should offer to be friends with benefits,' Isla giggled.

Melody laughed. Usually, in the cold light of day, Isla had quite a sensible head on her shoulders, but after a few glasses of wine anything could come out of her mouth.

'Do you know me at all? I'm more of a big white wedding, fairy tale happy ever after kind of girl, not the sort that has passionate sex with my friend that leads to nowhere.'

'I'm just saying, if Jamie isn't keen on a relationship, maybe a few weeks of hot sex with you would change his mind.'

'And if it doesn't?' Melody said.

'Then maybe you would have got him out of your system.'

'Or fallen in love with him even more.'

'But if it's not going to happen, at least you would have had some great sex with the man you love, rather than no sex at all. God, why am I so obsessed with sex? Being around Leo Jackson makes me horny as hell.'

'And are you going to jump into bed with him just to satisfy that need?'

'No, because that bloody man would break my heart if he walked away.'

'Exactly,' Melody said.

Isla sighed. 'God, we're rubbish, aren't we?'

'Falling in love is never easy, is it?'

'It would be if the men we fell in love with weren't so complicated.'

'This is all their fault,' Melody said, laughing at how quickly the conversation had gone downhill, from gratuitous sex to man-bashing. Maybe it was time to go home, before she declared she was going to become a nun and take herself off to a convent.

'Men!' Isla said with a groan of frustration.

'And on that hopeless note, I'm going to go and say goodnight to Elliot and then I'm going home.'

Isla lay back on the sofa as Melody stood up. 'Bloody men.'

She met Leo coming down the stairs.

'Is Elliot in bed?'

'Yes, magic trick learned, teeth cleaned, bedtime story read and now he's tucked up in bed.'

Melody smiled, and she put a hand on Leo's shoulder. 'You're a good man, Leo Jackson. I'm a little bit in love with you.'

'Whoa there,' Leo teased. 'I like you and everything, Melody, but I just don't think we would work.'

Melody laughed and swatted at him. 'Not like that, you daft oaf. I love you for how you are with Isla and Elliot. You're good for them.'

He frowned. 'I'm not but I'm trying to be.'

'You are. I wish you could see yourself through my eyes.'

He shook his head and walked down the stairs.

She pushed open Elliot's bedroom door and he was lying in bed, his toy rabbit held tightly in his arms as he dozed. Isla was right, Elliot was besotted with Leo.

She kissed Elliot on the cheek. 'Goodnight, beautiful boy. I'll see you tomorrow.'

'Night Melody,' Elliot mumbled. 'Love you.'

'I love you too.'

She went back downstairs, into the lounge, where she saw that Leo had joined Isla and was lying next to her on the sofa.

'Men are complex creatures,' Isla said, resting her head on Leo's shoulder and wrapping an arm around his stomach.

'I think you'll find women are the complicated ones,' Leo said.

'How so?' She looked up at him and Melody saw the look of love he gave her.

'Most women just want to get married, live in a big house by the sea, have lots of children, be financially secure, but you don't want any of that,' Leo said.

Isla smiled, sadly, and then put her head back down and closed her eyes. 'I think you'll find that what most women want is much simpler than that.'

It was evident that Isla was drifting off to sleep and Melody watched as Leo kissed her on the head.

Melody stepped up and Leo looked at her and smiled.

'I'm going to go,' Melody whispered.

'I'll walk you home,' Leo said.

'No, don't, it's five minutes down the hill. I've done that walk a hundred times before. I'll be fine. Stay here and look after my sister.'

Leo smiled. 'I always will.'

Melody gave him a little wave and left the house, stepping outside into the warm night air. A million stars peppered the darkness like tiny snowflakes. The moon was shining brightly and, out in the sea, a silvery blanket danced over the waves. The pale-yellow houses were lit up with gold as lights twinkled from the windows. Other houses were sleeping, the curtains closed, lights off. Even the animals were sleeping or tucked up inside at this time of night. It was completely silent.

As she made her way back down the lane towards Sunshine Beach she automatically looked over at Jamie's house, which was shrouded in darkness.

She really wasn't sure where she stood with him. The kiss that night had been amazing but after that he hadn't really given her any hope he wanted to make a go of things. If he had planned on dating her, the fact that she had poisoned him within the first half hour of the date would probably put him off her anyway. And even if that didn't put him off, her tendency for accidents and clumsiness would soon scare him away. Maybe they really were better off being friends.

Her phone beeped in her pocket and she quickly fished it out, hoping it was Jamie. It was a message from Leo instead. She opened it up and smiled when she saw it was a photo of Isla lying fast asleep on Leo's chest, her mouth open slightly, a tiny drip of drool on Leo's shirt. His arm was around her shoulders and there was a look of resigned amusement on his face.

Looking after your sister, the message said.

She grinned. Things might be hopeless for her, but they looked pretty good for Isla, if only she was prepared to take a risk. She just had to hope that Jamie was prepared to take a risk with her too.

CHAPTER 7

Jamie knocked on Melody's door early the next morning. He had spent almost the entire night throwing up everything he had ever eaten, and he intended to spend the day sleeping it off. He still felt awful, but he was better now than he had been the night before. He wanted to tell Melody not to wait for him in their usual spot for their walk to work and to apologise for the night before. He also needed to get his phone, which was probably still sitting in his jacket pocket on the back of one of Melody's dining chairs.

She didn't come to the door.

He knocked again and this time he heard Rocky yapping on the other side but still there was no answer. It was a lot earlier than their normal meeting time so maybe she was still in bed or in the shower. He peered through the window and there was no movement at all, beyond the wagging of Rocky's tail as the little puppy stood by the front door.

He could see through to her bedroom and he could see her bed was empty.

He rubbed his hand across his face. God, he needed to go back to bed. He'd eaten some toast this morning and it was lying heavy in his stomach. He wasn't hopeful of keeping it down.

He knocked once more but there was still no response. He turned to leave but, as he got to the front gate, he stopped.

There was Melody sitting cross-legged on a paddleboard a few metres out from the shore, keeping perfectly still, not moving at all. Her hair was tied up in that cute ponytail, though the early morning breeze was still gently moving it around her shoulders.

He watched as she carefully stood up, the paddleboard barely moving at all, as she raised her arms up in the air into a point above her head, then she stretched back, reaching them behind her head so she was a perfect C shape. With her arms still stretched out, she moved her arms back over her head, out in front of her and then touched her toes.

He realised he was watching her do paddleboard yoga. He knew she'd had paddleboard lessons when she'd first come down here and she had mentioned to him that she had started doing yoga on her board. After practising normal yoga for years in London, she was evidently quite flexible.

He watched her walk her hands out in front of her and then bring one leg off the board and high in the air. She looked magnificent. She was wearing a strappy blue vest and matching tiny shorts that showed off her legs beautifully.

He couldn't help but stare as she worked her way through a multitude of positions, gracefully and with wonderful poise and balance.

His stomach suddenly churned as if the toast he'd eaten earlier was having some kind of party in there. He groaned and turned back for home.

The apologies would have to wait until later.

Melody pulled up her little anchor and then hopped down into the shallows, tugging her paddleboard behind her.

She loved doing yoga on her paddleboard; nothing could be rushed; every move was slow and considered. She would often do yoga on the beach in the mornings if the sea or tides weren't paddleboard-friendly, but today had been a beautiful calm day.

She noticed Agatha, Emily and her daughter Marigold coming down the beach towards her. Marigold was holding the lead of her puppy, Leia, who was from the same litter as Rocky and Sirius. She seemed more sedate than her brothers, walking gently at Marigold's side. Maybe she would have to ask Emily and Marigold for some tips.

Marigold waved and came running over to talk to Melody, dragging Leia behind her.

'You looked like a ballerina out there, so beautiful and graceful.'

'Oh thank you.' Yoga and paddleboard yoga felt like the only time she had any grace so it was nice that someone had noticed it, even if it was a five-year-old girl.

'I'd like to be a ballerina when I'm older,' Marigold said, doing a little pirouette and getting tangled in Leia's lead.

'I bet you'd be marvellous at that.'

'Or a racing car driver.'

Melody smiled. There were no gender stereotypes when it came to Marigold. She loved *Star Wars* as much as she loved *Frozen*, wore jeans and dinosaur t-shirts one day and pink sparkly dresses the next.

'Or maybe even a pilot, so I get to fly to different countries.'

'That all sounds great. Maybe you can do all those things.'

'Being a ballerina takes many, many years of training. So does a pilot. I wouldn't have time for both,' Marigold said, putting Melody in her place.

'Well, lots of people retrain after spending time in one career so they can be something else. You could train to be a ballerina first and then when you're older you could retrain to be a pilot.'

Marigold nodded thoughtfully. 'Can I practise on top of your paddleboard?'

'Being a pilot?' Melody teased.

Marigold laughed. 'No, silly, being a ballerina.'

'You want to do it in the water?' Melody asked as Emily and Agatha approached them.

'No, I'd get my dress wet, I'll do it on the sand.'

Melody laid the board down, fin side up so they didn't snap off in the sand while Marigold was dancing on it.

'Keep down this end,' she pointed to the nose.

'You be careful on that board, Marigold Breakwater,' Emily said. 'We don't want to break it.'

'No Mummy,' Marigold said seriously and then proceeded to dance and spin like a loon on the back of the paddleboard, sticking the odd leg out here and there and waving her arms in the air.

Melody suppressed a smile and it was quite clear that Emily was trying not to laugh as well.

'Has she done much ballet before?' Melody asked innocently.

'Not one lesson, but that obviously doesn't matter when you have enthusiasm,' Emily said, dryly.

'Am I a beautiful dancer, Mummy?' Marigold said.

'The very best, darling,' Emily said.

'So I hear you had a date with my dear nephew last night,' Agatha said. She must have been biting her tongue till now and was clearly not prepared to wait any longer to bring it up.

Melody wondered how she could possibly know. Maybe Jamie had told Emily and she had told Agatha. She glanced at Emily, who shrugged her shoulders.

'Don't look at me, she told me about it this morning, I had no idea,' Emily said.

'My friend Elsie West from the chemist was in the chocolate shop in Starfish Court last night and she saw the two of you holding hands when you left work—'

'We weren't holding hands,' Melody protested, although she remembered that Jamie had caught her hand to stop her flapping them about while she was talking about sex. Oh god, had Elsie West heard that conversation too? Was nothing private?

'And then Frances O'Toole saw him going up to your front door wearing a suit jacket and tie. She said he looked very hand-some and very nervous. He was carrying a bunch of hand-picked flowers but then he seemed to change his mind before he knocked on the door and left them in your garden instead. So it obviously was a date.'

Melody felt herself smile. He had brought her flowers. He'd thought it was a date and he had picked flowers for her.

Emily shook her head in wonder. 'Wow, you really do have spies everywhere.'

'I shouldn't need them. I would have thought Melody would have told me herself,' Agatha said, haughtily.

'Gee, I wonder why she didn't,' Emily said, sarcastically.

'Well, I know now, that's the important thing,' Agatha said. Melody sighed.

'I hear it didn't go too well either,' Agatha tutted, as if it was Melody's fault. She supposed it was in a way.

'Well no, I managed to poison him,' Melody said. It really wasn't the best start to a date and she had no idea whether there would be a second one.

'A good hostess should always check dietary requirements of their guests,' Agatha said.

'Oh shush,' Emily said. 'It's not Melody's fault. Jamie doesn't exactly tell everyone he meets about his shellfish allergy.'

'I did know, but the jar just said Chinese sauce, it didn't mention oyster at all, at least not on the front,' Melody said, exasperated.

'It will be something you'll laugh at when you're married,' Emily said, encouragingly. 'A first date you'll never forget.'

'Are you marrying Uncle Jamie?' Marigold said as she kicked her leg out in front of her like she was doing a goosestep.

'No, I'm not,' Melody said.

'Not yet,' Agatha said.

'Not ever, according to you. Who would want to marry a bad hostess?' Melody said.

Agatha waved her hand dismissively. 'I don't think Jamie is going to care about that.'

Melody rolled her eyes, wondering why she'd had the lecture in the first place.

'I just think that it's a shame you didn't get a chance to take the date into the bedroom,' Agatha said.

'Why would you have a date in a bedroom?' Marigold asked as she touched the board with her hands and stuck one leg out behind her.

'I wouldn't,' Melody said, more for Agatha's benefit than Marigold's. 'I'd prefer to *talk* to someone on my first date.'

'What do you need to talk about?' Agatha said. 'You've lived down here for over a year now, been walking to work with him every day, I think you've done all the talking you need to do. You two are moving at the rate of snails. Time to speed things up a little or at this rate you'll be having your first kiss at the age of sixty.'

Melody didn't tell her that they'd already had two insanely hot kisses, admittedly over a year apart, but still, it was something.

'I've heard he's very good in that department,' Agatha went on.

'Urgh, Agatha, that's my little brother, I don't want to hear that,' Emily said.

'I'm just saying what I've heard. All the women he's been with say he was always a bit of a surprise in the bedroom. Very sweet and nice to talk to but once they got to that stage, he was a bit of an eye-opener in terms of how skilled he was. Polly Lucas says that was the only reason she stayed with him so long.'

'That's horrible,' Melody said. Poor Jamie.

'Of course it is; Jamie is wonderful. I'm just saying that skills like that are not something to shy away from. The only real way to see if you have a connection with someone is to… try those skills out,' Agatha said, trying to be vague around Marigold. 'Talking and having meals is all well and good but friends do that and you want to be more than that. Just grab him and…' She trailed off as she clearly had an idea and started rooting around in her bag. 'I got this from the library yesterday.

I thought I might show it to Stefano to see if it galvanises him into action, he's still refusing my requests for a date at the moment. But he'll cave eventually. I think your need is greater than mine. Aha!'

She pulled a book from her bag and passed Melody a copy of the *Kama Sutra*.

Emily burst out laughing.

'This one has pictures so you can see how to do them.'

'Aren't you a bit old for picture books, Agatha?' Marigold said, finally getting tired of her impromptu dance session and coming to look at the book. Fortunately the cover wasn't too offensive, just a couple, lying together on a sofa, the remainder of their clothes covering all the important bits.

'I think some picture books can be very informative,' Agatha said, knowingly. 'Many non-fiction books have pictures.'

'I don't need this,' Melody said, trying to give it back.

'Oh, I'm sure you don't need any tips,' Agatha said. 'I'm sure you know exactly what you are doing in that department.'

Melody bit her lip, because truth be told she was a bit lacking in experience. Two men was not a lot and the first time had been very underwhelming. There had been other men, of course, but none of them had got that far.

'But this can help to spice things up a bit, give you some ideas. Polly says that Jamie really loves… having cuddles. A lot. I'm sure he would appreciate having… lots of cuddles from you too.' Agatha pushed the book back towards Melody.

'Will you leave the poor girl alone,' Emily said. 'You want the two of them to get together, not make her run for the hills. She doesn't need this pressure.'

'There's no pressure,' Agatha said. 'I'm merely suggesting she takes a look.'

Melody knew it was better to take the book, than try to argue against Agatha. It didn't mean she would look at it. Well, maybe just a little peek. She shoved the book into her bag and picked up her paddleboard.

Leia yapped and chased a bird down the beach, her lead trailing behind her like a ribbon. Marigold gave chase, yelling the puppy's name, which Leia completely ignored.

'Thanks for the book Agatha; I'll see you at lunch time Emily.' Melody turned to walk away.

'Don't keep the poor lad waiting too long, he'll have balls as big as watermelons otherwise,' Agatha said.

Melody cringed. She knew she would have to endure some of the village gossip going out with Jamie, but she didn't expect it to be as bad as this. Hopefully it would all die down in a few weeks. Or in a few days if nothing else happened between them.

Melody stood at the bottom of the hill, waiting for Jamie, but there was no sign of him. She had already been waiting for fifteen minutes but it was clear he wasn't coming.

She pulled her phone out of her bag and tried his mobile but, after ringing several times, it went through to the answer machine. He hadn't replied to her text from the night before either. Part of her knew that he was probably still feeling rough, the effects of food allergies could last for a good twenty-four hours after the event, but the other part of her was wondering whether he was avoiding her after that amazing kiss.

She hadn't got the patience for that malarkey. If he didn't want a relationship with her then he needed to be a man and say it, rather than avoiding her.

She walked along the beach towards Starfish Court, though she couldn't help but look over her shoulder every few minutes to see if he was coming. Even Rocky seemed to be disappointed with the lack of Jamie, although it was probably the lack of Sirius more than anything.

She arrived at Starfish Court and peered into his art studio to see if he had perhaps gone into work early, but there was no sign of him there and Klaus was dealing with a customer so she didn't go in and ask him.

Melody settled Rocky into his basket and then leaned on the counter, wondering what to do about the whole Jamie situation. She dialled his number again, but there was still no answer.

Worry pushed aside frustration. What if he was really sick? She should have gone up to his house to check on him when he didn't show that morning, instead of coming into work.

She picked up her phone again and dialled Leo's number.

He answered after the first ring. 'Have you rung to tell me you love me again, because I've already said, this would never work,' Leo said.

She smiled, despite everything. 'Leo, have you spoken to Jamie since last night?'

'I ended up staying at Isla's last night. On the sofa,' he quickly added but Melody couldn't help wonder if he had spent the night on the sofa with Isla. 'But I popped round to his house this morning. He's OK, still feeling the effects but he said he'd managed to keep his breakfast down so that was a good sign. He looked a bit grey, but I don't think he's going to die any time soon. He said he planned to sleep it off today as he didn't get much sleep last night.'

Melody sighed with relief.

'He says he still intends to come to Isla's tonight for dinner so I'm sure you'll see him then,' Leo said.

'OK, thanks,' Melody said, quietly. So he was alive and well enough to talk to Leo, but he hadn't called her to say he wouldn't be meeting her. But then she supposed that their walk to work was a casual arrangement anyway. 'Did he... mention me at all?' she asked and cringed as she did so. She was better than this.

Leo paused before answering. 'I didn't ask. And Jamie defi-nitely isn't the sort to kiss and tell. He could have had the most amazing sex of his life and I wouldn't hear a word of it. You know what Jamie is like, his business is his own.'

Melody knew that was true.

'I do know that he's crazy about you,' Leo said.

'How do you know that?'

'Any fool can see that. He adores you.'

But was that enough?

'Don't let some stupid spell of bad luck ruin what you two started. Talk to him tonight and then maybe have a second attempt tomorrow. Don't give up on him yet.'

'You're right. It wasn't really anyone's fault it ended so badly. I just thought he would have been in touch today.'

'He was on the sofa asleep, when I walked in and woke him up. He probably hasn't been awake enough to call you. Stop overthinking this.'

Melody knew he was right. She would talk to Jamie tonight so there was no confusion.

A customer came in then so she said her goodbyes to Leo and helped them to pick out a lovely starfish necklace before turning her attention to her design for the Great Sculptures in the Sand Festival.

Jamie's idea of using sea glass was a good one. She had a ton of that, plus she had glass cutting and smoothing tools. Mosaicking couldn't be that hard. She could just glue the pieces down onto a piece of wood and add some grout. She could get Klaus to cut her wood for her into the right shape and then she could probably add some kind of stand easily enough.

Now she just had to decide what she was going to make.

The waves weren't a bad idea either. She doodled some waves on a piece of paper and they didn't look awful.

She thought about what Jamie said about making a sculpture that represented the thing he really loved the most. What she really wanted to do was a design of her and Jamie walking along the beach together. But she couldn't do any kind of real likeness of them, especially not in glass, it would look like a five-year-old had drawn it. And would it be weird to do a sculpture of her and Jamie as the thing she loved most in Sandcastle Bay?

But then she had an idea.

Sandcastle Bay was famed for its rare heartberries, which grew on Aidan's farm. They were supposed to bring luck in love to whoever ate them. The people of the village were supposed to be the happiest loved-up people in the UK. Every year in the spring there was a big love festival to celebrate the harvest of the special berries and people would share the heartberry cake with their loved ones, as well as little tokens of love. Love was a big thing in Sandcastle Bay, and also a huge selling point to the tourists. She could do a silhouetted couple together on the beach to show the thing she loved most about the village was love, and in her heart she would know that the couple represented her and Jamie, even if no one else did.

She sketched out a few rough drawings of couples together, but they looked crap, their entwined arms seeming oversized and not anatomically correct. Maybe she could persuade Tori to help her draw something; she was brilliant at stuff like this. She would ask her later.

The shop door opened and Aidan walked in.

'Hey, have you come back to buy a second engagement ring, because normally one will suffice?'

Aidan laughed. 'Actually I wondered if I could borrow you for half an hour.'

'Now?'

'If you have time and you don't mind leaving your shop.'

It was a little quieter today, mid-week was never normally as manic as the weekends.

'Sure, why not.' Melody called Rocky, who came tearing across the shop. She grabbed her bag and stepped outside, locking the door behind her. 'What do you need?'

She crossed her fingers, hoping that he wanted help with the proposal for Tori – anything with romance and love on the agenda was definitely up her street.

'I wanted to show you where I was planning on proposing to Tori, see if you think it's OK.'

Her heart soared that she would get to be involved, but she had to be honest with him.

'If you proposed to her in your kitchen over a bacon sandwich, she would be saying yes. She is head over heels in love with you, I've honestly never seen her so happy before. As much as I would love to see a proposal with all the bells and whistles for her, she doesn't need that for her to say yes to you. Whatever way you decide to do it, it will be perfect for her because it's you.'

Aidan smiled down at her. 'You have a romantic heart, which is why I knew you'd be perfect to help me with this. I want the bells and whistles proposal for her; I want it to be so unbelievably romantic, because I think that's what she really wants. I want to do this right.'

He opened the door to his jeep for her and she climbed inside, scooping Rocky onto her lap. He walked round to the driver side and they took off down the road. It wasn't long before they reached the end of the village and he parked next to a small wooden gate, which Melody knew led to the heartberry field. She climbed out and waved at Mary Nightingale who was waiting at the bus stop. Mary looked over at them, squinting her eyes, but she didn't wave back.

Aidan held the gate open for her as she walked into the field with Rocky dancing on the other end of his lead.

Two floods had swept across the field in recent months. One had been expected as it happened the same time every year but the other hadn't and, if it hadn't been for the whole village turning out to help, Aidan would have lost his entire crop of the rare heartberry. The bushes were no more than dead twigs now, but

Melody knew that, come April and May the following year, the bushes would be overflowing with tiny red heart-shaped berries.

'So what's the plan?' Melody asked as they walked through the rows of the dead plants.

'A romantic meal, just the two of us in the place where I realised I wanted forever with her.'

'Aww, that sounds very sweet,' Melody said as they reached the part of the field where it joined Orchard Cove, a tiny little secluded beach that was only really accessible from Aidan's field.

She stepped out onto the sand with him.

'We stood here, the night of our first kiss, looking out on the sun rising, so it is a special place for us.'

'You're going to propose here on the beach?'

'In the cave actually.' Aidan gestured to the little cave at the side of the beach. Melody stepped up to look inside and Aidan flicked on a switch on a nearby generator that she hadn't spotted before. Suddenly the cave was filled with hundreds of fairy lights, glowing silver and gold in the darkness. Origami paper flowers hung from the walls like bunting and she knew that was something that was kind of their thing.

'Ahh, it's beautiful,' Melody gasped.

'Is it, is it OK?' Aidan said, nervously.

'It's perfect.'

'I thought about doing it on the beach, but the cave is so protected from the elements. I've been down here at high tide and the water barely goes into the cave at all so I can get all this stuff ready and it shouldn't be affected by the weather or sea. I'm going to bring a table and chairs down here tomorrow and I have a double-bean-bag-type bed thing so we can lie here and watch the stars after dinner. I thought I would propose as soon as I bring her down here and then we can just enjoy the meal and the evening, just the two of us.'

'It sounds wonderful,' Melody said, dreamily. 'She will love it.'

'Good, I'm glad you like it,' Aidan said. 'I was wondering if I could ask a favour.'

'Of course.'

'She absolutely loves your Eve's Pudding; would you mind making some for us for tomorrow night?'

'I would love to,' Melody said.

'I'll have a warmer down here, so if you can drop it off around eight o'clock and then I'll probably bring her down about half past.'

'Great, shall I make some custard too?'

'If you don't mind.'

'Absolutely. Oh, I'm so excited. I can't believe tomorrow night Tori will be engaged.'

'She has to say yes first.'

'She will, I guarantee it.'

Aidan bent to turn off the generator. 'I hope she doesn't think it's too soon.'

'When you've found the one you want to spend the rest of your life with, why wait?'

Aidan walked out of the little cave and Melody followed him back into the field, with Rocky barking at a nearby bird.

'She was scared of getting involved in a relationship when she came here, we both were, but I know she belongs here now, with me. We were meant to be together, I just hope she sees that too.'

'She does, she loves you.'

Aidan nodded, a frown on his face as he escorted her back to the jeep.

They were silent as they drove back to the shop. Aidan was clearly deep in thought and she hoped he wasn't suddenly having second thoughts about the proposal.

'Don't doubt what you have,' Melody said as he pulled up outside Starfish Court.

He nodded. 'Thanks Melody, I'll see you tonight and remember, not a word.'

She crossed her heart and zipped across her lips for good measure and Aidan laughed.

She hopped down from the car and he drove off.

The love lives of her best friend and sister were slowly coming together, she just needed to sort out her own now.

CHAPTER 8

Melody knocked on Isla's door later that evening and she could hear lots of voices from the other side. Elliot opened the door, still wearing his top hat, and gestured for her to come in like a butler would do. Obviously, the hat had other uses beyond magician.

'Thank you, kind sir,' Melody said.

'May I take your coat?' Elliot said, trying to put on a posh voice.

'I'm not wearing one,' Melody giggled.

Elliot looked down at Jamie's jacket, which she was holding.

'Oh well, this isn't mine, but you can take it and hang it up anyway,' Melody said, handing him the jacket.

Elliot folded the jacket carefully over his arm and then gestured for her to follow him into the kitchen. Luke, Elliot's puppy, raised his head from the basket, saw that it wasn't anyone interesting and went back to sleep again.

'Miss Melody Rosewood has arrived,' Elliot announced loudly. Evidently Isla had him very well trained or they had been watching episodes of *Downton Abbey* together.

Isla and Leo were there and they were happily chatting to Aidan and Tori, but there was no sign of Jamie. It wasn't a direct route for her to go past Jamie's house on the way to Isla's, but she could see it from the road and there hadn't appeared to be any movement from inside to indicate he was still there. She had considered knocking on his door to check, but she had already texted and phoned him that day; knocking on his door as well looked a bit too stalkery.

Isla greeted her with a hug. 'You snuck off last night without saying goodbye.'

'You were asleep and in very safe hands,' Melody smiled.

Isla blushed a little and then turned her attention back to the curry she was cooking.

Tori and Aidan gave her a hug, Aidan giving her a little wink, reminding her of the secret they were sharing.

Leo gave her a hug too and whispered in her ear, 'He'll be here.' She smiled.

'Would Madam like a nacho?' Elliot said, formally. His hat had taken on a bit of a wonk, slipping over his eye, but like a true professional he wasn't going to let that affect him delivering the snacks.

She straightened his hat and took a handful of nachos, before he moved through the others, offering the bowl. Leo tapped the hat so it fell over his eyes again and Elliot went round offering the bowl of nachos to the others, clearly not being able to see. Isla took the hat off and popped it on the side before he injured himself and gave Leo a mock scowl.

'So are you all ready for the Great Sculptures in the Sand Festival on Sunday?' Melody asked.

'Ours is going to be amazing,' Elliot said. 'It's going to be a sea horse; not a proper sea horse but a horse made from the sea. It's going to be made from giant waves and will have lightning and fire and it's going to change colour so it looks like the clouds in a storm. We decided that the thing we love the most is the sea when it's stormy and churning with big crashing waves and thunder and lightning over the sea.'

'That does sound amazing,' Melody said. 'Is Leo helping you with this?'

'Yes.'

'Then I have no doubt it will be the best sculpture on the whole of that beach.'

Leo was crazy talented when it came to big models like this. In the spring, there had been a boat race event as part of the

Heartberry Love Festival where everyone had made their own boats. Leo's had been a giant water dragon that shot fire from his mouth and had wings that moved. It had been incredible. He owned his own firework display company, so he was a complete expert on pyrotechnics and utilised those skills whenever he could.

'Isla is helping us too and on Saturday we are going to take part in the Great Sandcastle competition together because we're a family,' Elliot said, excitedly.

Tori smirked at Isla and Melody arched an eyebrow.

Isla quickly waved it away. 'I think he thinks that because Leo is here all the time.'

'No, Marigold says we're a family,' Elliot said.

'Did she?' Aidan said. 'I may have to have words with my niece.'

'Marigold said that although I don't have a real mummy or daddy any more, Isla was like my mummy and Leo was like my daddy.'

'Oh no honey, Leo is wonderful and we're so happy to have him around, but he isn't...' Isla trailed off, awkwardly.

There was silence in the group. This was not a conversation to be had in front of everyone and Melody didn't know what to do or say to change the subject. She felt for Isla, as she visibly battled with not wanting to offend Leo with everything he did for Elliot, but not wanting to give Leo that label and responsibility if he didn't want it.

'I know he's not my daddy, Daddy is in heaven,' Elliot said, patiently. 'But Marigold said he was like my daddy because he came to the Daddy Day at school last week.'

Leo swore softly. 'And we agreed we wouldn't tell Isla, didn't we buddy?'

Isla stared at Leo. 'You went to Daddy Day?'

Leo cleared his throat awkwardly. 'I'm not trying to take Matthew's place, that's not what this is. Elliot said that everyone was bringing their dads to school last week and said he didn't have anyone to come in with him. And then he asked me if I would go instead.'

'You didn't have to—' Isla started.

'I know. But I couldn't bear the thought of him sitting there with no dad beside him.' Leo's voice broke a little.

Melody wanted to hug him. The grief for Matthew had affected them all and it hit them unexpectedly sometimes. She felt tears prick her eyes at this wonderful kind gesture from him.

'I was going to keep him off school that day as I didn't want him to feel left out,' Isla said. 'They were only going to play games and things so I knew he wouldn't miss out on anything important. Thought we'd go out for the day but he was insistent he really wanted to go. Now I know why.'

'I thought you'd be angry,' Leo said.

Isla shook her head and it was evident she was holding back the tears as well. 'I'm not angry at all. I just… We're… I feel very lucky to have you in my life.'

Tori grabbed at a tissue box, handed one to Isla and quickly took one herself.

'Have I made you sad?' Elliot asked Isla.

'No you haven't, honey,' Isla laughed through her tears.

Elliot turned to Leo. 'You should give her a hug. When I'm sad a hug from you always makes me feel better.'

Aidan grabbed a tissue for himself and theatrically dabbed it at his eyes. Melody giggled at him as he tried to lighten the mood.

'I don't think…' Leo started but Elliot had already taken his hand and led her over to Isla.

Leo wrapped Isla in his arms, holding her close, and Elliot put his arms around them both.

Melody thought her heart might actually burst as she watched them together. They *were* a family, even if Isla wasn't keen to define them as such. She glanced over at Tori as Aidan slid an arm around her shoulders. She couldn't be happier that her sister and best friend had good men in their lives, but it did seem to make the ache in her own heart hurt a little more.

As Leo continued to hold Isla, Aidan grabbed the nachos. 'Shall we go and sit down?'

Melody nodded her agreement and left the little makeshift family to hold each other in the kitchen. She moved into the dining area which was around the corner from them.

Aidan sat down with Tori, and Melody sat opposite them.

'What are you two making for the sculpture competition?' Melody asked.

'Well, making cakes and tarts is more my forte than any kind of sculpture,' Aidan said. 'And we all saw the terrible boat I made at the Heartberry Love Festival in the spring, but thankfully making models is right up Tori's street.'

'We're making a heartberry. A large version of Max actually,' Tori said, speaking of the main character in the animated adverts she had been making for the farm. 'It was the heartberries that brought us together so it's definitely the thing we love most about Sandcastle Bay.'

'What about you?' Aidan asked Melody.

'I thought I would make something to represent the Heartberry Love Festival,' Melody lied. Well, it was only a slight lie. 'I'm making a mosaic couple out of sea glass. Tori, I wanted to ask you whether you'd mind drawing me a few couples, maybe one walking hand in hand and one kissing and hugging, and I can then get a wooden template made for my mosaic.'

'Oh no problem, I can do that now.'

Tori grabbed her sketchbook, which she habitually carried around with her in her bag, and started sketching out a few different couples, her hand flying across the page as she added different details.

'OK, food is ready,' Isla said, bringing in a big bowl of curry, visibly brightened after her big hug with Leo. Clearly Elliot was right; hugs from Leo seemed to have medicinal properties.

Elliot trailed after her with a plate of naan breads and Leo followed with a big bowl of rice. Plates and cutlery were already on the table as everyone started helping themselves and then sat down, leaving an empty seat next to Melody.

Jamie clearly wasn't coming.

'And after the meal, Elliot has a spectacular magic show to share with you all,' Isla said.

'Great food, great company, great entertainment. What more could we want?' Aidan said.

Suddenly there was a knocking on the door. Isla got up to answer it, winking at Melody.

She opened the door and Jamie stepped in.

'I'm so sorry. I overslept, then I took a shower to freshen up.' He hugged Isla, briefly, his eyes finding Melody's over Isla's shoulder as if the apology was more for her than for Isla.

'It's OK, we've just sat down. Apart from an embarrassing episode a few minutes ago, where Leo made me cry, you haven't missed anything.'

Leo cursed softly again.

'Well, I won't ask you to repeat the episode. I'm not insensitive like my brother,' Jamie said. He moved into the dining area and kissed Tori on the cheek and then gave Melody a brief peck on the cheek too.

Melody didn't even know what to do with that. Twenty-four hours before, they had been lying on her sofa, kissing so passionately that she'd thought it was going to move to the next level, and now he was here, after not talking to her all day and giving her a polite kiss on the cheek. Of course he wouldn't grab her and kiss her passionately again in front of everyone, but she still hoped that there would be more than a peck later and she'd thought he would give her more of a sign that there would be.

He looked better than the last time she'd seen him, still a bit pale, but certainly not grey like he'd been when he'd ran out of her house the night before. He also looked a bit more relaxed too. No jacket or tie. Just a pale blue shirt that was rolled up at the sleeves and open at the collar. He obviously wasn't as uncomfortable with friends as he was when he was with her.

That made her feel a little sad.

Jamie dished himself up some food and Melody offered him the plate of naan breads. He took one.

She took a forkful of curry and popped it in her mouth, noticing to her horror that she had spilt a drip of the bright orange sauce down her top. She cursed softly. Why now, when her relationship with Jamie seemed to be hanging in the balance? She grabbed a napkin and started wiping at her top and noticed Jamie was suddenly doing the same. She glanced over at him in shock. She'd never had him down as being clumsy before but, sure enough, there was a small drip of curry down his shirt too. Had he done it deliberately to make her feel better? Or was it just an accident? Either way, her heart filled a little with love for him. When it was apparent the sauce wasn't coming off his shirt, he shrugged and turned his attention back to his curry and then fixed her with a meaningful gaze that quite plainly told her that the curry down *her* top didn't matter either. She purposefully put her napkin down and turned her attention back to him.

'So, how are you feeling?' Melody asked quietly as conversations continued across the table.

'Better, I've slept most of the day,' Jamie said.

'I'm so sorry.'

'Don't be, it wasn't your fault.'

Melody tore off a chunk of naan bread and dipped it into her sauce, not entirely sure what to say next. Why was it suddenly so awkward? They had been really close friends for the last two months; they had seen each other practically every day. They'd talked and laughed and it had never been awkward then. Now it was difficult.

'I brought your jacket.' Melody gestured over her shoulder.

'Oh good, my phone is in the pocket.'

Melody stared at him, pennies dropping into place. 'You left your phone at my house?'

'Yes, which has been a right pain. I couldn't phone you and I didn't have your number to call you from the landline. I even tried to call my own phone in the hope you would pick up, but I'd turned it to silent before I got to your house last night, I didn't want anything to disturb our evening.'

'Oh.' Her little bruised and fragile heart was suddenly healing.

He looked at her. 'You tried to call me, didn't you?'

'Yes, twice. I was worried. I wanted to know if you were OK and…' she trailed off.

'If we were OK?' he finished for her.

'Yes.'

'I came round this morning,' Jamie said.

'You did? When?'

'It was early, you were paddleboarding. I watched you from the beach, you looked… magnificent.'

She stared at him, a lump forming in her throat. 'Why didn't you come and talk to me?'

'You were completely absorbed. And I didn't want to do anything to cause you to lose your balance. Besides, I was still feeling rough and I had to rush home because I thought I was going to be sick again. I'm sorry I missed you and caused you to worry all day.'

The others were all laughing over a story that Tori was telling them and she got the impression that Isla and Tori were talking extra loudly so that she and Jamie could have some privacy.

She was aware that their curries were going cold as they continued to stare at each other. He hadn't been avoiding her at all. He'd even come to see her. So what happened now?

He slipped his hand into hers underneath the table, effectively answering the question. Her breath caught in her throat.

'Did you think I would walk away from you? Last night was incredible,' Jamie said, quietly.

She frowned in confusion. 'I poisoned you and made you sick.'

'And that kiss was the most amazing kiss I've ever had. There was no way I was walking away from that.'

'So... we're dating? We're really doing this?'

'Yes, if you still want to date a man who throws up at the merest sniff of oyster or any other shellfish.'

Melody smiled. 'We can't all be perfect.'

He laughed and she squeezed his hand.

'I want this to work, I really do,' Jamie said. 'I'm crap at relationships and knowing what to do or say with women. So I'm going to do my best to get this right.'

'I don't want you to change for me; I don't want you to wear a suit to go on a date with me, I want you to be comfortable. I don't want you to have to second-guess what you're saying or constantly be worrying about making the best impression on me. We were friends before anything happened between us and you were relaxed around me then. Things don't need to change. We can still be friends, but we'll be friends who kiss, and go on dates and spend time together and we'll talk and laugh like we've always done and if things go well... maybe there'll be *more...*' she trailed off, leaving what the 'more' would be to his imagination.

'I especially like the sound of that last bit.' He sexily ran his finger over her wrist. God, just that simple touch made her pulse race and he smiled because he felt it too. 'So... friends with a side order of dating?' he asked.

Melody cringed a little inside because it sounded like she had just agreed to friends with benefits and that wasn't what she wanted at all. She wanted to say that maybe if this *friendship* worked then one day they would get married and promise to be friends forever. But it was way too soon to think about that. He was scared of having any kind of relationship at all. It could end

in disaster after just a few weeks. She didn't want to scare him off
with talks of marriage and forever. And she'd never really had any
kind of serious relationship before either. She had dated several
men, some of them for a few months, but she'd never been in
love before, never thought that the men she'd dated were going
to be the one she would be with forever. Until now. This felt
different and exciting and she wanted to do it right. They had to
go slowly, she knew that. Maybe if he relaxed enough, he might
actually enjoy what they had enough to want to take it further,
to want to be in a serious relationship with her, and then they
could see where it led.

'Well, the dating will be the starter, the main course and the
dessert. The friendship will just be the plates and bowls the dating
is served on,' Melody tried, really not wanting to agree to friends
with benefits. 'We'll just take things slowly and you're going to
try to relax.'

'OK,' he nodded.

She wanted to reach out and stroke his face, but she knew
how much of a private person he was.

'I so want to kiss you right now,' Melody whispered.

'Believe me, when we leave here and I walk you home, we'll
be doing just that.'

Her heart soared, her stomach doing butterflies at that thought.

To her surprise, Jamie put an arm around her and pulled her
into him, kissing her head. She couldn't help the smile from
erupting on her face.

'Finally!' Isla said, holding up her glass across the table in
celebration. Melody laughed but she couldn't help echoing that
sentiment. Maybe, finally, her own love life was getting sorted too.

CHAPTER 9

They said their goodbyes to the others and then Jamie took her hand and started walking down the hill. It was a perfect night. The moon was shining over the sea, adding a silvery glow to everything it touched.

'That was a long night,' Melody said. 'I love hanging out with them but all I really wanted to do was kiss you again.'

Jamie quickened his pace. He needed to kiss her too. It had taken all his willpower to focus on the conversations around the table and not what it would be like to have his lips against hers again, to feel her body in his arms.

The thought of that now spurred him on to move quicker.

'Where are we going?' Melody asked as she jogged a little to keep up with him.

'Your home.'

'And why are we going there so quickly?'

'I really need to kiss you.'

He pulled her onto the beach and she tugged him to a stop. 'So kiss me.'

He turned to look at her. 'I kind of intended to do it somewhere a bit more private.'

It was dark down here on the beach, making them seem cut off from the rest of the world, but she seemed to glow in the darkness, the moonlight catching her skin, caressing her hair and causing her eyes to sparkle with mischief.

She stepped up to him, so her body was warm against his and he put his hands round her waist, holding her against him.

'Are you planning to take me home and make love to me, Jamie Jackson?'

He swallowed. She was teasing him, he knew that. There was a huge part of him that wanted nothing more than to do just that, but he wanted to get that part of their relationship right if nothing else.

'No, I... don't think we're there yet, it's too soon.'

'You have rules for when you sleep with a woman?' Melody played with the top button of his shirt.

Usually his rule for when he slept with women was whenever the woman instigated it or made it crystal clear that she wanted it. He'd never really thought there was a right or wrong time to have sex in a relationship before. But this thing with Melody, however she wanted to define it, was important, he knew that. He wanted her to trust him completely. He wanted it to be the natural next step to their close and wonderful friendship. He didn't want to rush things between them because of lust and need. Although there was a lot of that coursing through his veins right now.

He held her closer. 'I think if we're going to be friends who make love, there need to be certain rules for that.'

'What are the rules?' She popped open the button and placed a gentle kiss on his chest.

His mind went blank. He had no idea what rules there should be, all he could think about was her mouth on his chest. He stroked his hand through her hair, wondering why he was holding back from this. They had been friends for a while so maybe they had already done the early stages of a relationship, the getting to know each other and finding out if they were compatible. She trailed her mouth up to his throat as he tried to hold onto his self-control.

'I don't know... I'm sure they were good rules,' Jamie said, his voice rough.

Melody laughed. 'OK, I have rules too. We kiss often, whenever the feeling takes us.'

'Good rule.'

'There should be dancing, on the beach, under the stars.'

'I can do that.'

'Public displays of affection. If we're together, I'm not going to hide it. I'm not talking about having sex in broad daylight on Sunshine Beach, but if I want to hold your hand or hug you, I want to be able to do it. I don't care what the people of the town make of that, or Agatha or anyone else. I'm not going to pretend that we're just friends.'

Jamie wasn't totally happy with that. He preferred that any affection was behind closed doors. All of his previous relationships had been very private. He hated the townspeople talking about his life. But they were going to talk about them whether they were open about their relationship or not. Past experience had proved that. He was quite sure half the village already knew about their date the night before. And he liked the idea of holding hands with Melody so he wasn't going to say no to that.

'OK,' he said.

'And we're honest with each other,' Melody said.

'These are good rules, but my rules were more about... protecting you and what we have. I don't want to lose you and the very last thing I want is to do anything to hurt you. I want to do this right. I don't want to rush into this and ruin what we have.'

She nodded. 'I think taking it slowly is definitely the right thing to do. This is all new for us in many ways and, while we know each other well, we don't know each other intimately and when that happens, everything changes between us. I'd be lying if I said I'm not nervous about that part.'

He didn't want her to be nervous. He hated the thought of that.

'Why are you worried about it?'

'What if it's crap? I've slept with two men in my life and you've slept with... a lot more than that.'

'I haven't slept with any men.'

Melody laughed and he liked he could put her at ease.

'You know what I mean,' she said.

'Seven.'

'Seven men?' she teased.

He grinned. 'I don't think that's a lot. Certainly not enough to put me in the *experienced* camp. I'm confident that I know which bits go where.'

'Well that's a good start,' Melody giggled.

'I'm not really selling this, am I? If I was Leo I'd probably say something like, "Baby, I'm going to rock your world," or "I'm not going to stop until you've had twenty orgasms." But all I can say is the women I've been with seemed to enjoy themselves so I must have been doing something right. I hope you don't think it's crap.'

'What if we have zero chemistry?'

He smiled. 'That's one thing I'm definitely not worried about. After that kiss last night, we can absolutely put that fear to bed.'

She grinned. 'It was pretty hot, wasn't it?'

'Smoking.' God, he wanted a re-run of that kiss. He wanted to hold her body against his and kiss her until every fear and doubt in her mind drifted away.

'Let's do it again, here, now, under the stars,' Melody said.

Hell, he didn't need to be asked twice. He bent his head and kissed her.

She wrapped her arms around his neck and kissed him back. His heart soared, filling with so much joy and excitement. This was what kissing was supposed to be like. He ran his hands up her back, stroking her body. She slid her hands down his arms and round his shoulders. As she ran her tongue inside his mouth, he lifted her against him. But as she shifted her legs around him, he stepped back a little and stumbled in the sand, taking her with him as he landed flat on his back with her on top of him.

She barely took her mouth off his, though she did giggle a little against his lips. He ran his hand through her hair, feeling the silky softness slide against his fingers. She gave a little moan and the sound of it sent a kick of desire straight to his stomach.

He rolled so he was on top of her. As he ran his hand up her side and his fingers grazed against warm, bare flesh, he realised that her strapless dress had slid down and she wasn't wearing a bra.

The kiss continued, but he had no idea what to do with his hand. His brain battled with doing the decent thing and pulling her dress back up or doing what he wanted to do and stroking his hand across her breast. His desire for her won out and he filled his hand with her breast, stroking the nipple with his thumb.

'Oh god, Jamie,' Melody groaned. Her need for him was so clear with those words. It was such a turn-on. He kissed her bare shoulder and then kissed her breast.

Suddenly, a bright light was shone on them and Jamie looked up, blinking into a torchlight as he quickly yanked Melody's dress back up so she was decent.

'What's going on here then?' a man said, and Jamie recognised the voice of Trevor, the part-time village policeman.

Melody giggled as she no doubt recognised his voice too.

'Nothing Trevor, I mean, Officer,' Melody said. 'I just fell over in the sand and, um… Jamie was helping me back up.'

There was no way Trevor was buying that; Jamie had had his mouth on her breast for goodness sake. They couldn't even claim he was giving her CPR with those actions.

'It certainly didn't look like that from where I was standing,' Trevor said, obviously taking his job way too seriously. 'There are a number of laws surrounding having sex in public places. Outraging public decency is a law protecting the public from seeing lewd behaviour and—'

'Trevor, we were kissing, we're not having sex, not even close,' Jamie said, getting increasingly frustrated. He wouldn't have minded being told off for having sex if he'd actually been doing it. But all he could think of was that Trevor had interrupted the best kiss of his life.

'There are laws surrounding indecent exposure as well but, as I didn't see any genitals, I'm prepared to let you off with a warning,' Trevor said.

Under him Melody's giggles got louder, her whole body shaking.

'I suggest you get yourselves off home and in future, if you want to have outdoor sex, do it in your garden or somewhere that you are not likely to offend anyone.'

'Sorry for offending you with our kissing,' Melody said, clearly not taking this remotely seriously.

'I'll be having words with your mum about this, Miss Rosewood,' Trevor said, obviously not amused at being laughed at.

'My mum?!' Melody said, incredulously. 'I'm thirty-one. I don't think I'm going to worry about being grounded or losing my pocket money anytime soon.'

Jamie stood up and hauled Melody to her feet. 'Come on, let's go home.'

He didn't want to push Trevor any more in case he found reason to arrest them after all.

Melody was still laughing. 'And I'm not scared Santa is going to leave coal in my stocking either.'

Jamie put his arm around her shoulders and ushered her down the beach. Trevor watched them go, obviously to make sure that they didn't sneak off and have mad passionate sex anywhere else.

'Can you believe him?' Melody said when they were out of hearing distance. 'Did you know he's apparently going out with my mum?'

Jamie laughed. 'No I didn't, but at least this will give them something to talk about on their next date.'

Melody groaned. 'Why would my mum go out with someone as serious as him? I'd love to see her happy again, I just don't see that Trevor is going to do that.'

'He's a nice bloke, I think he's just a bit bored in his job, nothing happens down here. There is almost no crime in Sandcastle Bay, so whenever there's even the tiniest sniff of some wrongdoing, Trevor pounces on it.'

Melody grunted with annoyance. 'He stopped the most incredible kiss I've ever had. He's not exactly high up there on my list of favourite people at the moment.'

'Don't worry, there will be plenty more where that came from.'

'There better be.' She was silent for a moment. 'Is it wrong that I really want to have outdoor sex now?'

Jamie laughed. 'I'm sure we can find somewhere a little more secluded, when the time is right.'

He walked her to her front door and could hear Rocky yapping with excitement at having his owner come home.

She opened the door and scooped the puppy up in her arms, his whole body wagging with happiness. Jamie knew how he felt at being wrapped in her arms.

'Do you want to come in?' Melody asked.

He stepped up close and gave her a brief kiss on the lips. 'I really want to, which is why I think I'd better not.'

'Scared I might be into whips and handcuffs?' Melody teased.

'Scared you might pounce on me the second the door is closed and take advantage of me.'

She laughed. 'There might be an element of that. Though I think you could look after yourself.'

He wrapped his arms around her and gave her another brief kiss. 'Do you think I could possibly say no to that, turn down your advances? I'd be powerless to resist your wiles and the next morning I'd feel all dirty and used but very very happy.'

'Doesn't sound so bad.'

'Sounds amazing. Goodnight, my siren.'

She reached up and kissed him before she stepped into the house and, with a smile, she closed the door.

He leaned his forehead against the door for a second and sighed. God, being with her was going to be trouble and he was loving every single second of it.

CHAPTER 10

Melody was helping a customer the next day when Jamie walked in. She couldn't help the little flutter in her heart at the sight of him, which was crazy as she'd only seen him a few hours before when they'd walked to work together hand in hand along the beach. He'd kissed her goodbye before she went into her shop and everything just felt so perfect between them.

He winked at her and then pretended to browse. She smiled and tried to turn her attention back to her customer, who was having trouble choosing between a sea-horse necklace made from opal, or a starfish necklace made from turquoise.

'These are so beautiful, I really do like them both,' the woman said. Melody hadn't seen her before so she was probably a tourist. Most of her customers were unless it was someone from the village buying a gift for someone.

Jamie sauntered over. 'They're both very pretty.'

The woman looked up at him and her eyes visibly lit up at the sight of him. Melody smirked. He was very sexy and she knew a lot of women found him attractive, although that hadn't been what had drawn Melody to him. She had been attracted to his kindness, his sweet nature and his warmth more than anything else.

'Are they for you?' Jamie went on.

'Yes, a reminder of my lovely holiday down here.'

'Well in that case I think you should buy both,' Jamie said. 'Then you can alternate between the two for different outfits and always carry a piece of Sandcastle Bay with you, wherever you go.'

The woman looked at the necklaces and nodded. 'You know what, I think you're right. I'll take both.'

Melody smiled and rang up the sale and the woman left the shop, giving Jamie a little wave as she went.

Jamie waved back and immediately turned his attention back to Melody before the shop door had even closed.

'You're so smooth,' Melody said.

'Hey, I got you a sale, didn't I?' Jamie said, leaning over the counter and giving her a sweet kiss.

Melody smiled against his lips. 'Can I help you with something or did you just come in here to pester my customers?'

'You can actually. I'm looking for two gemstones, the same size, roundish, but I'm looking for an exact shade of blue.'

Jamie had bought different gemstones for his sculptures before so this wasn't an unusual request.

'OK, I have lots of different blue stones that I haven't used in any designs yet. What kind of blue are you looking for?'

She pulled out her box of stones, all laid out in different colours, and she started sorting through them with her finger.

'Blue-green like the sea.'

'OK, sparkly and polished like a sapphire or more of a flat colour like a piece of turquoise?' She indicated the two stones.

'Sparkly definitely.'

'OK.' She picked out a few different ones. 'We have blue topaz, spinel, zircon… The smithsonite has a nice blue-green hint.'

He stared at them but clearly wasn't convinced any of them met his needs.

'What about that one?' He pointed to one that had shades of blue and green but also streaks of purple and turquoise too. It was beautiful and one of her favourite stones. She was almost loath to give it away as she didn't get them very often. She knew she only had four or five of these left. She pulled it out anyway and laid it on the counter.

'This is called a mystic topaz and probably my favourite stone.'

He looked up at her and smiled. 'That is exactly what I'm looking for. Do you have two the same colour and size?'

She sorted through her box and pulled out one triumphantly. 'There we go.'

He smiled as he stared at them. 'These are perfect. Actually, do you have a third one a bit smaller?'

She looked through the box and pulled one out and laid it next to the other two to check for size. It was about half the size of the previous two.

The shop door opened again and Melody looked up, surprised to see her mum walking in. It had been over a year since she had opened her shop in Sandcastle Bay and her mum hadn't been in once.

She waited for her to look around, to perhaps make some comment about the shop or even for her to say something positive or even remotely nice about her jewellery, but she didn't.

'Hello Melody, how are you?' her mum said, trying to force a small smile onto her face.

'I'm fine, Mum, how are you?' Melody said. She could be civil too.

'I'm OK,' her mum said. She was always OK, never good or great, just OK. Either that or she had a list of moans a mile long. Today was obviously a good day.

There was an awkward silence for a moment or two and Jamie bravely stepped in and filled it.

'Hello, Carolyn.'

'Hello Jamie, how's it going over in the studio?'

'Good, business is good,' Jamie said.

'That's good,' her mum said.

God, this was awkward. Melody wondered if her mum knew she was dating Jamie or if she even cared.

'You know, I saw one of your sculptures the other day, in... a friend's house. You really have a wonderful talent.'

Melody felt a tiny stab of jealousy at that. She loved it when people complimented Jamie's sculptures; he was so talented and deserved any praise that was aimed his way. But this was the first positive thing she had heard her mum say in years and it was directed at someone else, not her.

'Is there something I can help you with?' Melody said, and she knew her tone of voice was cool.

'I just popped in because it's your Aunt Rosa's birthday next week and I was going to send her something. She likes jewellery. You sell jewellery, so…'

'You think Aunt Rosa might like something I make?' Melody said, and she knew she was fishing for some sliver of a compliment.

'She has very quirky, eccentric tastes and so do you. I'm sure you can help me find something suitable.'

Nope, not even a glimmer of a compliment was coming her way.

Melody took a deep breath. 'Aunt Rosa likes big statement rings, maybe you'd like to choose something from one of the cabinets over there.'

Her mum wandered off to have a look and Melody watched her for any sign of approval. Of course there wouldn't be, because her mum wouldn't be seen dead in a big oversized statement ring, or most likely in any of the jewellery that Melody made. Sure enough, she saw her mum wrinkle her nose with distaste.

She felt the stab of hurt in her heart.

She glanced at Jamie, who was hovering awkwardly. He must feel the tension between them. She had spoken to him a little about her relationship with her mum before.

Jamie walked over to the cabinet next to her mum. 'I love these rings, they're so expressive and bright and fun.'

Her heart filled with love for him.

'I prefer jewellery to be a bit more subtle myself,' her mum said.

'I think subtle jewellery has a time and place as much as these wonderful rings. I love this one,' Jamie said, pulling out one that looked like a cluster of M&Ms. Melody had made them out of Fimo clay and varnished them to make them look shiny like the sweets. They were so easy to make and the customers absolutely loved them. 'These are very popular with the customers.'

'They are?' Her mum sounded incredulous.

'People like to wear jewellery as a way to express themselves. Some people have a silly, fun sense of humour and that is reflected in the jewellery they wear. This is probably not really your thing, but what about something like this?' Jamie said, pulling out a ring that was made from rainbow pyrite, tiny speckles of gold like sand formed into the shape of a star. Melody loved that one and she thought Aunt Rosa would love it too.

'I suppose this one would be OK,' her mum said and Melody could tell she was done with this little impromptu visit.

Jamie brought it back over to the till, and Melody put it in a box and rang up the sale. 'Twenty-six pounds please.'

Her mum paid.

'Thank you, Melody.'

She left the shop with the quickest of waves and a tiny smile that held a glimmer of sadness and then she was gone.

Jamie didn't say anything for a moment. Well, what was there to say?

Melody groaned, and she let her head fall into her hands.

'Why, why do I always do it to myself? Why do I always seek her approval? I love the stuff I make here, more so than any of the jewellery I made in London. It makes me happy, it makes my customers happy and I make a good living from selling it. Why do I care what she thinks?'

'I suppose we always want our parents to be proud of us,' Jamie said, coming round the counter and taking her in his arms.

She leaned her head into his chest. There were no words he could say that would make her feel better, but his presence did.

'She hasn't said anything positive for nearly twenty years, since my dad left when I was thirteen. I'd almost given up hearing anything positive from her ever again. But since she's been dating Trevor Harris, she's apparently mellowed. Isla has seen it too when Mum's been with Elliot and when she came in today. I thought, maybe, just maybe, she might have something nice to say. And she did, to you. The first time she's been in my jewellery shop and she could have said how smart the shop looks or how proud she is of me or how she likes my jewellery but nothing. She couldn't even say that she thought Aunt Rosa would like the gold ring, just that the ring was OK.'

Melody let out a heavy breath.

'God, I'm sorry. I don't know why I let her get to me. I just saw her wrinkle her nose at my statement rings and I was right back to being fourteen years old and bringing home a painting I'd done in art. That exact same look. It hurt then and it hurts now.'

Jamie stroked his hand through her hair and she smiled. She didn't know why Jamie thought he was rubbish with women. He was here for her in exactly the way she needed.

'I was always really clumsy when I was a kid—'

'Just when you were a kid?' Jamie teased and she laughed.

'OK, now too, but Dad used to get really impatient with me. Mum was sympathetic, always sticking up for me when I'd knock something over or break something. I struggled at school too and my dad spent many hours sitting with me at the dining table trying to help me with my homework. When he left, for a while I blamed myself. If I was cleverer, smarter, better, less accident-prone, maybe he would have stayed. I spent years trying to be this A-grade student, trying to excel at every subject, trying to be less clumsy. I think partly in the vain hope that he would come back if he could see how smart I was, and partly to make my mum proud of me, to try to make her happy again. There was probably a tiny part of me that was scared she would leave as well.'

She sighed, and Jamie placed a gentle kiss on her forehead.

'But she wasn't proud. Nothing I did had any impact on her. She was angry, negative and dismissive with everyone, including me. And worse, whenever I'd knock something over or break something, that patience she'd had before was gone. I used to enjoy writing little stories which I'd give her and they lay on the kitchen table, unread, until she'd moan at us to clear our crap off the table. I won a prize in art and she didn't even come along to the award evening. Matthew and Isla were there and even my dad came, but she didn't. She simply didn't care about anything I did. It didn't help that there wasn't really anything to be proud of. I was never top of the class for any subject. I was average at everything. And I suppose I could have accepted her indifference, but it was the negativity that was the hardest. The little comments, the looks of disappointment and irritation. It hurt, and I started to lose faith in the person I was. Matthew and Isla were great, they were always so supportive, trying to build me up and reassure me, they'd tell me how proud they were of me. It wasn't until I left home to go to university that I realised I didn't need her approval; that living with her was so oppressive and damaging. I swore that she wasn't going to hurt me any more with her lack of interest or scathing looks, but I suppose I never resolved it, I just minimised the time I spent with her and that works except for when I have to see her.'

'It sounds like you had it rough. Your teenage years are such an important time for developing who you are as an adult. You need support and guidance and it sounds like you didn't get any of that,' Jamie said, gently. 'Her divorce obviously affected her greatly and she took that out on you. I wonder if she regrets that now.'

Melody sighed. 'I doubt that.' She looked up at him. 'What's your relationship with your mum like? I know you don't see her very often.'

'Only because she lives so far away. We're very close. She's always been very supportive about my art and encourages me to follow my dreams.'

'Isn't that what every parent should do for their children,' Melody said. 'Be proud and shout about their achievements to anyone who'll listen.'

He nodded. 'Some parents obviously didn't get the rule book.'

Melody sighed and leaned her head against his heart again. 'She wasn't always like this. She was a wonderful mum when we were little, and everything changed the day my dad walked out.'

'Maybe that other mum is still in there, but she has been angry for so long that she no longer remembers what it feels like to be that other woman. This has become her new norm. Have you spoken to her about it?'

'No, I always feel like I'm treading on eggshells with her. She blows up at the slightest thing, so prevention and avoidance has always worked so well. Some things are just better left alone.'

'I don't think this will ever change though, not unless she knows how much it hurts you.' Jamie stroked his hands soothingly down her back. 'Surely, it's worth a try? You don't have any real kind of relationship with her at the moment, so it can't make it worse. I could come with you if you wanted.'

She looked up at him and smiled. 'You're very sweet, Jamie Jackson. And I know you're right. Let me have a think about it and what I could say. Maybe I'll talk to Isla about it too. It's times like this I really miss Matthew. He would always talk me down when I'd get in a tizz over Mum. You've done a very good job of stepping into his shoes today.'

'I'm always here for you, Melody. Regardless of what happens between us, I'll always be here. I know how hard it is to lose someone close to you so if you ever want to talk about that, I'm here.'

She smiled sadly. He had lost his dad when he was a child, and although they didn't speak about that very often, she knew it must have been hard for him.

'I'm here for you too. I imagine the pain of losing a close relative never really goes away.'

'It doesn't, you just get better at dealing with it.'

'Well you can always deal with it with me.'

Jamie smiled and bent his head and kissed her, cupping her face in his hands.

Another customer came in then and Jamie gave her a kiss on the head and stepped back out of her arms.

'Thank you for being here for me,' Melody said, quietly, as the customer started browsing round the shop. 'Want to come for lunch today, I'm meeting Tori?'

'I really need to get on with my sculpture for the festival, I feel like it's never going to be finished. Or I'm never going to be happy with it.'

'OK, can I pick you up something?'

'A bacon sandwich would be great.'

She nodded and, as the customer had her back to them as she peered in the cabinets, Melody reached up and gave him a kiss on the lips. He kissed her back without even a trace of embarrassment. God, she loved this man.

He smiled as he stepped back. 'See you later, my siren.'

She watched him go with a big smile on her face and then realised the customer was patiently waiting.

'Sorry, how can I help?'

'Honey, don't apologise. If I had a man like that, I'd be kissing him all the time too.'

Melody laughed, knowing how very lucky she was to have a man like that in her life.

CHAPTER 11

Melody arrived at The Cherry on Top before Tori had arrived. She had spent the morning making a start on her mosaic for the Great Sculpture in the Sand competition. Klaus had cut out a template for her based on Tori's design and she had spent an enjoyable few hours cutting and gluing the sea glass into the right positions. Now she was starving. She ordered a chicken satay waffle and went and found a table in the corner, settling Rocky underneath the table. Agatha was at the next table but in deep conversation with Elsie West from the chemist, so she and Tori might be able to have their own conversation without being overheard.

She couldn't be happier right now. She was sure everyone must know that her and Jamie were seeing each other. If they didn't, the huge smile on her face would be a big giveaway. She didn't even care. They could talk and laugh and embellish all they wanted. She was dating Jamie Jackson and that was definitely something to be happy about.

She was just about to get her phone out of her bag and send Jamie a flirty text when Tori arrived, and Melody's heart leapt with excitement. Aidan was going to propose to her tonight. This time tomorrow, Tori would be wearing the moonstone ring and would have a fiancé and she didn't even know.

Tori arrived at the table and Melody realised she was looking a bit flustered.

Melody stood up to hug her. 'You OK?'

Tori nodded. 'Well, no, not really.'

'What's wrong?'

'Aidan is up to something.'

Melody's heart sank. Evidently, Aidan had not been as subtle as he hoped with his proposal preparations.

'What do you mean?' she asked, hoping her voice wasn't giving the game away too. She was a terrible liar.

'I don't know, he's behaving really oddly,' Tori said. 'He seems really nervous as if he's scared I'm going to catch him doing something. A few times, I've walked into the room and he's quickly put his phone face down, so I wouldn't see what was on the screen. The other day he said he was going down to the strawberry field and when I went down to find him to tell him about a phone call, he wasn't there. And… I've just seen Mary Nightingale and she said that yesterday she saw him going into the heartberry field with a blonde woman. What would he be doing down there? All the bushes are dead, there are no berries and who's this blonde he was there with?'

Crap.

'You know what Mary Nightingale is like, she never wears her glasses. Maybe she thought it was Aidan and it was someone else.'

'Who else would be going into the heartberry field? It's supposed to be private property.'

'Well, I don't think the villagers pay too much attention to that kind of thing. You know a lot of people go to the cave at Orchard Cove to have illicit sex.'

Tori's face fell.

'What if that's what he was doing?' Tori said, her voice suddenly tearful. 'Meeting someone else for sex.'

Crap. Crap. Crap.

What was she supposed to tell her? That she had been the blonde woman Mary Nightingale had seen go into the heartberry field with Aidan. How could she possibly explain what she was doing with Aidan without giving the game away?

'Aidan was not meeting someone else for sex,' Melody said, firmly. 'The man is crazy in love with you. You trust him, don't you?'

'Of course I do.'

'Then why are you getting upset with Aidan being seen with another woman? If he'd been seen kissing this woman then of course you'd have something to worry about, but just going into the heartberry field. It could be anything and nothing.'

'You're right, I know you are, but I know he is hiding something from me, he's been so vague and evasive over the last few days. It's not my birthday so I know it's not that. What is he up to? I've been here before with Luc. He was sleeping with someone else for six months before I found out. I had no clue. I trusted him completely and he was shagging someone else the whole time. But if I'm honest with myself, the signs were there, the secrets, the lies that tripped him up. I knew something was going on, but I just couldn't believe he was being unfaithful. I don't want to be ignorant to it again.'

'Aidan is different, he would never do anything like that to you. He loves you.'

Tori nodded but she didn't look so sure. 'I thought Luc was different.'

'When was the last time you and Aidan made love?'

'Last night, when we got back from Isla's.'

'And did he instigate it or did you?'

'He did. He's like a dog on heat most of the time, can't keep his hands off me,' Tori said, a small smile forming on her lips. 'I love how much he wants me.'

'Exactly. Would he really be going elsewhere for sex when he can get it from you anytime he wants?'

'True. I'm being silly, aren't I?'

'Yes you are,' Melody said, relieved the doubt seemed to have passed.

Tori looked thoughtful for a moment while she studied the menu. 'But that still doesn't explain why he was in the heartberry field with a blonde woman. Maybe I should ask him. If it's nothing then he'll just explain it.'

Melody stilled her friend's hand as she reached for the phone. If Aidan lied, which he undoubtedly would, Tori would be even more suspicious.

'It was me, Aidan was with me. God knows why Mary didn't recognise me, but she never wears her glasses. Aidan wanted to show me something.'

Tori stared at her in shock, probably wondering why Melody hadn't mentioned it when Tori had first brought it up.

'But… What did he want to show you?'

Urgh. This was getting worse.

'Look, he has a surprise for you.'

'A surprise?' Tori said in confusion. She was clearly trying to work out what the surprise would be. Then her eyes lit up.

'No, not that, nothing big or life-changing,' Melody hurriedly said before Tori got carried away and imagined a big romantic proposal. Exactly like the one she was going to get. 'It's nothing really, he just wanted to do something nice for you and I was giving him a hand.'

This conversation hadn't gone how she had wanted at all. She hadn't wanted to give anything away about that evening. But she couldn't let Tori continue to think he was having some kind of sordid affair. She certainly wouldn't be saying yes to the proposal later that night if she spent the whole day having doubts.

Tori visibly relaxed. 'Oh god, I'm such a tit. Why did I fear the worst?'

'Because you've been hurt badly in the past.'

'I know, but there was no reason to doubt him. I love him, I know he loves me. I've just been so emotional lately, I don't know why. I had this silly wobble this morning. I was lying in bed this morning, he was wrapped around me, holding me tight, and I was thinking I have never been so blissfully happy as I am right now and then I started thinking, what if it all ended, what would I do? And I literally had tears in my eyes as I thought about losing him… God, I'm getting emotional now just thinking about it. I don't know what's wrong with me. I suppose, coupled with his secrecy, it made me think the worst.'

Melody narrowed her eyes thoughtfully. She thought back to the night before and how much Tori had eaten. They had all laughed when she'd helped herself to a third portion of curry plus a large dessert. And the other day, when they'd met for lunch, Tori had eaten a ton then too.

She took Tori's hand and was just about to speak when Agatha leaned over from her table, making them jump. Melody had almost forgotten she was there.

'Sounds to me like you're pregnant, dear,' Agatha said, knowingly. Melody had just been about to suggest the same thing. Agatha's friend, Elsie West, nodded sagely.

Tori shook her head and laughed. 'No, no, I can't be, we always use protection.' She paled as a thought clearly occurred to her. 'Well, there was that time in the bath but… No, I can't be. That would be crazy. I mean, we've talked about having children and how it was definitely something we wanted but sometime in the future, not now.'

'Your boobs are bigger,' Agatha said, bluntly.

Melody tilted her head to one side and had a good look. Did they look bigger? Possibly.

'When is your period?' Agatha said, not caring that that was way too personal a question for the middle of a café, or any time in public really.

'Well I'm always a bit irregular,' Tori said. 'I'm normally around the fifteenth of each month but I can be a week late sometimes.'

'And today is the twenty-fifth,' Agatha said. 'So that would make you ten days late.'

'Well, as I said, I'm quite irregular,' Tori tried. She looked between Agatha and Melody in disbelief.

Tori looked down at her boobs and then stroked across her almost flat stomach as if the pregnancy would be obvious.

'Why don't you pop along to the chemist, dear?' Elsie leaned over from their table joining the conversation. 'We can do a test and then you'll know for sure.'

Tori shook her head. 'I'm not pregnant.'

'It wouldn't hurt to find out though,' Melody said. 'To be sure.'

Tori nodded. 'You're right. I'm sure I'm not, but it would be good to rule it out.'

'I have a toilet at the chemist, you can do the test there,' Elsie said, obviously keen to be there when Tori found out.

'Maybe Tori might want to do it somewhere a little more private,' Melody suggested.

'Yes, maybe I'll buy a test and do it at home, or I think the whole town might know before Aidan does.' Tori looked pointedly at Agatha.

Melody suspected it would already be too late for that. Even if Tori turned out not to be pregnant, half the town would hear that she was by the end of the day. Agatha started to protest about that slur against her character but then she shrugged and nodded in defeat.

Tori stared down at her belly again in shock.

'Are you OK?' Melody asked gently.

'Yes, of course.' Tori smiled, brightly, but Melody knew she was putting on a front. 'Do you mind if I skip lunch? I think I better go and take this test just to put my mind at ease.'

'Do you want me to come with you?' Melody offered.

Tori shook her head. 'I'll text you.'

She stood up and Melody stood up and hugged her. 'If you need me, just call and I'll be round in five minutes.'

'Thanks,' Tori said, giving her a kiss on the cheek and hurrying out.

Melody sat down just as her chicken waffles arrived.

Agatha shifted her chair, so she was now sitting down at Melody's table. A few seconds later, Elsie joined her on the other side.

Melody paused with her fork halfway to her mouth. 'Is there something I can help you ladies with? I'm not pregnant as well.'

'Well you might be,' Agatha said. 'We heard you were having sex on the beach last night with my dear nephew.'

Melody put her fork down. 'We were not having sex.'

'That's not what we hear from Trevor Harris. Caught you in the act, he says.' Elsie had a wicked glint in her eye as she spoke.

'We were kissing, nothing more than that.'

'So you admit, you two have overcome the first-date hurdle, something is going on between you,' Agatha said, triumphantly.

Melody sighed and took a mouthful of chicken, playing for time as she chewed. She swallowed and scooped up another forkful, but Agatha stilled her hand with a pointed look.

'It's very early, we're taking it slowly,' Melody tried.

'Trevor said it was getting very heated,' Elsie said. 'That doesn't sound like taking it slowly to me.'

Melody shook her head in disbelief. 'I think me and Jamie will be the judge of that. We will decide when the time is right for us to kiss or make love or anything else.'

'Quite right, dear,' Agatha said. 'If you want to have sex on the beach, you go right ahead and do it.'

'We weren't having sex. We've been on one date and that ended a lot quicker than it should, as you are well aware. Kissing Jamie is… amazing but we haven't progressed past that yet and, when we do, it'll be our business.'

'Well, if you have sex in a public place, you can't blame people for talking about it,' Elsie tutted, though Melody could see she was as invested in this conversation as Agatha was. 'If you want to keep it private, I suggest you do it in a bit more of a private place.'

'Nothing wrong with a bit of sex in public places,' Agatha hurriedly said, undoubtedly loving the idea of Melody having sex somewhere where someone would see them and report back to her. 'Adds a bit of a thrill to it. There's a nice alleyway at the back of The Mermaid pub. I had quite a lot of sex there when I was younger. I was dating the barman and we'd often meet round the back when he was on a break. If it's a bit chilly, the library is always a good place. The aisles where the encyclopaedias are kept is a good location. No one goes down there when they have computers with Google. Last time I was there, I even saw a box of condoms next to the C encyclopaedia, so I'm not the only one who goes there. Not sure if they're in date though. Might want to check that before you and Jamie go there. The cave at Orchard Cove is great, lots of people have sex there. Even the heartberry fields at this time of year as no one is there to do the berry-picking. The old deserted Tanner manor house up on the hill is another great place for outdoor sex. There's a gate round the back that is always open. The grounds are so overgrown now, you can't be seen from the road. There's the summer house at the bottom of the garden that a lot of people use. Some people have even found a way into the manor house and a lot of the old furniture is still there. Dusty, but a good place for sex, though if you get caught in there it would be breaking and entering. Getting caught in the garden is just trespassing, which is much less of a crime.'

Melody stared at her, open-mouthed.

'The Clover Woods are a great place for outdoor sex too, lots of secluded glades and trees you can have sex up against. Once I was dating a soldier and we—'

'Um… thanks for the tips.' Melody interrupted in panic, instinctively knowing that the words that would continue to flow from Agatha's mouth would paint pictures she absolutely didn't want or need painted by the older woman.

'My pleasure,' Agatha said. 'I have lots more suggestions. You just say the word. I could write a book on all the places I've had sex. I've almost never been caught, but the thrill of that possibility does add an extra layer of excitement to it. Cars are good too, more private but a bit small.'

'As I said, we're not there yet,' Melody said, desperately trying to end this excruciating conversation.

'Yes we know, but when you are, you must try a bit of outdoor sex, great fun. And make sure you have a look at that *Kama Sutra* I gave you, might give you a few tips too.' Agatha got up and scooped her sleeping puppy Summer into her arms. Elsie stood up as well. 'And don't keep the boy waiting too long, eh. Poor lad. It's been way too long since his last sexcapade. His willy might fall off from lack of use.'

Agatha walked away with Elsie cackling at her side and Melody let her head fall into her hands.

Maybe it would be better if the whole village didn't know about her dating Jamie after all.

'So the whole village thinks we were having sex on the beach last night,' Melody said, by way of announcing her arrival in Jamie's art studio. She let Rocky go off in search of his brother.

Jamie was working on his statue for the Sculpture in the Sand competition and he didn't want her to see it. He didn't like anyone seeing his unfinished sculptures, but he especially didn't want Melody to see this one.

He quickly stepped out the little screened-off area to greet her and closed the curtain behind him.

He pulled her into his arms and kissed on top of her scowl and then on the mouth. He felt the tension leave her as he held her in his arms.

'Hello,' he said, softly.

'Hi,' she smiled up at him.

Klaus came running out from the back of the studio. 'You two had sex on the beach last night?' he said, looking absolutely delighted with this piece of gossip.

Melody pulled back from Jamie. 'We weren't having sex. We were kissing, that was it. I'm going to kill Trevor Harris when I get my hands on him.'

'Oh, that's disappointing,' Klaus said, returning to his area of the studio.

'What's going on?' Jamie said, wondering if this had more to do with his beloved aunt Agatha than Trevor having told everyone.

'Agatha accosted me in The Cherry on Top and tried to get me to admit having sex with you last night. I tried to explain we were just kissing but she wasn't too convinced. Then she gave me a whole list of places we could have sex outdoors, just in case we fancied it.'

Jamie couldn't help but smirk. The audacity of his aunt would never cease to surprise him.

'Let them believe what they want, they will anyway. Who cares what they think? By tomorrow there'll be some other piece of news to excite them. You were the one that said you didn't want to hide our relationship.'

Melody visibly exhaled. 'You're right, I know you're right. I don't really care if they want to talk about us, I just wish they'd get their facts right.'

'Shall we have sex on the beach now so that the rumours are actually true?' Jamie said.

Melody laughed. 'That would give them all something to talk about.'

'If that's what you want,' Jamie teased.

'Yes! Do it,' Klaus shouted from the back of the studio.

Jamie smirked.

'I think we should do it somewhere a bit more private for our first time,' Melody said, quietly.

'That's probably a good idea. Come for dinner tonight.'

Melody arched an eyebrow and he laughed. 'Just dinner, I promise.'

'OK, but I have to drop something off for Aidan around eight. It won't take long, we could eat after.'

He nodded. 'OK, come round about seven thirty. I can come with you if you like.'

'Sounds good.' She leaned up to kiss him and then looked around the studio. 'What are you working on?'

'Oh, my statue for the Sculpture in the Sand competition.' Jamie tried to sound vague in the hope that she wouldn't want to see it.

'Oooh, can I see it?'

His heart sank. 'I'm… kind of a bit funny about people seeing my work before it's finished. It will change so much between now and then and I don't want people to see it when it's only half done.'

'Ah, OK.'

He could tell she was disappointed.

'I could show you a piece I finished earlier this morning,' he offered.

She brightened. 'OK.'

He took her hand and brought her over to the drying shelf where a little statuette was sitting, drying before he put it in the kiln.

'It's a mermaid,' Melody said, visibly enchanted by it.

He didn't do conventional sculptures and statues very often. The tourists liked their art a bit more predictable, so he would do these little sculptures of seagulls, seals, crabs, and sea horses from time to time. Some were accurate and detailed, some were a little bit comedic, and he would paint them and put them in the window to draw the tourists in. Once they were in the shop, many of them would become transfixed with his more abstract pieces and buy those instead of the conventional pieces. But this idea had sparked to life the first night he had kissed Melody on their date and he knew he had to make it.

'It's a siren actually,' Jamie said, and he watched the smile fill her face. 'I was inspired.'

'She's very beautiful,' Melody said.

'As I said, I had great inspiration. I'm going to paint her hair sunshine blonde and her scales a beautiful sparkling sea-blue-green to match her eyes.'

She swallowed. 'I think the tourists will love her.'

He shook his head. 'She's a gift for you and then you can always be reminded of how I see you. This incredibly beautiful, magical creature that has cast a spell over my heart.'

'Oh,' Melody said.

She turned to face him, wrapping her arms around his neck. 'I do like you, Jamie Jackson. I might even go so far as to say, I adore you.'

He smiled. 'I like you too.'

He knew that didn't even come close to describing his feelings for her.

'You're quite possibly my favourite person,' Melody said.

He bent his head to kiss her, hoping that actions would speak louder than words. He was crazy about her, even if he couldn't find the words to tell her. Kissing her was everything, she must feel that too.

She pulled back, slightly. 'See, this "friends who date" thing can actually work.'

'I'm enjoying our *sort-of* relationship very much,' Jamie said.

She smiled and gave him a brief kiss on the cheek. 'I'll see you tonight.'

She called for Rocky and then he watched her go, staring at her as she unlocked her shop door and disappeared inside. He turned back to face his competition sculpture. He just hoped she would feel the same way about him when she saw this.

CHAPTER 12

Melody knocked on Jamie's door later that night and when he answered he looked happy and relaxed.

Maybe there was a lot to be said for friends who date. He immediately bent and kissed her and then pulled her into his arms for a big hug. God, it felt so nice.

Harry, Ron and Hermione, Jamie's older dogs, came sniffing around, wagging their tails and Sirius could be seen chasing his own tail in excitement as he bounced off the furniture and skidded over the wood laminate floor. Harry looked at Sirius and then back at Melody with that long-suffering look of a parent who doesn't know what to do with their hyperactive child. Dobby the turkey was also wandering round, pecking at bits of dust on the floor and following the other animals around the room.

'Come in for a moment,' Jamie said, and she followed him down the hall into the bright and airy lounge with stunning views over the whole of Sandcastle Bay. She hadn't been to Jamie's house very often – they tended to meet at hers or on the beach on the way to work – but that view always took her breath away. The little houses tumbling down the hill towards the vast swathe of inky blue sea. The fruit fields from Heartberry Farm could clearly be seen, as could her little cottage perched on the edge of Sunshine Beach. A pink haze hung in the sky as the sun had already started its very slow descent and it left a pink glow over the water. It was beautiful.

Jamie was picking up a few things in an attempt to make the place look tidier for her. His house had a wonderful lived-in appeal. This was a home and the pottery and art magazines that littered the coffee table, the hoodie that had been strewn over the arm of the sofa and the bits of paper with his sketches on them scattered in messy piles on the floor just added to the charm of the place. This cottage was the epitome of Jamie Jackson and she loved it.

'Don't tidy up for me,' Melody said.

Jamie paused in picking up some of his sketches and then deliberately left them on the floor, in a perhaps slightly tidier pile than they were in before.

'I love your home, this view, the decorations, your dogs and Dobby freely wandering about the place as if they own it, I wouldn't change a single thing.'

Jamie smiled. 'The animals do own the house; they just let me stay here.'

'Isn't that the truth. I like to think I'm the one in charge in my house, but really Rocky's the boss and he knows it.'

'Come through to the kitchen a moment, I'll just check on the dinner before we pop out. How long will we be?'

'Probably only ten or fifteen minutes.'

She followed him into the kitchen where wonderful smells were coming from the oven.

'What are we having? It smells amazing.'

'Lasagne. It should be done by the time we've got back.'

He fiddled with the temperature on the oven and put the homemade garlic bread in the fridge.

'Don't want to leave this out, it won't be there when we get back,' Jamie said, giving a pointed glare at Sirius.

He grabbed his jacket and they left the house.

'I thought we'd go by bike.' Melody gestured to her beloved pink moped. She'd bought it not long after she'd moved to Sandcastle Bay to make navigating the narrow and twisty lanes a lot easier, but she never really used it. Walking was much nicer but, knowing they were a bit pushed for time that evening, it made sense to dig it out. She didn't want to be late for Aidan's proposal and, as lovely as the walk through Sandcastle Bay would be at this time of evening, she wanted to eat and talk with Jamie in a more intimate setting.

'OK,' Jamie said.

She smirked as she handed him a pink helmet. To his credit, he didn't even bat an eye as he pulled it over his head and fastened it underneath. She pulled hers on and got onto the moped. Jamie got on behind her, wrapping his hands around her waist.

She started the engine and moved off and his hands tightened slightly around her.

'So what are we taking to Aidan?' Jamie said over the noise of the engine.

'I've made him dessert,' Melody said. Apparently Jamie didn't know. Well, he would soon when he followed her to the cave.

'I'm sure Aidan's more than capable of making his own dessert, the man is a demon in the kitchen.'

'I'm sure he could, but my Eve's Pudding is Tori's favourite thing in the world.'

Jamie clearly thought about this for a moment as they zoomed along the sea front towards the heartberry field.

'Special occasion?'

She grinned. 'Yes, you could say that.'

She pulled up next to the gate that led to the heartberry field and they climbed off. She retrieved the wrapped pudding and a jam jar of custard from the box at the back of the moped. Jamie watched her carefully.

'He's going to propose, isn't he?' Jamie said.

'How could you know that?'

'Because you have the biggest grin on your face. You have such a romantic heart; it's obvious you're really excited and happy about this.'

'OK, he is, and yes, I'm beyond excited. You have no idea how happy it makes me to see Tori getting her happy ending.'

'Wow, that's early for them,' Jamie said as he followed her into the heartberry field.

'I know but I suppose when you've found the right person, there's no point in hanging around.'

Jamie was quiet for a moment. 'I suppose not.'

'He's going to propose as soon as he brings her to the cave, so they can enjoy the night after. I think he just wants to get it out the way as the nerves are probably eating him alive.'

'If I was going to propose, I'd be scared to death too.'

'Scared she would say yes,' Melody teased as she knew he was anti-relationships.

'Scared she'd say no. It's a big commitment and both parties need to be ready for that. Nothing worse than one half of the couple being more into the relationship than the other.'

It sounded like he was speaking from experience. Her heart ached for him if he'd been hurt that way.

She waited to see if he would talk about it some more, but when he didn't she decided to change the subject.

'So we just need to drop this pudding off in the cave and then we can go and have dinner,' Melody said as she walked along the edge of the field. 'Though it's a shame we can't stay and watch.'

'You want to watch their proposal?' Jamie said, slipping his hand into hers as he fell in at her side.

She looked up at him and smiled. 'Oh god, my little romantic heart would love it. My world is permanently rose-tinted. My bedroom has shelves of hundreds of cutesy romance stories, with sparkly happy, feel-good endings. I love all that sort of stuff.'

'It's not real though, is it?' Jamie said. 'Love isn't really like how they portray it in those stories.'

'Why not? When you find someone, the other half of your heart, your soul mate, why can't you have the happy ending?'

'In my experience, there is no such thing as the happy ending.'

'Then you haven't met the right person. Look at Tori and Aidan, they were both hurt in the past and they put that behind them and now they've found their forever.'

'I think what Tori and Aidan have is something special. I don't think everyone has that.'

'You just have to find your someone special too,' Melody said. 'I couldn't be happier for the two of them. She has found someone wonderful in your brother and I'm so happy they're getting engaged. So yes, I'd love to see it. But I will content myself with being a part of it in some tiny way,' she gestured to the pudding, 'and hearing all about it after.'

They had arrived at Orchard Cove by this point. The tide was out, the waves lapping gently on the shore as the sun set over the sea. The evening was perfect.

They walked into the cave and her heart dropped into her stomach. The table and chairs had been knocked over, the vase that had been filled with flowers was on the ground and the flowers lay scattered across the cave floor. It had been quite windy that afternoon so they must have got blown over. Thankfully the generator was still working as the fairy lights were twinkling and she could see that the warmer was on too.

She quickly put the pudding under the heat as Jamie moved to grab the table. She had a quick check on the other food that was in there, making sure none of it had dried out. It looked OK. She grabbed the chairs and rearranged them at the table. She found the tablecloth in the corner of the cave and put that back on as Jamie re-hung some of the lights and origami flower bunting that had fallen down near the front of the cave. She gathered up the flowers and placed them in the vase.

She stepped back to look at everything and it all seemed fine.

'OK, let's get out of here,' Melody said.

Jamie nodded and followed her back onto the beach. However, as they walked to the edge of the field, Melody saw that Tori and Aidan were already making their way through the heartberry bushes towards them, having come through the farm entrance to the field.

'Crap!' Melody said, pulling Jamie back onto the beach out of sight. 'What do we do? If she sees us, it might give the game away or ruin it.'

Jamie looked around and then grabbed her hand. 'Quick, back in the cave, there's some rocks at the back we can hide behind.'

'We can't hide there all night,' Melody said, searching the beach for some other kind of solution, but there wasn't anywhere else they could go.

'We don't have to. You said that Aidan planned to propose to her as soon as they got into the cave. We hide there until she says yes, give them a few moments to hug and kiss and then we come out, offer our congratulations and leave them to enjoy their evening. They'll be too loved-up after the proposal to care that we were actually there and we get to watch the proposal, just as you wanted. Then we can be back at my house in a few minutes and be eating that lasagne that's in the oven.'

'OK, good plan. Do you have your phone? We could even record the happy moment for them.'

'Good idea,' Jamie said, tugging her behind the rock. They knelt down so they were out of sight and Jamie pulled out his phone. Melody peered over the top of the rock, but they were in complete darkness there and, because of the brightness of the fairy lights in the front of the cave, it was very unlikely they'd be seen.

A few moments later, Aidan and Tori arrived.

Melody couldn't help squeezing Jamie's arm in excitement.

Tori gasped when she walked in. 'Is this for us?'

'For you,' Aidan said.

'It's beautiful,' Tori whispered.

Melody checked on Jamie and he was already filming it all on his phone.

'I wanted to do something special for you, here in Orchard Cove, because it was here, as we watched that sunrise, the first night we kissed, that I realised I wanted to watch every sunrise with you.'

'Oh,' Tori said quietly, and Melody thought she might be cottoning on to what was happening.

'You have changed my life, you've filled it with colour and joy and I simply cannot imagine my life now without you in it. I love you, with everything I have. You are forever for me,' Aidan said, dropping down to one knee and offering out the ring box. 'Would you do me the honour of becoming my wife?'

'Oh god, Aidan,' Tori said, her voice barely a whisper as she stared at the ring. 'It's beautiful.'

And with that Tori burst into tears.

Melody looked at Jamie and he pulled a face. 'Not the best reaction,' he whispered.

'Just wait,' she hissed. She had a pretty good idea why Tori was crying and it wasn't just the proposal.

'What's wrong?' Aidan asked uncertainly.

'I'm just so happy,' Tori sobbed.

'It doesn't look like it. Is it too soon? We don't have to do this now, I just thought...' Aidan said, clearly not having expected this reaction at all.

Tori shook her head, still crying. 'I love you, this, all of this, is perfect.'

Though she still hadn't said yes yet. Poor Aidan.

He stood up and pulled her into his arms, holding her close. 'What's wrong?'

'Nothing is wrong, I'm happy, I promise.'

He stroked the tears from her face and Tori caught his hand and moved it down to her stomach. Melody felt the grin almost split her face. They had been right after all.

'Aidan, I'm pregnant.'

He looked confused for a moment. He definitely hadn't been expecting that. 'What?'

'I'm carrying your baby,' Tori said, laughing through her tears.

If Melody thought her own grin was huge, it was nothing to the smile that lit up Aidan's face at this wonderful news.

'We're having a baby?'

Tori nodded.

Melody chanced a quick glance at Jamie, not wanting to miss anything but wondering what he thought of this news too. He was grinning as well.

Aidan hugged Tori, laughing as he lifted her off her feet. 'Oh god, this is the best news ever. Second only to you saying yes to my proposal.'

'Oh, I can't believe I didn't say yes,' Tori laughed through her tears. 'Of course it's a yes, I love you so much. You are my forever too.'

Aidan sighed with relief. 'Can I put it on? See how it looks?'

Tori nodded, and it seemed like everyone held their breath as he slid the ring onto her finger. From where Melody was crouching, it seemed to fit Tori perfectly.

'I love it, you couldn't have chosen a more perfect ring,' Tori said as she angled her hand around so it caught the light. 'I really do love you, Aidan Jackson, you make me so blissfully happy. I cannot wait to be married to you and have your baby.'

Aidan kissed her. Melody's heart filled with joy. Her friend had found her happy ever after.

The kiss continued and it was clear it was very passionate and Melody felt a bit guilty for watching.

She turned to Jamie and motioned for him to turn off the video. They had captured the proposal. This was private.

Jamie looked at his phone and frowned.

'Did you get it?' Melody whispered. They obviously couldn't ask Aidan and Tori to do it again.

Jamie pressed a few buttons and then nodded. 'Yes I have. I didn't think I had for a moment. I can't believe they're going to have a baby. They are going to make such brilliant parents.'

'I know. That was so romantic.' Melody was smiling happily as she sat down and leant against the rock, her hand over her heart.

Jamie sat down next to her. 'Even I have to admit that was pretty much perfect.'

'That's what a true love story is supposed to be like,' Melody said, in a dreamy whisper.

'Is that what you want?' Jamie said, a note of worry entering his hushed tones.

'With the right man, at the right time, yes.'

Jamie leaned his head back on the rock, looking thoughtful.

'You don't need to worry, I'm not expecting that from you,' Melody said.

He turned to look at her again. 'I'm not the right man?'

She paused before answering. She couldn't tell him yet that she'd fallen head over heels in love with him and that she'd been in love with him for months. She had to remember she needed to take this slowly.

'I think you could be,' she said, carefully.

He continued to watch her and she knew she needed to add more.

'But now is definitely not the right time.'

He nodded as if he accepted that and she decided to change the subject.

'Let's see if they've finished kissing and then we can offer our congratulations and get out of here,' Melody said, kneeling up and peering over the rock to check.

To her horror, however, Tori and Aidan had moved to the beanbag bed that Aidan had brought down to the cave so they could watch the sunset over the sea together. Tori was naked and quickly wrestling the last of the clothes from Aidan as the kiss continued urgently.

Melody ducked back down before she saw anything else.

'Are they finished?' Jamie said.

Melody shook her head. 'I don't think they are going to be finished any time soon.'

Jamie looked at her in confusion and then his eyes widened in shock. 'You're kidding.'

'No, I wish I was.'

'We need to stop them before they get too carried away,' Jamie said.

A moan drifted down the cave.

'I'd say it's too late for that.'

Jamie scrabbled to his knees and peeped over the rock for a second before quickly ducking back down. 'Crap, you're right.'

Melody giggled. 'You didn't have to look.'

'I thought you might be exaggerating.'

'That's one hell of a successful proposal.'

'When I propose to you, I want that kind of reaction,' Jamie said.

'Make sure you don't do it somewhere public then.'

'Duly noted.'

Melody replayed his words. *When* I propose to you, not *if*. Her little romantic heart soared with happiness. While the rational side of her brain knew it was just an off-hand comment, her romantic side won out and she couldn't help the smile that spread across her face.

Another groan came down the cave, this time from Aidan, which burst her little happy bubble.

'What are we going to do? We can't go out there and interrupt them, but I can't sit here and wait till they've finished. It's embarrassing listening to that,' Melody said.

'It's worse than that. When they've finished, we can't even go out there then. They'll know we were here the whole time and heard or saw them at it. We're stuck here all night now, until they've gone.'

Melody realised he was right. 'Your lasagne is in the oven.'

'Yes, that isn't going to be fit to eat by the time we get back. I'll ask Leo to swing by and turn the oven off so it doesn't burn.'

His fingers raced across the screen on his phone as he texted and the moaning got louder.

Jamie pulled out some earphones from his pocket and plugged them into his phone, then passed her one earpiece.

She sighed and put it in her ear. Jamie turned on the music and Ed Sheeran started playing. The moans got louder and Jamie turned up the volume. Melody snuggled into his shoulder, trying to get comfortable on the cold stone floor. It was going to be a long night.

But as he put his arm around her and kissed her head, she thought it might not be too bad after all.

CHAPTER 13

Jamie leaned his head back on the rock and smiled. The evening hadn't gone anywhere near as planned. He was cold and stiff, his bum had gone numb, he was hungry. He had listened to his brother have sex three times, which was three times too many as far as he was concerned. He hadn't had a chance to properly talk with Melody; although they had been whispering a little, they were conscious that they might be overheard, so had sat in relative silence most of the time. The battery on his phone had died as well so they were left without any music. They had resorted to playing a silent game of Rock, Paper, Scissors for the longest time, which wasn't ideal. It had been a bit of a disaster.

Except, right now, Melody was fast asleep, snuggled against his chest with his arm around her, and it just felt so right. Her head was rolled back slightly, as if she was looking up at him, and her warm breath on his neck was the most wonderful feeling in the world. He looked down at her, at her long blonde lashes casting shadows on her sun-kissed cheeks. Little freckles had started to appear over the last few weeks on her cheekbones and on the top of her nose. They were cute and he had an urge to kiss every one of them. This close up he could see almost every detail of her skin, the tiny laughter lines around her eyes, the faint, silvery scar just above her eyebrow, probably from some childhood injury – he wanted to kiss that too. Her face was unadorned with any make-up, so she had this natural glow. Her lips were a perfect peony pink, parted slightly now as she slept.

He heard movement from the other side of the cave. He didn't think his brother and Tori had sat down to eat yet, preferring to spend the night making love under the glow of the moon and stars instead. But if the woman he loved had just said yes to his proposal, he imagined he'd want to spend the night making love to her as well.

'Let's go home,' he heard Tori say.

Jamie's heart leapt. Finally.

'But the food,' Aidan said.

'All I want is you and it's getting a bit chilly now,' Tori said.

'Let's take the food home and we can eat some of it in bed,' Aidan suggested.

'Good plan. This is all so beautiful, I'm sorry we didn't get to sit down and eat dinner properly.'

'Tonight has been the best night of my life,' Aidan said. 'I wouldn't change a single second of it.'

Apart from letting his brother overhear him have sex, Jamie thought.

He heard them move around for a few minutes, presumably getting dressed and gathering the food, before the lights were turned off, plunging him and Melody into darkness. He heard them talking and giggling as they left, until there was only silence in the cave and the sound of the waves lapping onto the beach.

He waited a few more minutes to be sure that Aidan and Tori had definitely gone, before he decided to wake Melody up.

He stroked his hand through her hair, which was like silk, but she didn't stir. He hugged her gently and kissed her head.

'Melody,' he said, quietly.

He felt her stir in the darkness and then her body tensed as she was probably a bit confused where she was. It was pitch black here and he couldn't see her at all; no wonder she was a bit scared.

'It's OK, you're OK,' he said, softly.

He felt the tension leave her immediately and he liked that she knew she was safe with him.

'Jamie?' she said, groggily. 'What's going on?'

'Aidan and Tori have just left. I thought we could go home.'

'Oh.' Realisation entered her voice as she clearly remembered where she was. 'I didn't think they would ever leave.'

'They didn't even eat anything; they just kept having sex again and again and again. It was torture,' Jamie said.

'My Eve's Pudding? They didn't bloody eat it after all that? We came here for nothing.'

He smiled at her indignant anger. She hadn't really minded being stuck here because the proposal had been so romantic, but not eat her beloved Eve's Pudding and there was hell to pay.

'They took it home with them,' Jamie said.

Melody made a noise of annoyance. 'I should think so too.'

'OK, stay here, I'm going to switch the generator back on so we can at least get out of the cave safely.'

'I'll come with you.'

'There's no need for both of us to fall arse over tit trying to get out. And don't forget, I have a reputation of being a nice guy to keep up. I couldn't let you go and fumble around in the darkness while I sat here on my butt.'

'Fair point,' Melody laughed.

As he moved, he felt his coat, which he'd draped round her, slip off her shoulders. He quickly felt around to pull it tighter around her and accidentally grazed her breast.

She burst out laughing.

'Groping me in the darkness definitely doesn't fit with your nice guy image.'

He laughed. 'No, it doesn't. I'll be getting a reputation as a bad boy. All the women will be falling over themselves to be with me.'

Melody fell silent and he knew immediately it was the wrong thing to say. Of course it was. Why could he never say the right thing? He knew that this friends with dating thing was supposed to make it easier for him, make him relax more and not worry about what he did or said, but then he made some stupid off-hand joke about other women. He didn't want anyone else. He wanted Melody. He knew he needed to say something else.

'And then I'll be fighting them off with a stick. "Sorry ladies, I've already found the woman of my dreams, you're too late."'

The woman of his dreams? Shit. That was way too much, too soon. They'd been on two half dates, if this could be classed as such, and he'd just told her she was the woman of his dreams.

But to his surprise he felt her lean into him. 'I think if we're going to cement this bad boy reputation, you grabbing me and kissing me in the cave would go some way towards achieving that.'

He nearly sighed with relief. He'd somehow pulled it back. He reached down to stroke her face and poked her in the eye.

'Ow,' Melody cried.

'Shit, sorry. It really is dark in here.'

'It's OK,' Melody said, though it really wasn't.

'Shall I try again?' Jamie said.

'Yes.'

He reached out again to find her face and aimed his hands a bit lower to try to cup her cheeks. This time he ended up shoving his finger up her nose.

Seriously? What the hell was wrong with him?

'Sorry,' Jamie said again but Melody was laughing, which was something of a relief.

'Why don't we wait until we get home?' Melody said.

'Good idea,' Jamie said. 'Stay here a second.'

He scrabbled up and slowly, with his hands out in front of him, felt his way around the rock. Once round the other side, there was some natural light coming in from the entrance to the cave and he was able to see a bit better. He moved gingerly across the cave floor, navigating his way around the table and chairs until he came to the generator, and then spent a few moments feeling around until he found the switch.

Light filled the cave and he blinked against it briefly before he saw Melody emerging from the rocks at the back, blinking against the lights too. She looked adorable, her hair a bit mussed up, tumbling in curls over his jacket she was wearing. There was something very sexy about Melody wearing his clothes. Despite his promise to wait until they got back to his house, he moved across the cave towards her, cupped her face in his hands and kissed her. She started a little at the unexpected gesture before kissing him back, circling her arms round his neck, pulling herself tighter against him.

He pulled back slightly. 'I like you in my jacket.'

She grinned. 'This do it for you, does it?'

'Strangely, it does.'

'It's not that strange, lots of guys like the women they're with to wear their shirts. Well, at least in the books I read they do. I presume that's based on some kind of fact.'

God, the thought of her wearing only his shirt made his stomach clench with need.

'I love the idea of you in my bed, wearing only my shirt.'

That was too soon as well, but her eyes widened with a mixture of fear and excitement.

She swallowed.

'I'd rather be naked in your bed,' Melody said, clearly trying to show more confidence than she felt.

He smiled. 'That would work too. When you're ready. There's no rush.'

She opened her mouth as if she was going to insist she was ready now, but she seemed to change her mind.

He stroked her shoulders. 'Let's go back to mine. With any luck Leo will have got to the lasagne before it turned black and it will just be a case of reheating it.'

She nodded. 'I'm starving.'

He took her hand, switched off the generator on the way out and they left the cave behind.

The lasagne was black. Worse than that, it looked like a tray of molten tar. There was an apology note from Leo saying sorry for not getting there in time.

Melody sighed. As second dates went, this one wasn't turning out to be a big success either.

Except she had got to spend the evening cuddled up in Jamie's arms. And he had told her he wanted her in his bed. That had to count for something.

'Beans on toast?' Jamie offered as he poked at the burned mess. 'That's quick and easy.'

'Sure, let me give you a hand.' She grabbed a tin of beans, emptied it into the saucepan and put it on a low heat on the hob.

Jamie picked up the bread bag and pulled out four slices and placed them under the grill.

'So, you have your first jewellery workshop next week. Are you nervous?'

'I am really. I don't know if anyone will turn up. I kind of wanted to leave it open and flexible for the first one. It's just a taster and then if they like it they might want to sign up to do a six-week course, focussing on a particular area. I've got some leaflets printed off explaining what kinds of methods they will be learning over the different six-week courses and I'll do a little demonstration of a few different things at the end. I just have to engage them enough in this session for them to want to come back for more. That's if anyone turns up.'

'I'm sure you'll get lots of takers,' Jamie said. 'Lots of people will be interested in that sort of thing. I've run one-day courses myself in the past, focussing on pottery, and I've had loads of people attending.'

'Really? Oh, that makes me feel better. It'd be awful if no one turned up. What sort of people came?'

'Mostly the older ladies of the village, they love a bit of craft.'

Melody smiled and wondered if it was the lure of being taught by the sexy Jamie Jackson that had the old ladies turning up in their droves.

'I am a bit nervous. I have no idea about their capabilities and experience. I might get people who have done lots of this kind of thing before and others who will have no clue so I'll have to tailor the course to suit.'

'OK, why don't you practise on me? I have never done anything with jewellery before so I will be utterly clueless. You can then see what the worst-case-scenario student will be and cater accordingly when it comes to the real thing. I'll tell you if your explanations and demonstrations are clear enough or give you suggestions if I think the course is lacking anything.'

'OK, that's a great idea. Thank you.' She watched Sirius careen into the table leg, bounce off and chase an imaginary foe across the room. 'And then we have our puppy training class Saturday.'

'I think half the village will be turning up for that.'

'I think it's lovely that all eleven puppies were rehomed here in the village. It means that Rocky and Sirius still get to see their brothers and sisters. And Beauty still gets to bump into her children.'

'I think it will be chaos with all the siblings meeting each other again, all together in one room. I don't think there will be much training done in that first session. And we have the sandcastle competition on Saturday afternoon. Fancy being on my team?' Jamie said.

Melody smiled. 'I'd love that. I've heard it gets super competitive though.'

He laughed. 'Oh it does, especially between families and friends. Everyone wants to prove they are the best at building sandcastles.'

'You know you're not likely to win if I'm on your team.'

'Oh, I don't know about that. You can be my lucky charm.'

'I'm not particularly lucky.'

'Well I feel very lucky being with you.'

She felt her smile grow at that.

'Toast is ready,' Jamie said.

Melody peered at the beans. 'These are done too.'

He placed the toast on two plates and she poured out the beans while he got two glasses of water and took them over to the table.

She picked up the two plates and carried them over just as Jamie sat down. As she leaned over the table to hand him his plate, she stubbed her toe on the table leg and jerked the plates she was holding in shock. The two slices of beans on toast slithered off the plate, flipped over and landed on Jamie's lap.

'Oh my God, I'm so sorry,' Melody said, quickly running round to help him.

'It's fine,' Jamie said, grabbing the empty plate and somehow scooping the toast and most of the beans back onto the plate in one swoop. She started picking up the stray beans from his crotch. 'Oh I see, you did this just because you wanted to have a grope of me too,' he teased.

Melody smiled. 'I'm sorry, I've ruined your dinner.'

Jamie cut a bit of toast off on his plate, scooped some beans onto it and popped it in his mouth.

'If the five-second rule applies to food that's fallen on the floor, it sure as hell needs to apply when it's fallen on your clothes too.'

'Are you OK? You're not burnt? Maybe you should take your jeans off.'

'Oh, that's your game,' Jamie said, continuing to eat his toast. 'It's fine. I'm sure everything is still working down there.'

She sat down tentatively so she could eat as well and she watched him eat, hungrily. He wasn't bothered at all and her heart swelled with love for him because of it. All their dates had been a total disaster so far and he didn't seem to care.

He caught her looking at him. 'What's wrong?'

'Just thinking you must have the patience of a saint to put up with all this crap.'

He swallowed his mouthful of food. 'What crap? I love spending time with you. So what if things don't go exactly to plan? Life isn't like that, perfect with no mistakes, why should love be like that too?'

Melody thought about this for a moment. In the books she read, love always seemed perfect, sweeping the heroine and the reader off their feet, but Jamie was right, real life wasn't like that. Real life was beans on toast at midnight with your favourite person in the world.

She reached out and took his hand. 'I really bloody like you, Jamie Jackson.'

He grinned. 'I should hope so. I wouldn't eat dirty beans on toast for anyone.'

'You said it was fine,' Melody laughed.

He laughed too. 'It is, a bit gritty and fluffy, but that's extra protein, right?'

She laughed, shaking her head.

'It's perfect, I promise. Because I get to share them with you.'

Her breath caught in her throat. Maybe it was time to redefine her perfect. He was right, being together was the only thing that mattered.

CHAPTER 14

Melody looked out on the sea as she stood in the shallows. It was calm today, barely a ripple on the surface. The perfect day for teaching Elliot how to paddleboard. She had taken him out a few times before, sitting on her paddleboard while she did all the paddling so he had some idea about how the paddleboard felt on the water and that when it wobbled it wasn't the scariest thing in the world. Today he was going to try it for himself.

She looked around as he stood next to her, ankle-deep in the water as he fastened the clips on his lifejacket.

'You ready?' Melody asked, kneeling down to check his lifejacket.

Elliot nodded keenly.

Melody pushed his child-sized board out a little bit deeper so he would be up to his knees in the water when he got on. Elliot followed her.

'OK, hands either side of the board.' Melody indicated where he should put them. She held the paddle for him; he would learn how to get on while holding a paddle at a later stage.

Elliot did as he was told.

'Now place your knee here, that's it,' Melody said. 'Now lean on your hands slightly and bring your other knee up next to the first one.'

She held the board steady for him as he got himself comfortable in a kneeling position.

'OK, kneel up and we're going to paddle for a little while on your knees. Hold your paddle like I showed you before. Dip the paddle straight into the water towards the front of the board and then pull it back towards you.'

'Hey Elliot, you look good,' she heard Jamie call from the beach. She glanced round and smiled at him, one hand still on the back of the paddleboard as if teaching Elliot to ride a bike. Jamie was wearing only shorts and her grip nearly slipped as she enjoyed the sight of his tanned, muscular body in all its glory.

'Hi, Jamie.' Elliot waved madly with the paddle and the board rocked precariously. Melody tightened her grip on the back, to stop it tipping over. 'Look at me, I'm a paddleboarder.'

'You certainly are,' Jamie said.

To Melody's surprise, he waded out to join them.

'Want a hand?' he asked quietly.

'If you've got the time, an extra pair of hands wouldn't hurt. Some of us need to learn that poise and balance is the key.'

Jamie smiled. 'I've always got time for you.'

Her heart filled with love for him. She had mentioned the night before that she was looking after Elliot for a few hours the next day and that Elliot had asked if she could teach him how to paddleboard. She had also told Jamie that she was a little nervous about letting Elliot do it on his own for the first time, so she loved that Jamie had turned up here to support her.

'Well, I'll follow your lead,' Jamie said. 'You're the expert.'

She'd had several lessons when she first moved down here and she had been out on her own many times, but she wouldn't call herself the expert.

Jamie moved to one side and she moved round to the other.

She turned back to Elliot. 'OK, put your paddle back in the water. No, the paddle is backwards, turn it round the other way. That's it. Push down and pull backwards, gently, you don't need to do it hard.' She glanced over at Jamie as he stood opposite her and saw he was smiling at her. 'Try to remain straight, you don't need to lean into the paddle too much, it's about finding your balance. OK, now swap sides with your paddle. Well done Elliot, you're doing great.'

They moved up and down the shore for a while, still staying where she and Jamie could stand easily. After the first few shaky minutes, Elliot seemed to get into his stride. He was good at following instructions and Jamie kept giving him gentle words of encouragement.

'Shall we try standing up?' Melody said, gently.

'Yes, I bet I will be brilliant at that,' Elliot said, and Melody smirked at his confidence. This was a kid who had been raised to believe he could do anything.

'So hand Jamie your paddle and lean forward and put your hands at the sides of the board.'

Elliot did as he was told.

'Now bring each foot to where your knees are on the board so you are squatting and slowly stand up.'

She held the board steady as Elliot followed all those instructions at top speed. There was no worry in his mind that he might fall. He clearly trusted in his own abilities, completely.

Jamie passed him his paddle and Elliot went straight into paddling without any hesitation. Melody smiled. Children were completely fearless. They would climb trees and play in the sea and run through woods without any fear of falling or getting hurt. She wondered when those fears started to creep in, when getting hurt physically and emotionally was a worry with almost any activity, from paddleboarding to being in a relationship. Maybe this carefree, confident attitude towards the world was something to be adopted herself.

'Straighten up a bit,' Melody said.

She decided to release the board and see how well he could do on his own. For a few moments, Elliot glided across the water perfectly, holding a textbook stance. He really could do it.

'Look, there's Marigold,' Elliot said, suddenly waving vigorously.

The board toppled in the water and, though Melody reached out to grab it, Elliot fell sideways and landed straight into Jamie's arms.

Elliot laughed, completely unfazed by his fall, wiggled down from Jamie's grasp and splashed ashore, then ran up the beach to greet Marigold and Emily. Melody noticed Isla was with them, obviously having returned from her shopping trip.

'You're so good with him,' Jamie said, steadying the board between them.

'Thanks. He has no fear, does he?'

'That's because he trusts in you.'

She didn't think that was entirely true, but it was a nice idea. She looked up the beach and saw Elliot was chasing Marigold around with a water pistol Isla had just given him. Marigold and Emily had one each too.

'I'm not sure if our lesson has finished or not. That looks much more fun.'

Jamie laughed. 'Well, why don't I go and get some ice creams for all of us and we'll see if he wants to continue after?'

She nodded, and he helped her pull the board ashore, even though it was very light, before walking off to the little ice cream shack. She waved at Emily, who was definitely not going easy on the children in their water fight, much to their delight.

Melody took off her lifejacket, which she'd only worn to set a good example to Elliot, and sat down on the sand. Isla left Elliot to play with Marigold and Emily and came and sat down with her.

'How was he, did he listen to instructions?' Isla said.

'He was very good at listening. He has so much confidence in his abilities. There is no slow and steady approach when it comes to Elliot,' Melody said.

Isla laughed. 'No, slow is not in his vocabulary.'

'Did you get everything you needed at the shops?' Melody asked. She knew if you wanted to go clothes shopping it involved a trip to the next town. Sandcastle Bay was too small to have any decent clothes shops.

'Yes. Thank you for having him. I would have taken him with me but it's much more fun for him if he can stay here. He loves spending time with you. And now Tori and Aidan are throwing this impromptu barbeque this afternoon, there was even less time for me to go shopping, so I needed to get round the shops quickly, not stop and look in toy or sweet shops.'

'It was my pleasure. I love being with him too.'

Isla looked over to where Jamie was queueing. 'It's nice of him to come and help. How are things going with the two of you?'

Melody couldn't help but smile. 'Really good.'

She looked out over the waves.

'But?' Isla said, insightfully.

Melody looked at her. 'There's no but.'

'Melody, I know you better than I know the back of my hand. I know when there's a but.'

Melody sighed. 'I'm scared I'm going to push him away.'

'Why on earth would you think that?' Isla said in surprise.

'Because I'm a disaster zone. I'm clumsy, accident-prone, I spill things. I keep thinking he'll tire of it at some point.'

'Jamie knows you really well; he's known you for a long time. This is not brand-new information for him. If he was really that bothered by stuff like that, he wouldn't be going out with you in the first place.'

'But before he got to witness it occasionally, now he bears the full force of it every day.'

'He doesn't care about stuff like that. He's so laid-back, he's practically horizontal. What kind of asshole would he be if he dumped you because you're too clumsy.'

Melody opened her mouth to say her last boyfriend was that kind of asshole, but Isla got there first.

'I know Kevin did exactly that, but he was an utter twonk.'

'Twonk?'

'I'm working on not saying swearwords around Elliot.'

'Twonk works,' Melody said, looking at Elliot who was way too far away to hear them. 'Cockwomble is better.'

Isla nodded her agreement. 'The point being, Jamie is a million miles away from assclown Kevin. Jamie is not going anywhere, he adores you.'

'I just wonder if Jamie knew what he was letting himself in for.'

'Don't say that like he is dragging the bottom of the barrel going out with you. He knew exactly what he was getting when he went out with you. Someone who is wonderful, funny, kind and he's very lucky to have you.'

'Oh, I wasn't putting myself down. I just meant the clumsiness is a lot to take. Even Mum's patience wore thin with it eventually.'

'Is that what this is really about? You know her negativity and anger had nothing to do with you and everything to do with her.'

'I know,' Melody said, sadly.

'Don't put those fears on him.'

Melody looked over at him as he got to the front of the queue. 'Do you think he really knows me?'

'I bet he sees more than you see yourself. Did you tell him what flavour you wanted?'

Melody shook her head

'Let's see if he passes the ice cream test,' Isla said.

'Because that's conclusive proof?' Melody said.

'Do you think Shithead Kevin would know your favourite ice cream flavour? You guys were together for three months.'

'No, he wouldn't.'

Jamie came over with a tray loaded with different ice cream flavours.

'I didn't know what everyone wanted so I took a lucky guess with chocolate for the kids, and then I got a selection, coconut, honeycomb, pistachio, oh and rocky road for you Melody.'

Her heart leapt into her mouth and, as he sat down and placed the tray carefully in the sand, she leaned over and kissed him, ignoring the smug smirk on Isla's face.

Jamie pulled back slightly and smiled against her lips. 'What was that for?'

Because I love you, Melody thought. 'Because I really love rocky road.'

He grinned. 'You're easily pleased, Melody Rosewood.'

She picked up the rocky road and the pistachio, as she knew that was Jamie's favourite. She passed him his and leaned her head against his shoulder as she started eating her own.

Maybe Isla was right. Maybe they would be OK.

A drip from her rocky road landed on his chest but before she could apologise, Jamie immediately scooped it off with his finger and sucked it into his mouth.

She looked up at him and smiled.

I really bloody love you.

CHAPTER 15

The barbeque was in full swing, Aidan was busy flipping burgers and Tori was going round making sure everyone had a drink. Everyone else was sitting back on their sun loungers, enjoying the warm weather and chatting to each other.

It was a very small family affair, Melody noted, just the Jackson brothers, Isla, Emily and her husband Stanley, Agatha and the two children. Melody suspected they were gathered there to hear Tori and Aidan's big surprise news and, by the way that Agatha was fidgeting impatiently in her seat, Agatha obviously thought the same – although she didn't know about the proposal so Tori and Aidan still had some surprises up their sleeve. Agatha had tried to corner Tori on several occasions to cut to the chase, but Tori had managed to sidestep her with hostess duties.

'Stop fidgeting,' Melody said to Agatha.

Agatha let out a sigh of exasperation. 'Do you know?'

'What?'

'You know perfectly well what. Is she pregnant?'

'I have no idea,' Melody lied. 'I've not really spoken to her.'

'Why else would we be having this barbeque?'

'Because the sun is shining and it's nice to get us all together for a change. We're all so busy that we don't get the chance to catch up together very often,' Melody said, innocently.

Agatha rolled her eyes.

Jamie came and sat back down next to Melody, which she was thankful for. He passed her a burger and she quickly took a bite before Agatha could ask her any more questions.

'How are you two getting on?' Agatha asked, and then carried on as if Jamie wasn't there. 'Have you looked at that book I gave you yet?'

Melody choked on her burger. Crap, she really didn't want to have this discussion in front of Jamie.

'What book?' Jamie asked.

Melody quickly swallowed.

'The *Kama Sutra*,' Agatha said, simply.

Jamie stared at her and then burst out laughing. 'I think we'll be fine at that side of things.'

'I think we all could do with a little bit of inspiration now and again,' Agatha said. 'Spice things up a little.'

'What's a Kama Supra?' Elliot asked as he stood nearby, working his way through an entire box of raspberries.

Agatha had the grace to blush. 'It's a book about… birds and, um… bees.'

'No it isn't,' Marigold said. 'I saw Agatha give it to Melody on the beach and it had a man and a woman on the front and they were kissing and cuddling and they didn't have many clothes on. There were no bees or birds on the cover.'

Elliot giggled. 'Is it a book about kissing and cuddling?'

'Sort of,' Agatha said.

'What are you teaching my godson?' Leo came and sat next to Jamie and stole a crisp off his plate.

'About the Kama Supra,' Elliot said, simply.

Leo arched an eyebrow and Melody couldn't help giggling over how this conversation was going.

'I think Mummy and Daddy have been reading the Kama Supra,' Marigold said. 'I saw them in their bed yesterday. Daddy was on top of Mummy just like on the cover of the book and he was kissing her and moving around. Mummy kept saying to him, "Harder," and Daddy said he didn't want to hurt the baby.'

There was silence for a few moments.

Jamie cleared his throat. 'Well, that was information I really didn't need to hear,' he said, quietly. 'What is it with my family and their oversharing?'

Melody laughed as she remembered the night before.

Emily came and sat down with her plate of food, completely none the wiser that her daughter had just been discussing Emily's sex life.

'What did I miss?' Emily said, ironically biting into a sausage.

'You don't want to know,' Leo said. 'But maybe you should invest in a lock on the bedroom door.'

Emily paused with the sausage halfway to her mouth and then her cheeks flooded with colour as she looked at Marigold.

Marigold shrugged. 'Come on Elliot, let's go and see the dogs.'

Elliot followed her across the grass to where all the puppies were playing.

'Oh god,' Emily said.

'Don't be embarrassed. Nothing wrong with having sex and kudos to you for doing it when you're pregnant. Sex shouldn't stop just because you're having a baby,' Agatha said.

Emily stared at her in shock.

They were saved from any further talk on the subject by Tori chinking on a glass.

'Finally!' Agatha muttered.

'We want to thank you all for coming today at such short notice,' Tori said, slipping an arm round Aidan's waist. 'But we wanted you guys to be the first to know, although there are some here who have already guessed, but… we're expecting a baby.'

There was a roar of approval and cheers from the small gathering as everyone rushed over to congratulate them.

After a while everyone sat back down and was just picking up their plates and talking between themselves about the happy news when Aidan cleared his throat.

'We actually have more news.' He smiled at Tori with a look of complete love. 'Last night, I asked Tori to be my wife and, after many tears, she said yes.'

There were more cheers and even Agatha looked shocked at this piece of news. Evidently her spies weren't *everywhere.*

As Melody and Jamie joined the queue of wellwishers to congratulate them again, Jamie whispered in her ear. 'Do you think we should ever tell them we have the proposal on video? They might enjoy looking back on it.'

Melody laughed. 'Maybe one day. But did you see how embarrassed Emily was at the thought of Marigold simply telling us she saw them have sex? Let's not put Tori and Aidan through that. Let them enjoy tonight. For now, at least, I think we might have to keep that video under wraps.'

She hugged Tori and felt a surge of happiness for her best friend. This was real progress for her, someone who had never wanted a relationship, let alone a family.

She turned away and Agatha was waiting for them. 'You two will be next, you mark my words. You'll be married before the year is out.'

Melody laughed and then checked Jamie's reaction to Agatha's crazy predictions. To her surprise, he was laughing as well. That was progress for him too.

He put his arm round her and they walked back to their seats. 'When I do propose, I'm going to damn well make sure I do it in private.'

❀

There was a knock on her shop door at the end of the day, just as she was getting everything ready for her trial workshop with Jamie. Rocky leapt up from his basket, barking gleefully at having a visitor.

She turned to see Jamie smiling at her from the doorway and she went quickly to answer it. She threw her arms round his neck and kissed him before he'd even had a chance to speak. His large hands spanning her back as he held her tight against him was a wonderful feeling and, for a glorious few seconds, she allowed herself to think about what it would be like if he was holding her like this when they were both naked.

She pulled back before she could get too carried away.

He cleared his throat awkwardly. 'I, um… I'm here for the jewellery-making workshop with Melody Rosewood.'

She giggled and tugged him inside.

'I hope you're not going to greet your real students like that,' Jamie muttered as he followed her inside.

She laughed, knowing he was teasing her. 'Why not, I'm sure I'd get great feedback if I do. OK, sit down here.'

'Bossy too,' Jamie said. He gave Rocky some fuss and seeing nothing exciting was happening and no food was involved, the puppy went back to his basket.

She shushed Jamie, flapping her hands at him. 'The class is about to start.'

Jamie sat up straight and focussed all of his attention on her.

'Welcome to my beginners' jewellery class. Today we are just going to learn the basics of a few different techniques to give you a sample of the different courses I'm going to hold in the future. We will be learning how to use beads and pliers, and on future courses you will use these tools and materials to make earrings, pendants and bracelets. A very simple way to make jewellery, and one of my favourites, is to use silver clay. You can get some great results with this. Another thing I'm going to demonstrate for you today is sandcasting. We can create moulds in the sand and melt down old bits of silver with a blow torch and—'

'Ooooh, blow torch?' Jamie said, reverentially, sitting up in his chair.

She smiled. 'You'd like to use that, would you?'

He nodded, keenly.

'Well we can come on to that shortly, we also use the blow torch for the silver clay. Let me show you a bit of wire work first. You'll need three different pairs of pliers. We have the side-cutter.' She held up the small pliers with a blue handle and Jamie found a matching pair laid out in front of him. 'This is used for cutting wire.'

'Does what it says on the tin,' Jamie said.

'Yeah exactly. These green ones are the round-nosed pliers. You will use these for making loops, which will be useful when making the ends of bracelets or earrings or the chain loops for the pendants. And this pink pair are the chain-nose pliers, which you use to bend, twist, straighten or crimp the wire, depending on your design. You have a few strips of practice wire in front of you so you can experiment with what you can do with the different pliers.'

'Just have a play?' Jamie asked, looking at the wire dubiously.

'Yes, see what each one does.'

Jamie looked at the pliers. 'I think you need to demonstrate this part, show us some examples of what you can achieve using these tools.'

'OK,' Melody said, doubtfully. 'It's quite close intricate work, I'd worry that the students wouldn't be able to see what I was doing. I was going to wander around at this point and give little pointers to each of the students.'

'You could rig up a projector and a camera so you could zoom in on what you were doing with your hands and it would be projected onto the wall. If you have say, fifteen students all at once, you couldn't get around to them all in any decent timeframe and that means the students on the other side of the room from where you start would have a long wait before they could be shown how to use the pliers. When you introduce the pliers, give a little demo using the projector then, before you move onto the next set of pliers and then give them time to play once they have been shown what they can do.'

Melody thought about this. 'That's a good idea, though I'd have no idea on the technology side of things.'

'I have some idea about that, but Klaus would be your best bet, he'd come round and set it all up for you.'

'OK, thanks.'

'And for now, you can come here and give me a personal demonstration.'

She grinned and walked around the table towards him. She stood next to him and picked up the pair of side-cutter pliers. Jamie looped his arm round her and pulled her onto his lap.

'Hey! I don't expect this kind of behaviour from my students,' Melody protested. 'It's supposed to be a professional relationship.'

'You said it was close, intimate work,' Jamie said, placing a kiss on her neck.

'Intricate, not intimate,' she laughed.

'Well, it doesn't get much closer than this.'

Melody smirked but didn't get off his lap. She loved this affectionate side of him.

She demonstrated how to use the different pliers and the different effects he could achieve with round-nosed and chain-nosed pliers especially. Though she wasn't sure how much attention he was paying to her instructions as he kept kissing her and somehow her top had slid off her shoulder during her demonstrations and he was now kissing that too.

'You need to behave; my boyfriend would not be happy if he saw me cavorting with one of my students like this.'

'No he wouldn't,' Jamie said.

'I'm going to let you have a play with the wire for a few minutes while I get the silver clay ready. If you're good, I'll even let you use the blow torch.'

'Now that is motivation.'

She climbed off his lap and gathered together the tools and materials for using the silver clay. She watched him playing with the pliers and the wire quite efficiently so he must have been paying some attention.

Deciding that close work was what was needed for the next part of the demonstration, she pulled up a chair next to him and laid out the silver clay, the blow torch, a damp tea towel, a bowl of water and the other tools, just as Jamie was finishing an intricate spiral that was part braided. She wondered if he'd ever done anything like this before in his sculpture work; he had a natural flair for it.

'OK, this next bit should be right up your street, working with clay. This is just like working with any of your clay sculptures. It's soft and malleable like clay, only this stuff dries out really quickly, so you need to have a good idea of what you're going to make before we make it. Sometimes I practise with plasticine first.'

'Maybe you should give your students a small lump of plasticine to work with so they can get used to modelling something and making the shapes they want. For some, this might be the first bit of clay they've touched since they were kids.'

'That's a good idea. I'm sure you'll be OK if we miss that stage for now, seeing as you're an expert in all things clay.'

Jamie nodded. 'I'm sure I'll cope.'

'So, we can make whatever we want then we stick it in a kiln or use a blow torch and that removes all the clay elements and the binder so all you are left with is silver. For my demonstration I'm going to make a leaf, which is simple and easy. I'm sure you can create something suitably amazing.'

He grinned. 'Show me the leaf.'

Leaving the plastic wrap over the clay so it didn't dry out, she rolled out a section of clay about the size of a fifty-pence piece until it was really thin, using the spacers either side so that the clay was the same thickness throughout. She carefully peeled the plastic wrap away.

'We should lubricate our hands when using the clay, so it doesn't dry out too quickly. I use olive oil.' She blobbed a few drops into her hands and rubbed them together, then offered the bottle to Jamie. He took it and did the same.

'I'm going to use this leaf I picked from outside to imprint into the clay.' She pressed the leaf into the soft clay, pressing down the edges and around the veins to get the pattern of the leaf. 'Now we're going to cut around the edge using this knife. So we're just left with the leaf shape. Keep any clay you cut away and rewrap it. You can use it next time. You might want to leave the leaf in the clay until it dries to get more of an imprint.'

Using the round-nosed pliers, she made a loop of wire which she pressed into the back of the leaf so she could thread a chain through it and sell it as a necklace once it was finished.

'And that's it. Now we need to leave it to dry, normally for about ten minutes on the warming plate.'

'And what should we do in the meantime?' Jamie asked, leaning forward to kiss her.

She batted him away. 'Fortunately, in true *Blue Peter* fashion, here's one I made earlier.' She showed him the clay leaf she had made the day before that was now solid but very brittle. 'I'll show you the next stage when you've had a go at moulding the clay.'

Jamie played with the wrapped clay in his hand for a moment as he clearly thought about what to make with such a small piece and then his fingers started moving, poking the clay through the plastic until he had a rough shape, then carefully removed the plastic and continued his sculpting. She watched him. He was obviously in his element, enjoying the feel of the clay against his fingers. She realised he was making a couple embracing in a hug, very similar to what she was making for the Sculptures in the Sand Festival. Although he hadn't seen her design, it was possible he might have seen the template that Klaus cut out for her. She was surprised at how much detail his couple showed as the piece of clay he was using was so small. Finally, he placed the clay couple back down on the table.

'It's beautiful,' Melody said.

'I had inspiration,' Jamie said.

She smiled. 'Well, that will need time to dry on the warming plate before you use the blow torch on it, but you can have a go at using the blow torch on this sun that I made yesterday.'

She turned the blow torch on and moved it over her clay leaf, side to side to show him what to do.

'It depends how thick your piece is, but normally you're going to use the blow torch on it for around two minutes. Your couple might need around five minutes because it's thicker, but you can tell when you need to stop because the clay will be a slightly different colour. You can use the wet tea towel to turn the piece over when you need to and then, when it's finished, just pick it up using the towel and throw it into the bowl of water. That will immediately cool it down enough to touch without having to wait a long time.'

He nodded, taking it all in, and she turned the blow torch off and passed it over to him. She placed the sun on top of a block that was non-flammable and slid that in front of him too.

He rubbed his hands together with excitement

'How do I turn this on?' Jamie looked at the blow torch.

'Just turn the knob and press the ignition button at the back.'

He turned the knob more than she would have but at least he would get a big flame, which he would probably enjoy. He pressed the ignition button and the huge flame shot out. But the next second the whole of the bottom of his shirt caught fire. He leapt back in shock, but she was already on him, instinctively grabbing the bowl of cold water and throwing that on him and then the wet tea towel and smothering the blaze, patting him to put the flames out. The fire were out in what felt like less than a few seconds so she grabbed his shirt and ripped it open away from his stomach, relieved to see that he was wearing a t-shirt underneath. Although the t-shirt was wet, it wasn't burned in any way. She lifted the material carefully to make sure and revealed perfect unblemished skin underneath.

She was vaguely aware that Rocky was whimpering and barking, obviously traumatised by the fire too.

Jamie stared at her in shock, his breath heavy, and then he looked down at his stomach, rubbing it and checking for injuries himself.

'Are you OK?' she asked, grabbing the blow torch and quickly turning it off.

He nodded. 'I think so. Thanks to you.' Satisfied he wasn't injured, he turned his attention back to her. 'What the hell was that?'

'I don't know, it's never done anything like that before. The flame wasn't anywhere near the shirt. I'm not sure…' She could smell something that was beyond the smell of burnt fabric. Something chemical. 'Did you have something on your shirt?'

He shook his head and then froze. 'I was using a spray-on varnish on one of my pieces just before I came here.'

She groaned. 'I'm guessing it's very flammable.'

'I imagine so yes, I've never tested it before.'

'Well now you have.'

'That's not something I ever want to repeat,' Jamie said, shakily.

'Me neither,' Melody said, feeling the tears smart her eyes now the adrenaline was leaving her body. 'Are you sure you're OK?'

He nodded. 'Are you?'

'I think so.'

'You reacted so quick.' Jamie took her hands and examined them for any injury, but they didn't hurt.

'It was just instinct.'

'Instinct that saved my life.' He kissed both of her palms and then pulled her in for a hug, wrapping his arms around her and holding her tightly.

After a while he pulled back slightly. 'Let's leave this lesson for tonight, let's go home.'

She didn't even ask whose home he meant. There was no chance she was leaving him tonight.

She nodded.

He let her go and she tidied up a few things before turning the lights off. She grabbed Rocky's lead, took his hand and they left the shop.

Melody was lying on Jamie's sofa, being kissed so intimately, so intensely, she'd barely had chance to draw breath since they'd walked back into his house.

Kissing Jamie was always so passionate, he was obviously going to be the same in bed too, which made her a little nervous. What if she really was crap in bed and he was some kind of sexual god? He wouldn't get the same enjoyment out of it as she did. She'd had a little peek at the *Kama Sutra* that Agatha had given her and quite honestly that had made her feel worse.

So when they'd burst through his front door and he had kissed her hard, manoeuvred her to the sofa and started removing clothes, she'd stopped him while she still had her underwear on and he was still wearing his jeans. To his credit, he hadn't seemed bothered at all and had spent the last few hours just kissing her, his hands stroking her arms and shoulders, or trailing through her hair, but she knew he must be secretly annoyed. She was annoyed with herself too; she had no idea why she was holding back. She had thought about what it would be like to make love to Jamie for many many months.

Her stomach gurgled loudly and he chuckled against her lips before pulling back slightly.

'I really need to feed you.'

She reached up to stroke his face. They hadn't spoken about her turning him down for sex. She'd simply stilled his hand as he started to tug down her knickers and he'd barely missed a beat as he continued to kiss her, keeping his hands above her waist from that moment on.

'I'm sorry,' Jamie said, just as she had been about to say the same thing.

She frowned. 'What are you sorry for?'

'For trying to take it too far.'

'God, don't apologise for that. Do you know how wonderful it is that you want me like that? I want you too, I'm just a little nervous about it.'

'There's no rush. I want to do this right too and grabbing you and mauling you on the sofa is not the right way to do it.'

'I don't know; it was pretty bloody hot.'

He grinned and sat up and looked around the room. Her dress was flung across the other side of the room, so he picked up his shirt and passed it to her. She slipped it on and did up the buttons as he got up and wandered into the kitchen.

'Pasta OK?'

'Yes, that's fine,' Melody said, following him in. 'So, marks out of ten for my course?'

'Well, as a paying customer, I had a bloody great time tonight.' He gave her a mischievous grin over his shoulder as he was chopping a pepper.

'I set fire to you,' Melody protested.

'I set fire to myself. That was my own stupid fault. Anyone with half a brain would think about the possibility of the spray-on varnish being flammable. Besides, I was talking about the special one-on-one attention I got before the incident and the amazing conclusion to the lesson after I set fire to myself.'

She smiled at him. 'You always see the positive in our dates.'

He turned to her and frowned. 'And you always focus on the negatives.'

'It's hard not to, they've been a disaster.'

His frown deepened even more. 'I don't see that at all. I've had three dates which have included kissing you and holding you, time spent with you chatting and laughing. That sounds pretty perfect to me.'

She smiled sadly that he was kind enough to look past all her imperfections, clumsiness and inherent ability to somehow attract accidents and hazards everywhere she went.

'You don't see your worth, do you?' Jamie said, softly. 'Why is that, I wonder.'

She flinched inside. That was a sore nerve she hadn't really thought about for many years. She didn't realise that wound was still there.

'Is this to do with your mum?'

'No, why do you think that?'

'I don't know. Maybe because she had nothing positive to say to you since you were a teenager, you started to think there is nothing positive about you at all.'

'I'm happy with who I am,' Melody said, but she couldn't help the defensive tone seeping into her voice.

He cocked his head slightly as he studied her. 'But you're not, are you? You don't see what I see at all.'

'A walking disaster zone?'

'You have so many more qualities than that.'

'Being clumsy and accident-prone is not a quality,' Melody said.

He smiled. 'It is, it's very endearing. But as I said, there is so much more to you than that.'

'I'm good at making jewellery.' Melody tried to see what Jamie could see. She did have good points, she knew that.

'You are, but that is the tip of the iceberg.' He paused as he stepped up to her. 'I'm going to show you what I see, but not today. I have a plan. But this…' he laid his hand over her heart, '…is the thing I adore most of all.'

Her little romantic heart soared at that.

'Come here tomorrow night, I have an idea for a date that can't possibly go wrong,' Jamie said.

She grinned. 'Now that, I have to see.'

CHAPTER 16

Jamie stood outside his shop the next day in the tiny courtyard, kissing Melody goodbye. They'd been there, kissing for the last five minutes. Other shop owners had walked around them to get to their own shops and he didn't care. He was more than happy taking his time with it because he really bloody enjoyed kissing her. It didn't matter that he was going to see her tonight; he could honestly spend the whole day kissing her and never get tired of it.

She pulled back slightly with a big smile on her face. 'I need to get to work and so do you.'

'Spoilsport,' Jamie said, giving her another brief kiss.

She waved goodbye to him and he watched her go. It was safe to say he was well and truly smitten.

He walked into his art studio knowing he was wearing the biggest grin on his face. Klaus was already waiting for him, two mugs of coffee in his hands, a huge smirk playing on his lips.

Klaus handed him his mug. 'Happy Birthday!'

Jamie's smile slipped slightly. He never really wanted to celebrate his birthday so he tried to keep quiet about it, but that didn't stop his friends and family wanting to celebrate for him.

'Thank you.'

'It seems like you've already had a great start to your day.' Klaus nodded towards Melody's shop. 'God, I thought I might have to surgically separate you both, you guys were kissing for so long.'

Jamie smiled and sat down at his desk, noticing the neatly wrapped present. Klaus hovered; evidently this conversation was nowhere near finished.

'So it's going well then?' Klaus said, grabbing a chair and sitting down opposite Jamie.

'It's so much better than I could possibly have imagined. I don't know why I held back for so long.'

'Tell me everything, what's the sex like? Is it amazing? With a smile that big she's got to be good in bed. Does she...' He made an obscene gesture.

'I'm not telling you those details,' Jamie objected. He wasn't a prude, but he didn't talk about his sex life with anyone. That was private.

'Ah come on, my sex life is completely lacking at the moment, but I can live vicariously through you. What was the first time like? I think you can tell a lot about a relationship from the first time you sleep with someone. Was it passionate, sweet, was it swinging from the chandeliers?'

Jamie laughed. 'My relationship with Melody is wonderful and she makes me very happy, but it's also private.'

'You just snogged her face off for the last five minutes in front of everyone; you were caught on the beach the other night in the throes of passion. This doesn't sound very private to me. Just tell me something, one little snippet, anything,' Klaus pleaded.

'No.'

'Please. Pleeeeeeeeaaaase!' Klaus begged.

'There's nothing to tell,' Jamie said, getting frustrated.

Klaus's face fell. 'Nothing to tell? You haven't slept together yet?'

Jamie sighed, wishing he hadn't said that. 'We're taking things slowly.'

'Do you not want to sleep with her?' Klaus pushed.

'Of course I bloody do,' Jamie snapped. 'But we... have this friend arrangement.'

'Friends with benefits?' Klaus asked, in confusion.

'No, sort of. No, it's not that—'

'Not if you're not shagging it's not, it's just friends.'

Jamie rubbed his head. 'No, we're friends who are dating so there's no pressure to try to be super romantic or wear a suit on a date. We're just going to be ourselves and have fun as we always do and date as well.'

'And have sex, right? If you're going to have a friends with benefits arrangement, you have to have the benefits as well.'

'She wants to wait.'

His face fell even more. 'Till marriage?'

'No, just… we've not even been dating a week yet, and none of our dates have exactly been smooth sailing. I think she's just waiting for the right time.'

'There is no right time. It's sex, not buying a house.'

'The right time is when she is ready for it,' Jamie said, defensively. 'And I'm happy to wait as long as she needs.'

Klaus obviously realised this conversation was over as he stood up. 'All right mate, no need to get tetchy. Clearly the lack of sex is making you really frustrated.'

Jamie decided not to mention that it was Klaus that was making him really frustrated, not Melody. He motioned his head towards the present.

'Thank you for this.'

Klaus shrugged but Jamie could tell he wasn't really upset.

'Can you do me a favour actually? Melody is doing her workshop on Monday. Could you go over and set up a projector and camera for her so she can do close hand work?'

'Yeah, no problem. I can do that, I'll pop over later.'

'Thank you.'

Klaus went over to his side of the studio and started work. Jamie sipped his coffee for a few minutes as he thought about his new addition to the sculpture he was working on for the competition that weekend.

The studio door opened and Jamie looked up and saw that it was Carolyn, Melody's mum. Well, that was a bit of a surprise.

He stood up and went over to greet her. 'Hello Carolyn, how are you doing today?'

'I'm good. I'm looking to buy one of your sculptures for a friend. We came past here the other day and he mentioned how much he loved the horse in the window. I thought I'd buy it for him.'

'That's very nice of you,' Jamie said, noticing that his tone of voice held an element of surprise. He cleared his throat. 'Do you want to take it now or shall I have it delivered?'

'Oh, a delivery would be great,' Carolyn said.

He gestured for her to come over to the till and took payment from her, writing down her details.

'Thank you, he's going to be so pleased when he sees it,' Carolyn said, excitedly.

She turned to go but Jamie suddenly had an idea.

'Carolyn?'

She turned back to face him.

'I wonder if I might trouble you for a few moments of your time.'

She looked surprised but she nodded.

'I'm doing a sculpture for the competition this weekend.' He paused because no one ever saw his work before it was finished, but this would work so much better if Carolyn saw it. 'It's not finished yet but… would you like to see it?'

She nodded keenly. He pulled back the curtain and she stepped up to look.

She gasped when she saw it. 'Oh… God, it's… beautiful.'

He knew straight away that he had done the right thing.

'Thank you. It's not quite finished and I have an idea for what I can do to finish it off. Maybe you can help me?'

⁂

Melody added the last piece of glass to her mosaic for the sculpture competition on Sunday and stood back to admire it. It looked great and she was really pleased with how it had turned out.

She had been glad of the distraction that morning. All she had been able to think about was that incredibly hot kiss the night before, the way Jamie had tugged her clothes off with a desperation for her. No one had ever done that before. In fact Kevin had taken his own clothes off and folded them neatly on the chair, encouraging her to do the same. But with Jamie, there had been this urgency to be with her. Her dress flung across the room, he had ripped his own shirt off in his need to be skin to skin with her. And when she had stopped him from taking off any more clothes, he had spent hours kissing her, caressing and stroking her all over. God, she wanted to be with him now, but she wanted it to be the right time too. In her mind, it would be super romantic and perfect, though she wasn't sure what she should do to achieve that.

The shop door opened and Emily walked in. She was always so busy in the café that Melody didn't see her outside of it very often, let alone two days in a row. She knew Emily would be taking a few days off here and there over the summer to spend with Marigold; fortunately, as Emily owned her own café, she had the flexibility to do that.

'Oh hey, has your boss given you another day off?' Melody teased as she mixed the grout ready for applying to the mosaic.

'She's a hard taskmaster, that one,' Emily said. 'Always works me to the bone, but today I've managed to wangle a day off. We're going to the fun pool over in Meadow Bay. Marigold is very excited because there's a slide called the Death Star which apparently we have to go on.'

Melody laughed. 'Where is she?'

Emily pointed over to Jamie's studio and Melody could see Jamie playing with her.

'I just popped in because I need some gemstones for my sculpture for Sunday.'

'Oh, OK, what are you thinking of?'

'Well, gemstones have different meanings, don't they?'

'Yes, they do. What are you looking for?'

'Do you have one for happiness?'

Melody nodded. 'Alexandrite is for joy.'

'That works.'

Melody pulled out her box of stones and fished out an alexandrite stone.

'That's lovely. I also need one for creativity and imagination.'

'Um, citrine is supposed to represent imagination and diopside is good for creativity.'

'I'll take both. And can you label each one somehow, so I know which one is which?'

'I can wrap each one in tissue paper and write on that.'

'That sounds good, I'll have forgotten which one is citrus and alexander by the time I get back home.'

Melody smiled and didn't bother to correct her.

Emily pulled out a sheet of paper from her pocket, which looked like it held a list.

'I'll also need one for bravery and courage, one for friendship, generosity, patience, passion, persistence, compassion, warmth, wisdom, empowerment, integrity, loyalty, honesty, energy and—'

'You want a gemstone for each of these meanings?'

'Yes.'

'What are you making?'

Emily visibly panicked. 'It's a surprise. You'll see it when it is revealed to the village along with everyone else's.'

'Right, OK.'

'This is kind of something for Marigold. These are the qualities I hope for her,' Emily said, vaguely.

'Oh, that's lovely,' Melody said, not entirely convinced that Emily was telling the truth. 'This is going to work out quite expensive though.'

Even if she charged Emily cost price, it would still cost her a lot.

'Oh, it's OK, money is no object apparently,' she said, dryly, as if she didn't entirely agree with that sentiment.

Melody started fishing through her stones pulling out the relevant ones. The Jacksons were not a particularly affluent family. They weren't poor but definitely not rich either. She knew that Leo lived in a very large house, but she also knew he'd received a really big pay-out after his accident in the fire brigade cost him his job. His job in his own firework display company also gave him a good income. Jamie earned a ton of money for his sculptures and deservedly so, but she didn't think that Emily was that well-off that she could afford to spend a few hundred pounds on gemstones for a sculpture that was only going to be on the beach for a few days. Unless this sudden generosity had come from her husband Stanley. She didn't see Stanley very often because he worked out of town, but she knew he absolutely adored his daughter. Maybe this was his idea.

'Can I see the list?' Melody said, and her eyes widened when she saw how long it was. But doing something like this for Marigold was a lovely idea, even if the little girl might be a bit too young to appreciate it.

'I can't wait to see your sculpture,' Melody said. 'All of them actually. It will be interesting to see how different people have interpreted the theme.'

'I think you'll be surprised. People love Sandcastle Bay for lots of different reasons,' Emily said. 'I think you'll love Jamie's.'

'He's showed you?'

'No, he never shows anyone, but I have a good idea what he's done from the brief information he told me this morning.'

Melody nodded. She couldn't wait to see it; she knew it would be something amazing.

'It's exciting. What time does it all kick off on Sunday?' Melody said, slowly working her way down the list.

'Seven o'clock is the big reveal and the party and entertainment will happen after that.'

'It should be a great night.'

'I bet it will be super romantic as well,' Emily said, dreamily. 'The moon, stars, the fireworks, the sea lapping on the sand. It's definitely a night for love and romance.'

Melody looked at her, wondering if she was saying that purely for her benefit. But she was right. Sunday would be perfectly romantic and maybe, after a night of romance and dancing under the stars, it would be the perfect time to take her and Jamie's relationship to the next level.

Melody was just walking back from The Cherry on Top after lunch when she bumped into Klaus. He had the biggest ice cream she'd ever seen, a pale pink whipped affair with sprinkles, and fruit and marshmallows covering it. She was surprised it didn't have a cocktail umbrella too.

'Hello my darling, you're looking beautiful today.'

Melody grinned. She really liked Klaus. He was completely over the top and as bad as Agatha for interfering, but he had a good heart.

'Thank you, you're not looking bad yourself.' Melody nodded towards his bright turquoise Hawaiian shirt. Nobody looked good in a Hawaiian shirt any more, but somehow Klaus managed to pull it off.

'Ah thank you, the sun is shining, the birds are singing, it's definitely time to dig out the summer shirt. Have you tried these new ice creams from Sprinkles? They are to die for.' He shoved it towards her for her to take a lick but she smiled and waved it away.

'Thanks but I just had a big lunch with Tori.'

'Ah, how are the young love birds?'

'Very happy.'

'And you and Jamie?' He waggled his eyebrows mischievously. 'Are you very happy too?'

Melody couldn't help the grin from spreading on her face.

'I'll take that as a yes. He's been telling me all about your little friends with benefits arrangement,' Klaus said, taking a big lick of his ice cream.

Her heart sank a little. 'Is that what he called it?'

'Um…' Klaus said, clearly trying to think back. 'Well yeah. Friends who date. I'm not totally sure I understand it myself. I mean, he's not actually getting the "benefit" part, is he, so are you just friends that kiss?'

Melody felt her cheeks flush that Jamie had discussed their lack of sex with Klaus.

'He told you that we haven't had sex yet?' Melody asked, quietly, mortification crawling over her.

'The boy is desperate to get you into bed; he's like a rabid dog foaming at the mouth for you. He was very snappy with me this morning, obviously sexually frustrated,' Klaus said knowingly. 'Nothing worse than walking around with wood in your pants for days on end and not being able to do anything about it. You should totally put the poor boy out of his misery.'

Melody stared out at the turquoise waters for a moment, embarrassment turning to anger.

'Excuse me, I need to talk to Jamie.' She marched off.

'Oh no, wait, did I say something wrong?' Klaus called after her. 'Don't listen to me.'

She ignored him and walked straight into Starfish Court and into Jamie's art studio.

Jamie looked up when she walked in. He was mixing what looked like paint in a small pot. His whole face lit up at seeing her but the smile quickly fell from his lips when he could quite clearly see how angry she was.

'What's wrong?'

'You told Klaus we haven't had sex yet?'

He cringed and swore under his breath. 'It wasn't like that—'

'Did you tell him all about last night, about how we kissed and I stopped you from taking it any further? Did you have a good laugh about it?'

'What? No!'

'You said you were OK about it, that there was no rush and you wanted to do it right. And then you come in here and tell Klaus that you're sexually frustrated and how much you're desperate for me. He said you were like a rabid dog. Is that all this is to you, just sex? I thought we had something special that went way beyond that.'

'Firstly, I'm going to kill Klaus and, secondly, I never said any of that. He was going on and on, begging me for details of our sex life and in my frustration to get him to shut up, I told him there was nothing to tell. And being the big tart that he is, he was horrified that we hadn't jumped into bed with each other after the first kiss. He asked me if I didn't want to sleep with you and I said of course I did, but was happy to wait until you were ready. And he's bloody translated that to me being desperate to have sex.'

She shook her head, angrily, although what he said did seem totally plausible. It sounded exactly like something Klaus would say.

He took a step towards her but she stepped back out of his reach.

'Don't. I'm so embarrassed right now. You discussed our sex life with one of the most indiscreet people in the village. You might as well have taken out an advert on a huge billboard and told everyone that we're not doing it.'

'I'm sorry, I really am.'

Klaus appeared in the shop doorway then, looking horrified.

There was nothing left to say so she turned and walked out of the studio and back into her own shop.

CHAPTER 17

'Helloooo, can I come in?' Klaus said, peering round the shop door waving a white flag a few hours later.

A smile twitched on Melody's lips. He was one of those annoying people who it was impossible to stay mad at.

'I suppose,' she said.

'Jamie sent me round to help set up your camera, so I'm here to save you from technological despair.'

'And?' Melody prompted.

His face fell. 'And to apologise for being a complete ass,' he said, staring at the ground like a forlorn child.

'You are an ass. You coerced Jamie into telling you something he didn't want to tell you about and then exaggerated it wildly when you told me. How many people have you told?'

'No one, I swear,' Klaus said, running his finger in a cross shape over his heart.

'Well make sure you keep it that way,' Melody said, hoping she sounded suitably stern enough that this time this piece of juicy gossip would remain between them.

'I am sorry. You two are so perfect together and I just thought maybe with a little nudge you might…' he trailed off. 'I'm sorry. Jamie really did do his best to fend me off when I was pushing him for details. He was the perfect gentleman and told me he wasn't discussing your relationship with me but then I kept pushing anyway. He also said he was more than happy to wait for you, that it would happen when you were ready and he was fine with that. Don't blame him for me shooting my mouth off.'

Melody sighed.

'OK, tell me where everyone is going to be sitting during this wonderful course of yours?' Klaus said, clearly hoping to change the subject.

As he had apologised profusely, she decided to let it go.

'There will be small tables there and I'll be standing over here. Probably behind this cabinet,' Melody pointed.

'OK, so we can set up the projector here and it will project what you are doing with your hands on the wall behind you. We'll get a throw or something to cover the cabinet, so it's not distracting with what's inside.'

'I have the exact thing,' Melody said, going to her small storeroom at the back and pulling out a sparkly cream tablecloth. She laid it over the cabinet and Klaus placed his projector and camera down and started rigging them up to each other.

'So what did you get Jamie for his birthday?' Klaus said, as he untangled wires.

Melody stared at him. 'When's Jamie's birthday?'

Klaus looked up. 'Oh honey, it's today.'

'Oh no. Crap.' She cast her mind back to the previous year. She had been away with Isla and Elliot for two weeks and she had totally missed the Sculptures in the Sand Festival the year before. She had clearly missed Jamie's birthday at the same time. She hadn't really been friends with him then. They'd been in that stage of awkwardly trying to avoid each other after that amazing first kiss. 'Why didn't he say anything?'

'He hates celebrating his birthday. He's had a bad run of them and I think he would just prefer to bypass them now. His birthday always fell in the school summer holidays and all the children of the village were away on holiday. One year he had a birthday party and no one turned up.'

'Oh no, how awful,' Melody said, her heart breaking for him. That must have been a terrible thing for a child to go through.

'It gets worse. One year his dog died and they buried it in the back garden – that was a pretty crappy way to spend your birthday. When he was thirteen he went to that big theme park in the next town. One of his so-called friends thought it would be funny if he gave Jamie some shellfish without him knowing. I think he found this bottle of oyster sauce in the supermarket and added it to his burger. Jamie went on one of the rides with this girl he liked and threw up at the top of the loop – all over him, all over this girl. Poor Jamie was so embarrassed. Oh and one year, when he was fifteen I think, no maybe sixteen, he had a party and invited this girl he fancied. She asked if she could bring a friend and then she only bloody well turns up with her boyfriend in tow. I think it was another teen birthday party, maybe his eighteenth, when another girl he was dating told him she just wanted to be friends and then went off and promptly snogged his best friend, on his bloody birthday. She could have at least waited until the next day. All in all, he's not got a great track record when it comes to successful birthdays.'

'And I've just shouted at him,' Melody groaned. Another cherry to add to the cake of birthday disasters. 'I haven't bought him a gift either.'

'I don't think he'll care. Wait, that can be your birthday gift to him, lots of hot sex,' he winked at her.

Melody rolled her eyes. 'I'm not jumping into bed with him just because it's his birthday. We're waiting for the right time.'

'And when is that?' Klaus started attaching the camera to a small stand.

Melody sighed. 'I don't know.'

'What is it that's holding you back, honey?' Klaus gave her his fullest attention. 'Some asshole of a man hurt you?'

'No, nothing like that.'

'Was it really bad sex?'

Melody thought about this. 'I don't think it was great. The first guy I slept with I never saw again.'

God, why was she discussing this with Klaus? No wonder Jamie had spoken to him about their relationship, he had this power to make you talk.

'Ah, the first time you have sex is always tricky. Not only do you have to find out what you like but you have to get used to each other's body too. Find where the other person likes to be touched, what they like in bed. It takes time to get sexual compatibility with a partner. It's never going to be amazing the first time you sleep with a partner and even less so when it's your first time having sex. What about your second serious boyfriend?'

'Well… it was better. Nice, it was nice.'

'Oh shit, nice sex? No one wants that. You want bodice-ripping sex.'

Melody laughed. 'Not much call for wearing bodices these days. Anyway, Kevin always seemed to enjoy himself, but I don't know if I really contributed to that enjoyment.'

'You slept with a guy called Kevin, this is getting worse.'

Melody laughed again. 'He was a nice bloke. Well, to start with.'

'There's that word again, Jesus, I hope none of my ex-partners describe me as nice. Do you think Jamie's nice in bed? Is that what you look for?'

'No, I imagine Jamie knows exactly what he is doing in the bedroom. I'm sure he's very passionate if his kissing is anything to go by.'

'Passionate, that's definitely the sort of sex you want.'

'Oh yes,' she said, excitedly. She pressed a hand to her stomach at that thought. Every time she imagined making love to Jamie, her stomach did this little summersault of joy and excitement. She couldn't wait to take that step with him.

'So what's holding you back?'

'I'm guess I'm just scared. I want it to go right. Everything else seems to be going wrong on our dates and I just want this to be perfect. I suppose I'm scared that it will be crap and he won't want to do it again.'

His face softened. 'There's no way Jamie is walking away from this. He is crazy about you. He could have the worst sex of his life and he'd still be coming back for more. As I said, it takes time to get to know each other sexually, but you guys have plenty of time, neither of you are in this for a one-night stand. And you both have so much chemistry, it's bound to be hot. Those nerves you have now are never going to go away – whether you date for a few weeks or a few years, that first time together is always going to be nerve-wracking. So you might as well enjoy it now. When I spoke to Jamie this morning, he said things were going so well that he wished he hadn't waited so long. Don't look back and regret the time you waited.'

Melody thought about it. It was a good philosophy. She just had to find the courage to do it.

Jamie was busy painting the mermaid statue he'd made for Melody, concentrating on the fine detail of the scales. Klaus had gone home a while before, but Jamie wanted to get this finished.

He had no idea whether his date with Melody was going to happen that night but it didn't look likely. Yet again, he'd ticked the box for another crappy birthday.

'She looks beautiful,' he heard Melody say behind him.

His heart leapt. He turned round and something in her eyes told him she wasn't here to shout at him again.

He swallowed. 'I don't think I've done it justice. I haven't captured the warmth that I get from my muse. There's no glow or that happiness that she gives me.'

Her mouth twitched into a smile and he let out a small sigh of relief. They were going to be OK.

'I also haven't captured her generous ability to forgive.'

She smirked. 'I don't think there's really anything to forgive. Klaus has a way of making you talk even when you don't want to say anything. He told me you were being the perfect gentleman in refusing to say anything to him about us. I'm sorry I shouted at you.'

He stepped forward quickly and took her in his arms. 'You have nothing to apologise for. I've known Klaus for a long time, I should be better at telling him to piss off rather than let him keep tapping away at me until I crumble. I'm sorry.'

She reached up and stroked his face. 'Let's stop apologising. Are we still on for our date tonight?'

He grinned. Maybe this birthday would have some redeeming features after all. 'You can count on it.'

She leaned up and kissed him, smiling against his lips.

'I have to meet Aidan first but that shouldn't take long,' Jamie said. 'Come round about seven. I'll leave a key under the mat just in case I'm a few minutes late.'

'And this is the date that can't possibly go wrong?' Melody said, stroking her hands up his back.

'I have a few ideas.'

She smiled. 'I do too.'

He kissed her briefly. He didn't know what she had planned but this birthday was sounding better and better.

Condoms. Where the bloody hell were the condoms? Melody scanned the shelves of the tiny supermarket to try to find them but no luck. She prayed that she wouldn't have to go to the chemist to buy them. Elsie West, who owned the chemist, would be sure to tell Agatha that Melody had bought condoms and then the whole town would know she was having sex, or at least planning to.

She didn't know when she was going to do the deed yet but at least if she had condoms, then she was ready. Maybe tonight, on Jamie's flawless date, the right time would suddenly present itself. And if not, then at least she would be ready for it when they did.

Finally, she found them, next to the hairbrushes and hair ties, because that was the logical place to put them.

She studied the shelves for a moment. There were so many different sorts. She picked up a box to look at just as Agatha came round the corner. She quickly fumbled to put it back on the shelf and managed to knock three other boxes off in the process. She bent and grabbed those and one more box fell on her head.

Agatha was suddenly there, bending to pick up the last box. Melody cringed. Her carefully laid plans had gone awry.

'Looks like Jamie is in for a fun birthday,' Agatha said, putting the box in Melody's basket, then perusing the shelves and adding two more different boxes.

'We're not... I was just looking,' Melody tried.

'Less looking, more doing,' Agatha said. 'I think you should strip off naked, tie a big ribbon around you and give yourself to Jamie as a birthday present.'

'Klaus said more or less the same thing,' Melody grumbled.

'I've always liked that Klaus, wise man.'

'I think Jamie might be a bit disappointed with that birthday gift. I'm sure he would much prefer a nice jumper or a book about sculptures,' Melody said. 'At least he can take those back with the receipt if he doesn't enjoy them.'

'Now you listen to me,' Agatha said, linking arms with her and guiding her away from the condoms so she couldn't change her mind and throw all three boxes back on the shelf. 'It is not your responsibility to make sure he has a good time during sex. The only thing you need to worry about is your own happiness.'

Melody felt her eyebrows shoot up. 'That sounds a bit selfish.'

'Men can find their happiness very quickly and easily, women need a little more help and time.'

Melody cringed that they were actually talking about this. She needed to change the subject fast. But actually she didn't, she just needed to humour her. If Agatha thought she was going to go along with her mad idea then she wouldn't spend the next half hour trying to persuade her.

'OK, if I'm going to give myself to Jamie as a gift, where would I get a bow big enough?'

'The little wedding shop might have something, or the card shop,' Agatha said practically, as if they were discussing where to get something much simpler. 'You could even get those little adhesive rosettes to stick over each nipple.'

'Ouch, I wouldn't fancy Jamie trying to remove those,' Melody said.

'No, fair point.'

They got to the till and Agatha insisted on paying. Hell, if Agatha was going to humiliate her in front of the whole village by telling everyone this huge piece of gossip, then Melody wouldn't feel bad about Agatha paying for the condoms.

Agatha escorted her outside. 'I'm so excited for the two of you. I think you welcoming him home wearing nothing but a smile and a big bow is going to be the best birthday present of all. Birthdays should always hold good memories and now you're going to give him one. Ha-ha, literally.'

Agatha gave her a hug and walked away cackling to herself.

Melody watched her go. Maybe Agatha was right. Maybe she could do this for Jamie. Maybe sex didn't need to be all romance and candles and perfection. They were supposed to be having fun on their dates. She wanted Jamie to relax and not worry about what to do or say all the time and she needed to take some of that medicine herself. This would be a silly, fun way to get over her nerves and just enjoy herself instead of holding the moment to such high standards. She smiled with excitement at what the night would hold and what Jamie's face would look like when he came home. It certainly would be a night to remember.

CHAPTER 18

Melody stood nervously in the lounge, completely naked, waiting for Jamie.

She had arrived at his house a bit earlier than he'd asked her to come round. Fortunately, he'd left the key under the mat as he'd said he would, which made her plan easier. When she had pushed the door open and the dogs and Dobby had greeted her, she had felt a little embarrassed as she had started getting undressed in front of them, which was ridiculous considering her plans for the evening. So she'd hurried off upstairs to undress in his bedroom, leaving some condoms by the bedside table just in case they managed to make it to the bed. In fact she'd left the condoms everywhere, in the shower, next to the sofa, in the kitchen, not sure where the passion would take them. And then she'd sat down on the sofa to wait for Jamie. But now she had been waiting for over half an hour and, with each minute that ticked by, her doubts got bigger and bigger.

This was a mistake. If she was going to make love to Jamie for the first time, she could have done it in many romantic ways. She could just have kissed him after another one of their disastrous dates and not stopped until they were both naked and sweaty. All their kisses were very passionate, any one of them could easily have led to that.

But no, she had to be swayed by Agatha and Klaus and, instead of something sweet, she was here, naked, ready to leap out at him in the vain hope he would immediately sweep her off her feet and carry her to the bedroom, or just ravish her here on the lounge floor. In reality, she was probably going to scare the crap out of him. This was most definitely the worst decision she'd ever made.

There was still time to change her mind. She could put her clothes back on, light some candles, surprise him in a different way. Yes, candles, some nice music; that was much more up her street.

Except they were definitely footsteps she'd heard outside, and that was Jamie's shadow walking past the window.

Crap.

OK, she just had to brazen it out.

The door opened.

'Surprise!' Melody yelled, waving her arms in the air, which made other parts of her wobble somewhat.

And it was a surprise. For Aidan.

Aidan stood there in shock, beers in his hands, large packet of Doritos falling from his fingers, before he quickly shielded his eyes and turned away. The dogs and Dobby all leapt around him in excitement, making the situation worse as they nudged him, demanding attention.

She yelped and dived behind the sofa. To make matters worse, she could hear Leo talking as he walked up the path too. And was that Elliot? Oh shit, she was going to scar the poor boy for life. She could even hear Emily and Marigold in the distance. Good lord, the whole Jackson family was going to be here. All she needed now was Agatha to complete the set. It was obviously going to be a big family party and she was going to have to hide naked behind the sofa the whole time.

She peered under the sofa to see them arrive. But Sirius had come round the back of the sofa now, wagging his tail proudly that he had managed to find her in this game of hide and seek she was playing.

'Change of plan,' Aidan said, grabbing Leo by the scruff of the neck and turning him around.

'Hey! What do you mean?' Leo said.

'Jamie's going to have a quiet night in, by himself,' Aidan said.

'I am?' Jamie said, in confusion.

Oh god, he was there as well, to witness her embarrassment.

'Yep,' Aidan was saying. 'I think you'll have a much more enjoyable night without us.'

'But I was going to thrash him on Gran Turismo on the Xbox,' Leo said.

'That will have to wait for another night,' Aidan said, handing the beers to Jamie. 'Happy Birthday, little brother.'

Aidan frogmarched Leo down the path. Presumably Elliot and the others followed because Melody could see Jamie standing in the doorway alone and looking utterly confused. The dogs all surged around him but then Sirius came back to her again, clearly intent on giving the game away.

Jamie came in and closed the door, plonking the beers on the table as he looked around.

Taking a deep breath, because she couldn't stay behind Jamie's sofa all night and because Sirius would probably reveal her location soon, she popped her head up over the back of the sofa.

'Hello.'

He stared at her and then his face broke into a smile. 'Hello. What are you doing behind there?'

'I'm kind of naked.'

His smile grew. 'You are? How naked?'

'As the day I was born.'

He laughed. 'You can't get much more naked than that.'

'I'm so embarrassed.'

Jamie cottoned on to what had just happened. 'Did Aidan see you?'

'I shouted "Surprise!" I'm not sure who was more surprised, me or him.'

'Well you've seen him naked in the cave, so I'd say you were even. I'm sorry, they weren't supposed to be here. I had a nice romantic evening planned for the both of us, but they insisted on coming over.'

'They want to celebrate your birthday with you.'

'Yeah, they always do. Are you going to come out?' he said, gently.

Melody shook her head. 'I think there's been enough surprises for one night.'

Jamie smirked and took his shirt off and passed it to her.

She smiled. He was such a gentleman.

She slid it on and it swamped her. She did a few buttons up in an attempt to preserve her modesty, although that was kind of redundant. Any dignity she did have had been thrown out the window the second she had decided to get naked in his house and give herself to him on a plate.

Thankfully the shirt came down to mid-thigh, so she was semi-decent, although certainly not respectable.

She stepped out from behind the sofa. 'Surprise,' Melody said, with none of the excitement she had shown before.

His eyes softened as he appraised her. 'And what a lovely surprise it is too.'

He took her hand and pulled her to the sofa, then sat down and tugged her down beside him. She let her head fall into her hands and she groaned.

'Want to tell me what's going on?' Jamie said, rubbing her back. 'Did you just come round and all your clothes fell off accidentally?'

'Yes, let's go with that version of events,' Melody said, peering at him through her fingers. 'It was some kind of vortex; that stripped me of my clothes. That sounds much better than me coming round here, stripping off and shouting surprise, giving myself to you as your birthday present.'

His eyes widened. 'You came round here to have sex?'

Melody smiled weakly. 'Surprise.'

'Well it is a bit. I thought you wanted to wait.'

'Well, I did. But after speaking to Klaus and Agatha—'

'Wait, what? After everything that happened today, you let Klaus bully you into this?'

'No, I didn't mean—'

'And you know you shouldn't listen to a word that Agatha says, meddling, interfering old woman. You should never have let them or anyone pressure you into doing something you don't want to do.'

'I didn't—'

'Have I made you feel this way? Have I done or said anything that made you think, I couldn't go one more second without sex?' Jamie said.

'No, you have been the perfect gentleman—'

'I know last night got a bit heated, but I was very very happy just kissing you. I could kiss you forever and never get bored by it.'

'Will you listen for a second? You can climb down from your high horse and just listen.'

Jamie closed his mouth, suitably chastised.

Melody sighed. 'I want this. I want you. Our kiss on our first date was so heated and passionate, if you had stripped me naked right there on the sofa and made love to me, I wouldn't have cared. There was an element of wanting to go slowly. This, what we have, is so important to me and I didn't want to do anything to screw it up. And I didn't want to lose you as a friend either. I thought we should wait for the right time, but I have no idea when that would be or what that right time actually looks like. I really wanted to make love to you and I realised that I was holding back because I was scared of things changing between us, because I was nervous about what it would be like. Klaus pointed out that those nerves are always going to be there whether we wait a few weeks or a few years. But I really do want this with you.

And yes, I might have let Agatha persuade me into this ridiculous farce of giving myself to you as a birthday present. She suggested I tie a bow around myself, but I drew the line there. And you're right, this is not me at all. I'm more of a candles and flowers and romantic music kind of girl. But the end result would have been the same. Us making love for the first time.'

He stroked his thumb across the palm of her hand. 'Then let's do this right. Tomorrow night, I'll cook you dinner, no distractions, no sudden caves we have to go to, no food poisoning or beans on toast disasters. Or we can go out for dinner, someone else can take care of all that. And after, there will be flowers and candles and music and we'll do this properly.'

She smiled at him. He was so sweet, one of the many things she loved about him. She stroked his face.

'That all sounds lovely, and we can still do all that tomorrow night, but I would rather you took me upstairs to bed and made love to me now. Then all my embarrassment would have been worth it.' She looked down and tugged at the collar of his shirt she was wearing. 'This was what you wanted, me in your shirt, in your bed. Let's go make it come true.'

'To be honest, if you were in my bed, wearing only my shirt, you wouldn't be wearing the shirt for very long,' Jamie said.

She grinned. 'That works too.'

Jamie let out a long, heavy breath as if preparing himself for something he really didn't want to do. Had she read this completely wrong?

He stood up, still holding her hand, and she allowed herself to be pulled to her feet. He looked down at her and smiled. But he didn't kiss her, to her surprise he wrapped her in his arms and hugged her tight. There really was no finer feeling in the world than being here in his arms like this.

He bent his head and kissed her and she wrapped her arms round his neck. Without taking his lips from hers, he bent and scooped her up into his arms. The kiss continued as he carried her upstairs to his bedroom.

He laid her down on the bed and was right there over her, surrounding her as the kiss continued. She ran her hands over his bare back, feeling the muscles in his shoulders. His kiss was so sweet, gentle and soft, adoring her.

He pulled back slightly, fishing his phone from his back pocket of his jeans.

'Let's have some music, I can give you that at least,' Jamie said. 'What's your perfect love-making music?'

'I don't know. If I'd had more time, I could have a very romantic playlist for you. Think this will do for now.'

He pressed play and put the phone down on the drawers before he carried on kissing her. She smiled against his lips as 'Just the Way You Are' by Bruno Mars came drifting out of the speakers. The lyrics that Bruno was singing, about how amazing and perfect his girl was, made her heart soar that Jamie had chosen this song for her.

He moved his hands down the shirt she was wearing, slowly undoing the buttons and placing a gentle kiss on her skin underneath. She cupped his head, stroking his hair as he adored her body.

He undid the final button and pushed the shirt apart, shifting back onto his knees so he could look at her properly.

'That is definitely very naked,' Jamie said, appreciatively.

He came back over her, caging her in as he kissed her hard. The kiss was slightly different now, urgent, needful. She was vaguely aware that the music had changed to some other Bruno song she didn't know, though it was something soft and sweet.

She moved her hands down to his jeans and undid his button and zip, then slid her hands round his back and pushed them down his legs, taking his shorts with them. He wrestled himself out of them as she quickly slipped her arms out of the shirt and threw it across the room. When he kissed her again, they were both naked and she could feel how much he wanted her from his kiss and the way he held her against him.

He ran his hand up the inside of her thigh and she moaned softly against his lips as he touched her between her legs. He was gentle but confident as he stroked her, taking care of her. Her orgasm rocked her as she clung to him, his mouth on hers as he captured her moans.

He moved back to grab a condom as she was trying to catch her breath. Her body felt limp, sated as he moved back around her, scooping his hands underneath her back and lifting her on top of him so she was straddling him. She leaned her forehead against his and, with his hands on her hips, he moved inside her and then held her there, eye to eye for a moment.

He moved forward to capture her mouth just as the music changed again. This time Bruno was singing 'Marry You'.

He stilled, and she giggled against his lips.

'One orgasm and you're already proposing?' Melody said.

He laughed. 'Well it seemed like the right thing to do.'

She kissed him briefly, sliding her hands to his chest as she started moving. He moved his hands to her lower back, pulling her tighter against him.

'This music is really distracting,' Melody giggled.

'Surely a proposal is what every woman wants to hear the first time they make love to a man.'

'I think most women would prefer to wait. At least until the second time they make love.'

He kissed her. 'Duly noted. I'd get up and turn it off, but I'm way too bloody comfortable where I am right now.'

'There's no way I'm letting you get up either,' Melody groaned as he moved deeper inside her.

'So you can endure it?' Jamie said.

'Believe me, I'm not enduring anything right now.' She wrapped her arms around his neck again, kissing him hard as that delicious feeling started building inside her.

He shifted her slightly, sensing the change in her breathing, and that feeling seemed now to be just out of reach, pleasure spiralling through her but never taking her over the edge. He was so responsive to her needs, to her body, everything he was doing was for her.

He lowered his mouth to her breast, his fingers gently massaging her back and it was too much sensation all at once, that wonderful feeling thundering through her so hard she could barely catch her breath. He stopped to watch her lose control and that look of love in his eyes was something she hadn't expected to see. She kissed him, holding him tight as he took what he needed, which sent those feelings tumbling over her again.

She stared at him, her breath heavy, as he stroked up and down her back. She didn't want to move or break this incredible connection between them. Something had passed between them that was way more than just sex.

'I think I want to marry you, Jamie Jackson.'

He laughed, thinking she was referring to the song that had long since finished. But as he rolled her back onto the bed and kissed her hard, she knew that there was a huge part of her that was speaking the truth.

The sun was setting, filling the room with a warm pink glow. The window was open, letting in the warm sea breeze. Life felt pretty perfect right now for Jamie and, to top it all off, the woman of his dreams was lying in his arms, her head on his chest.

'That was definitely not nice sex,' Melody said.

He frowned in confusion. She certainly seemed to enjoy herself. 'It wasn't?'

She propped her head on her hand so she could look at him, the biggest smile on her face.

'Definitely not. It was incredible, amazing, passionate sex, nothing nice about it.'

'Ah, I see.'

'Klaus and I were talking about my last boyfriend. I said sex with him was nice and he said there was nothing worse than *nice* sex. After what we just shared, I'd have to agree.'

'Klaus sometimes says the right thing.'

She kissed his chest. 'He told me about your history of crappy birthdays.'

'And sometimes he doesn't know when to keep his mouth shut,' Jamie said. How to turn a girl off; tell her all about his sad and pathetic history.

She ran her fingers over his heart. 'Maybe now you'll have some nice memories of your birthday.'

'Definitely not nice.'

She grinned and then bit her lip. 'Was it OK?'

He stared at her incredulously. 'Are you kidding? We've finally had a date that was perfect in every single way. Regardless of what happens between us, I'm always going to look back on this night as my best birthday ever. It was utterly wonderful.'

She smiled and then put her head back on his chest. He stroked his hand through her hair, sweeping it off her shoulder, and for the first time he spotted the small tattoo.

From his point of view it was upside down but he soon realised it was a small green Yoda, wearing his trademark cloak and brandishing a light-sabre.

He ran his fingers lightly over it and, when she looked up and gave him a sad smile, he knew that this was something she'd had done for Matthew.

'I love your tattoo,' he said, softly.

'It felt right to get Yoda. Matthew loved everything about *Star Wars*. Plus he was always there with some wise words of advice or comfort, especially whenever Mum would upset me. I suppose he was my Jedi Master. He was the oldest twin by seven minutes and he took those seven minutes very seriously. It always felt like I had this older brother I could turn to whenever I had any problems. I had the tattoo done to show that he's always with me.'

'I bet he is, watching over you,' Jamie said. 'Although I really hope he isn't here now.'

Melody laughed. 'You don't think he would approve?'

'Of one of his friends sleeping with his sister? I don't think he would be overjoyed.'

'Well, I'm sure he would like to be spared the intimate details of our relationship, but I think he would be delighted.'

'Really?'

'He would see how completely and utterly happy you make me and he knows you, he knows I'm in very safe hands.'

'Well, I'm going to take that responsibility very seriously too. I'll be your Obi-Wan.'

She laughed. 'I'd rather you were Han Solo.'

'That works too. I'm very good with my *hans*.'

She laughed. 'That's a terrible pun.'

'I'll try harder next time.'

She reached up and kissed him. 'Well if you're responsible for my happiness, why don't you put your *hans* to good use and we'll see if we can make more happy birthday memories?'

He rolled her over, pinning her to the mattress, and she squealed against his lips. He intended to do just that.

Jamie lay in bed watching Melody doze next to him, the moonlight casting a silvery glow over her back as she lay face down on the bed. God, he wanted her again, which was crazy as they'd already done it twice that night. Sex with Melody was amazing. He had always enjoyed sex, but this was something so much more than that and he didn't know why it was so incredible. Well, he had a pretty good idea why. This was Melody, the woman he loved with everything he had. There was no point denying those feelings any longer. This love for her had been there for years but he had always pushed it away before. He'd convinced himself she didn't feel the same way and that relationships were something to be avoided, but those feelings for her had never gone away. The past few days those emotions had intensified and now, tonight, they had all seemed to bubble over as he had made love to her.

He stroked down her back, not wanting to wake her but desperate to be with her again, maybe just touching her would be enough.

She stirred slightly but she didn't wake. That was OK, he could wait until morning, but he could kiss her now while she slept.

He placed a gentle kiss on her shoulder and then one on the tiny freckle at the base of her neck. He moved slowly over her, surrounding her as he placed a kiss on the top of her spine.

'Jamie.'

His name was no more than a whisper on her lips. She still seemed to be asleep. Maybe dreaming of him. He grinned. Maybe he could give her amazing dreams.

He trailed his mouth down her spine, giving gentle kisses, stroking and caressing her skin, but when he reached her tail bone, she arched her hips off the bed towards him. He glanced up. Her eyes were awake and alert, a small smile on her lips. She shifted her hips higher and that was the only invitation he needed. He grabbed a condom and was buried inside her a moment later.

Oh god, she felt so good.

He leaned over her, kissing her spine, he wrapped his arm around her, stroking her breasts, stroking everywhere, wanting to touch every part of her body at once. He moved his hands greedily across her soft skin. Her breath was already changing as little moans and pants fell from her lips. He started moving faster, needing more, and she arched back against him, taking it all, her pleasure getting louder. God, it was such a turn-on knowing that being with him like this could have such an effect on her. He watched her unravel, gripping the pillow as his name fell from her lips. He leaned over her fully, linking her fingers with his own as he pinned her to the bed, pushing into her deeper, harder, and as she let out a groan that was purely animalistic, he felt every emotion, every feeling for her come thundering out of him. If this was what making love was really like, there was no way he could ever walk away from it.

CHAPTER 19

Melody stood in the shower letting the hot water pour over her, soothing her aching bones. They had their first puppy training class later that morning and she needed to be more awake for that.

God, the man was insatiable. He couldn't keep his hands off her and she loved that.

She felt so silly to have waited, wanting the perfect moment. There had been no candles or flowers, the music had been hilariously inappropriate, she had embarrassed herself by jumping out on Aidan, stark naked, and she'd still had the most amazing night of her life.

Klaus was right. Why would anyone want nice sex when you could have passionate, hedonistic, incredible sex? But Klaus was wrong about first-time sex. There had been no faltering, trying to get to know each other's likes and dislikes. Maybe it was because she knew Jamie and trusted him completely, maybe it was because she loved him, but every touch of his hand, every kiss had been beyond flawless. They fitted together perfectly, two halves of one whole.

She looked up as he walked into the bathroom, sleepily rubbing his face, his hair dishevelled, looking absolutely adorable. And gloriously, impressively naked. Evidently ready for round four.

He opened the cubicle door and climbed inside, a big grin on his face. The shower was easily big enough for them both, though that didn't stop Jamie from moving closer towards her.

'No more sex,' Melody said, holding out a hand to stop him. She was met with a solid wall of muscle. 'I haven't got the energy for any more.'

'I've worn you out already? We'll have to work on your stamina,' Jamie said, his large hands spanning up her rib cage and then running his thumbs over her nipples.

'My stamina is just fine, thank you,' Melody squeaked. How could he turn her on so quickly?

'We don't have to have sex,' Jamie said. 'We can do other things?'

His mouth was mere centimetres away from hers and she was having trouble concentrating on anything but what it would be like to kiss him again.

'Like cuddling?' she teased.

His dark look of intent softened. 'I think I'd very much like to cuddle you right now.' He wrapped his arms around her and simply held her against him.

She rested her head against his damp chest and sighed blissfully as he stroked his hands gently up and down her back.

She had never felt so completely and utterly happy as she did right then.

'You know what I can't figure out?' Melody said. 'Why any girl would ever let you go.'

'I don't know, boredom, I guess,' Jamie said.

She looked up at him. 'How could anyone get bored of being treated like this? Of being held in your arms like I'm something precious and adored. I could stand in your arms forever and never want anything more.'

His eyes flickered with something, though she didn't know what. Was it too soon to be talking like that? They were supposed to be taking things slowly.

She opened her mouth to try to backpedal, but he cupped her face and kissed her softly.

'I adore you Melody Rosewood, right from the top of your head down to your sparkly blue toes.'

She smiled and leaned up and kissed him.

'I wonder if any woman has regretted finishing with you. I once dated a guy who dumped me and then got upset when I didn't beg him to reconsider.'

Jamie laughed. 'What an idiot. He finished with you as some kind of test?'

'Yes, I guess so. I wasn't really that bothered when he ended things with me, so I certainly wasn't going to try to persuade him otherwise.'

'I think that's the crux of it. I suppose if it's someone you really love, you'd fight tooth and nail for them,' Jamie said.

'Have you ever fought for someone?' Melody asked.

He shook his head. 'I'm not into playing games like that. If someone finishes with me, I'm not going to humiliate myself even more by begging them to change their mind. If I argue with a girl and we finish then I don't think there's any coming back from that. If I loved someone, I would never let them go in the first place.'

She looked up at him and vowed that she was never letting this man go. Something in his eyes said he felt the same way. Something unspoken passed between them, a mutual determination to make this work because it was important.

He bent his head and kissed her.

She let out a sigh of need as she wrapped her arms round his neck and kissed him back. One kiss led to another, his lips against hers like an addictive drug, his tongue touching hers, tasting her, enjoying her. It was so hot. He moved his arms around her, holding her tight against him. Despite her previous protests and the fact that she ached in parts she had never ached in before, she wanted him now with a sudden desperation that she had never felt with her previous boyfriends.

She hooked one leg around his hip and reached around for the condoms she had placed on the shelf the night before. She pressed one into his greedy hands as they explored her body.

He pulled back slightly from the kiss, tearing at the wrapper with his teeth and then sliding it on.

'I thought you said no sex,' Jamie said, lifting her. She wrapped her legs around him.

'I changed my mind.'

'I'm so glad,' he said, pinning her to the wall as he slid deep inside her.

She gasped against his lips as he shifted his hands to her hips, holding her in place as he moved against her. His kisses were relentless, his tongue searching, tasting, exploring. It was so much deeper like this, so much more intense as he moved inside her harder and faster.

She pulled back slightly from his mouth, barely able to catch her breath, and stared into his eyes as that feeling started to build inside her.

'Jamie… this is…'

'I know.'

Did he know? Did he realise how incredibly special this connection was between them? Did he understand this was way more than just great sex?

'I love you,' she whispered.

His mouth closed over hers a split second later and she wasn't sure he'd heard over the sound of the water or whether she'd even said the words out loud. She felt his movements get more urgent as he raced towards his release, his hold on her getting tighter, and she said the words again in her head, let the words dance in her heart as her orgasm thundered through her, and as he groaned against her lips she felt him tumble over the edge too.

✴

'OK, let the puppies just get to know each other. For many of them, this might be the first time socialising with other dogs,' Felicity the dog trainer said.

Felicity was very zen, Melody decided. Wearing a long pink flowing skirt, a pouffy flowery top and standing barefoot in the village hall, she didn't look like she could be fazed by anything. Although her peaceful mindset didn't fill Melody with any hope that these puppies would finish the six-week course any more disciplined than they were now. Melody had been hoping for some ex-army major to be taking the class in the hope that Rocky could learn some manners.

'These dogs have never met each other before so they have to sniff each other to get to know the other dogs,' Felicity was saying. Clearly no one had told her that three-quarters of this class had come from the same litter. Although Melody would have thought that was obvious: they were all large and black with curly hair.

The puppies were gambolling and jumping over each other, tugging each other's ears, chewing each other's tails, and the hall was filled with lots of delighted yapping as Beauty and Beast's offspring were reunited again. Rocky and Sirius were chasing each other around the room. Agatha's puppy, Summer, who had a pink bow over the top of her head, was being humped by Luke, Isla's puppy, who obviously wasn't worried about a little bit of incest. Spike, Aidan and Tori's puppy, was chewing on a ball and apparently not worried by anything going on in the room, and Emily's puppy Leia was sleeping through the whole thing. There were two other puppies in the room that were not from that batch of reprobates, a spaniel and a chocolate lab and they were running around chasing the other dogs too, plainly having the time of their lives. This had been going on for ten minutes or more and the lesson was only supposed to be an hour long. So far, Felicity's methods left a lot to be desired.

'OK, now call your puppies back to you,' Felicity said and Melody nearly laughed that she thought it was going to be that simple.

The room was filled with twenty-odd voices all at once – many people had brought their whole family to the class to help learn the puppy training skills. Names were called out, people tapping the floor to get the attention of the wayward puppies, squeaking toys, whistling and the puppies paid not a bit of notice to any of it. Except Summer who seemed to be so traumatised by all the sudden noise she peed on the floor.

Agatha scooped up Summer, hugging her to her ample chest, and placed a hanky over the pee zone, before going back to her place.

'OK, maybe call your puppies one at a time,' Felicity said, her zen slipping ever so slightly. 'Jamie, why don't you try calling yours?'

Jamie chuckled, probably at Felicity's optimism.

'Sirius, Sirius Black,' Jamie called. To his credit, Sirius actually looked over in Jamie's direction, but then so did Rocky, Leia and the chocolate lab puppy too. Sirius wagged his tail at Jamie and then continued trying to chew on the spaniel's ear.

'Let me show you how a pro does it,' Leo said, trying to outdo his brother again. It was a common theme between the Jackson brothers. He let out an ear-piercing whistle and every dog in the room looked over in his direction and then tore over to him in a kind of non-scary puppy stampede. Leo shrugged and somehow managed to grab Luke between all the waggy tails, scooping him up and passing him to Elliot to hold onto. 'It worked, didn't it?'

One by one they all tried various methods to recall their puppies, with various degrees of success, but not one puppy returned to their owner straight away. Many of the owners had to physically stand up and go and retrieve their puppies from the other side of the room.

'So that's the first thing you need to practise at home, calling your puppy and when it comes you reward it with a treat. Start off small, just a few feet away, and see if you can get it to come to you, then slowly start increasing the distance.'

'What if you can't get it to even look at you when you're calling its name?' the owner of the spaniel puppy asked. This was clearly a man exhausted with his puppy already. Melody didn't know a lot about different breeds, but she did know that if you'd never had a dog before, then starting off with a spaniel puppy was a big mistake. They were like hyperactive chimpanzees on speed.

'Then your puppy doesn't know its name. You need to teach it.'

'How do I do that? Write her bloody name on a piece of paper and make her read it?' the man said.

Felicity just ignored this question and addressed the group again.

'High value treats are the way to encourage your puppy to come to you.'

'I've taken a piece of steak out with me on walks,' Spaniel Man said. 'She couldn't give a shit.'

'We're going to play a little game,' Felicity said loudly, obviously deciding that the best way to deal with difficult clients was to ignore them. 'This is a game of control. You put some treats on the floor and every time your puppy goes to eat the treats, you place your hand over the top of it. The puppy will soon learn that they have to wait patiently in order to get the treats. This skill can then be applied to other areas of training too.'

'This should be interesting,' Jamie mumbled. Other families or couples started doing as they were told. Jamie poured some treats into a small pile in front of Sirius but before Jamie had a chance to put his hand over it, Sirius had snaffled it up.

Melody laughed. 'Why don't we work together? I'll pour out the treats, you hold your hand over it to stop Sirius from eating it.'

Jamie nodded. She held onto Rocky, who was straining at his collar to eat Sirius's treats too as she poured out a small pile on the floor. Sirius went for them straight away and this time Jamie managed to get his hand over the pile. Sirius licked Jamie's hand, trying to get at the treats through his fingers, and when he realised he couldn't get them he went to run off. Melody reached out to grab him, accidentally letting Rocky go in the process. Rocky bounded across the room, distracting Luke from staring at his treats, before crashing into Ted the Labrador puppy, who yelped and ran across the room, skidding in the pee that Summer had left on the floor and slamming into the fire exit door which then set off the alarm. This sent all the puppies into a tizzy and Felicity's zen visibly slipped another notch as she flounced over to the fire alarm panel and spent several minutes trying to figure out how to turn it off.

Melody quickly got up to retrieve Rocky, but the puppy clearly saw this as a game and went zooming across the room, bounding away every time she came anywhere near him. He spotted her bag where she'd left it in the corner and raced up to it, emptying its contents all over the floor before she could get to him and stop him. Spike obviously thought this was a great game as he came over too. To Melody's horror, he grabbed a box of condoms and gave it a good shake, tossing condoms all over the floor in front of everyone.

Melody felt her skin burn red as she quickly tried to gather all the condoms up, but other puppies were now attacking the condoms too, some tossing them around, some chewing on them and releasing the condoms from their foil packets. Summer got one stuck over her nose and was running around trying to get it off. Luke and the spaniel puppy, Delilah, started playing tug of war with one, stretching it to proportions Melody didn't even think were possible. Elliot picked up one of the packets and Melody could hear him asking Isla what it was, which caused Leo to laugh hard. Melody grabbed a few and shoved them in her pockets then tried to get a few back from the dogs, but they were enjoying their new toys way too much.

The alarm finally fell silent, but the carnage was still continuing. Melody glanced over at Jamie and saw he was laughing so much he could hardly breathe.

'You could help,' she hissed at him, though she was starting to laugh too.

'I'm having way too much fun for that; besides, why did you bring condoms to a puppy training class? Did you think we would be able to slip off for a quickie while people were teaching their dogs to sit?'

Melody grabbed Rocky and sat down next to Jamie, giving up on the condom retrieval as other owners managed to wrestle their dogs back under control.

'Agatha bought me three boxes. She had high hopes for last night.'

Jamie laughed. 'That woman will never cease to surprise me.'

They looked across the room at Jamie's aunt as she removed a condom from Summer's nose and then quickly straightened the puppy's bow. Melody smirked at her priorities.

'OK, the next thing we are going to learn is the command "Sit", and once we have mastered that we will extend that to a "Sit and Stay",' Felicity shouted above the noise, obviously thinking that the previous activities had been so successful and undeterred by the chaos that was ensuing so far.

Melody felt a little smug at this next part. Rocky had already learned how to sit. Everyone stood up and started encouraging their dogs to sit by holding their treats up to their chests. But Rocky had realised that the fire exit door had been left open after Ted had crashed into it the first time. After speeding over to it, he shoved the door open the rest of the way with a little nudge of his paw before Melody could stop him and ran outside onto the village green. Every single puppy followed, and now there were new distractions to contend with: cars, bunting, flowers, birds, butterflies, a marmalade cat sunning itself on the grass who let out a wail and darted up a tree. Melody hurried outside after Rocky, as did the other owners, and a big game of chase started.

As she wrestled Rocky under control, Jamie came up to her with a struggling Sirius in his arms and inclined his head to the other side of the green. There was Felicity getting in her car and Melody felt her mouth fall open as she watched her drive away.

'I think that's the end of the first lesson,' Jamie laughed.

'I don't think there will be a second,' Melody said. Clearly Felicity's zen had got up and gone too.

Jamie placed a kiss on Sirius's head and the puppy stilled in its struggling. She smiled at how sweet Jamie was.

'Come on, let's get these puppies home before the sandcastle competition this afternoon.'

They went back inside and grabbed their things and then stepped outside into the warm sunshine. The poor spaniel owner was still trying to chase a delirious Delilah around the village green.

Jamie slipped a hand into hers and she smiled up at him. She had found a new peace since spending the night making love to him. He hadn't said that he loved her, but she knew that he cared for her a great deal. The connection they had shared went way beyond just great sex. She felt suddenly so safe with him now. He wasn't going to leave. All of their crappy dates, her bumbling disasters and he was still here, holding her hand, smiling at her with complete adoration. He didn't seem to care about any of that. And here they were, after another disaster of a date this morning at the puppy class, and he was smiling and laughing about it all. She had told Jamie he needed to relax about dating her, but she needed to start taking some of her own advice too.

CHAPTER 20

Jamie looked around at the little mounds of sand that were placed the length of Sunshine Beach. Little teams; couples, families, friends, were already starting to gather, claiming their little mound of sand. He'd taken part in the Great Sandcastle competition every year since he was a child – before he was old enough to take part in the main event, the sculpture competition – and to this day he'd never won. Something his brothers always gave him great abuse over as he was the artist of the family. Even more so two years before when Leo had won, he had taken great pleasure in lauding it over him for months. But sand was such a hard substance to sculpt into anything impressive. It was volatile and fragile and one gust of wind would destroy hours of hard work. Give him clay to work with any day, it was much more reliable.

This year, though, he felt sure he would win. He had Melody on his side. He felt the luckiest man alive to have her in his life. Maybe she would bring him luck in the competition too. He smiled as she tripped over one of the buckets they'd bought for the competition. God, he loved her so much.

He hadn't told her that though. He'd heard her whisper it in the shower that morning and his own declarations of love had got stuck in his throat as he remembered the last time he had uttered those fateful words and Polly's reaction to them. He had kissed Melody instead, hoping to show her how he felt through his actions rather than words.

'How do we play this?' Melody said seriously, bending to pick up the sand and letting it fall through her fingers. He was glad she was taking it seriously; he couldn't allow Leo to win again.

'There aren't many rules. It has to be a castle but other than that we can tick that box any way we see fit.'

'So turrets and towers and moats and a moveable drawbridge,' Melody said, clearly getting into it.

'Yes, we can use props and shells and flags or whatever else we want to embellish our castle, that part is up to us.'

'And what do we win *when* we win?'

'When. I like your conviction. The knowledge that we're better than Leo, also free ice cream from Sprinkles.'

'Well that seems like a prize worth fighting for,' Melody giggled and he wrapped his arm round her shoulders and kissed her head.

She seemed so much more relaxed today, as if making love to him the night before had released all those fears and tensions she had been holding onto. Hell, if making love to her could make her this happy, he would gladly oblige her and make love to her every day.

'It looks like Leo has a plan,' Melody said.

Jamie looked over at his brother and smiled as he saw him squatting down in front of Elliot, Isla bending over to listen to this little family pep talk. Leo was such an unlikely father figure – Jamie had never thought that his brother would settle down and have a family of his own. But he had stepped into this role of godfather and had not only embraced it, but seemed so happy because of it. He was relaxed, he smiled a lot and he was such a natural with Elliot. He just needed to get his act together with Isla and then the little family would be complete. It was quite obvious she was besotted with him, he must see that.

He glanced over at Aidan, whose life was already complete, with his wonderful fiancée and a baby on the way. There was no pep talk or plan here. They were just standing quietly next to each, arm in arm, basking in the love they had for each other. They obviously didn't care about winning, they were just here to enjoy being with one another. Aidan stroked his hand across her stomach as he whispered something to her and Jamie couldn't stop the grin from spreading on his face.

He turned and looked at Emily and her lovely family. Stanley was receiving a lecture from Marigold about how to make the perfect sandcastle. Emily was sitting down, watching the two of them fondly as she stroked across her belly.

Suddenly Jamie could see his future so clearly, marriage, children of his own with the woman standing by his side. He had been so fearful of relationships for too many years, he had been hurt so much by Polly Lucas that he had shied away from anything serious and he had missed out on something beautiful and wonderful with Melody. But not any more.

The mayor stepped up to the podium, and started thanking people for coming, officially opening the Great Sculptures in the Sand Festival with the Great Sandcastle competition. He explained the rules, or rather the lack of them, and then started the countdown for the beginning of the competition. The crowds and competitors joined in as the last few stragglers quickly made their way to the empty mounds of sand.

An air horn pierced the air, announcing the competition had started and they now had thirty minutes to produce a sandcastle masterpiece.

'I think we should use this mound as our base,' Melody said. 'We'll dig a moat around it and then we can start adding our turrets on top of this mound.'

'Sounds good.'

They picked up their brightly coloured spades and started digging, starting in the same spot and working away from each other, creating a moat around the outside of the mound until they met again on the other side.

'Another round?' Jamie said and Melody nodded as they went back over the moat, making it extra deep and wide, patting the sides to keep it in place.

'Twenty minutes!' the mayor announced over the loudspeaker.

'Crap,' Jamie said.

'We got this,' Melody reassured. 'Let's take some of this sand off the top for the towers and then use the rest of the mound to make the hill which the castle will sit on.'

He nodded and started filling up the buckets and making a smaller mound of sand to use in a few minutes' time, while Melody started patting the side of the larger mound trying to make a hill with a flat top for the castle. He joined her and they soon had an impressive hill to build the castle on.

'Fifteen minutes!'

They desperately filled the three buckets and placed them carefully in towers all around the top of the hill before going back to fill them up and add more towers. Melody started shaping the tops of some of the towers into pointy spires as Jamie added a few more towers to the middle of the castle. It was starting to look quite impressive. He didn't dare look over at Leo's – he was exceptionally talented at stuff like this and with Isla helping him and her experience as a window dresser, theirs was bound to be good this year.

They started adding flags, shells for windows and then Melody started cutting a hole in the side of the castle for the drawbridge.

They patted and shaped and carved and Jamie knew that it looked good.

'Five minutes!'

'We need to fill the moat,' Melody suddenly said.

Jamie shook his head. 'It will just sink into the sand, it's not wet enough.'

But she had already grabbed the bucket and was just about to make a run for the sea when her foot caught in the well-tended moat. She went flying into the castle, landing on her stomach smack bang in the middle of the hill, flattening the castle completely. Jamie stared at her in shock, at the towers that were no more than misshapen lumps, the hill that was definitely more of a valley now and the flags that were fluttering across the beach as they had been freed from their structure.

Melody quickly pushed herself up onto her knees and looked in horror at the devastation that she had caused.

Then something wonderful happened.

A big smile spread on her face and that smile turned into a huge laugh that rumbled through her whole body and came out so loud and heartfelt, he couldn't help but join in. It burst from him so loudly that other people even looked around. The castle was completely ruined and he didn't even care. He stepped over the debris and offered out his hand to help her up. She was laughing so much she could barely stand and when he pulled her to her feet she held her stomach helplessly as the laughter bubbled over her. This was a new side to her and he absolutely loved it.

'Do you think that we might still win?' Melody giggled, when she could speak again.

'We might still have a chance,' Jamie chuckled.

'One minute!' the mayor announced over the speakerphone.

Jamie smoothed down the mound as much as he could, grabbed a stick and, in the last thirty seconds, he drew the best goddamned picture of a castle he had ever drawn.

Melody burst out laughing and, as the air horn sounded to end the competition, he pulled her into his arms and kissed her hard. She giggled against his lips and then returned the kiss.

'Well, this is a new approach.' Leo interrupted their embrace as he came to study their impromptu sculpture.

Jamie pulled away from the kiss, flinging an arm around Melody's shoulders.

'Why bother with all that silly sculpture stuff when I can just draw what I want?' Jamie shrugged.

He glanced across at his brother's sandcastle and groaned. Leo and his little adopted family had produced an amazing sand dragon, which miraculously had teeth and scales and massive claws. The man was a genius when it came to stuff like this – quite why he had never explored it as a career Jamie didn't know.

'It's supposed to be a castle,' Jamie said.

'There's a castle there.'

Jamie looked closer and saw that there was a tiny castle next to the dragon, so they had fulfilled that brief. It was down to the competitors to decide what kind of extras they wanted to add to the castle; some had even added little Lego men and horses in the past.

'Our castle has charm.' Melody squeezed Jamie.

'What happened?' Tori said as she came over to investigate.

'*I* happened,' Melody laughed. 'And these feet which are obviously way too big for me.'

Jamie smiled at her fondly, so happy that she could finally laugh at herself.

The judges started walking around all the different sandcastles, making notes on their clipboards.

'Do you think we should wait to see if the judges award ours the winner?' Melody giggled.

'Nah, let's give somebody else a chance. I have a much better use of our time.' He gave Melody a dark look which she quickly interpreted. She grabbed his hand and they ran off the beach, giggling and kissing like teenagers.

'Get a room,' Leo shouted after them.

'We intend to,' Jamie called back and it couldn't happen fast enough.

Jamie watched the voile bedroom curtains blowing gently in the summer breeze. The sunlight lay in ribbons of gold across the room, causing Melody's hair to glitter and shine. He ran his fingers through it and she snuggled into him tighter as she lay on his chest.

'Do you see children in your future?' Jamie asked.

Melody propped her head up on her hand so she could look at him. 'Is this your way of telling me you might be pregnant?'

He laughed.

She put her head back down and he thought that might be the end of the conversation. It was way too soon in their relationship to be thinking about that, it was ridiculous to even bring it up. It was just that seeing his brothers and sister so happy with their little families had made him think about his future too.

'I always thought that I would have children someday, in that kind of vague way when that day would probably never come,' Melody said. 'I think, since Isla has taken custody of Elliot, that has changed. Having a child is a massive commitment. It's not just about feeding them, clothing them, putting a roof over their heads – which comes with its own financial worries. It's developing their minds, so they are constantly learning, seeking answers, and helping to provide those answers. It's showing them the world and helping them to find their place in it. It's about educating them about different cultures, beliefs, traditions. It's keeping them safe without making them fearful. It's teaching them right from wrong. It's showing them that it's OK to be different or to like different things. And spending time with Elliot over the last year, I want that now. I really do. But I wouldn't want to do it alone. I know there are many single parents out there who do an amazing job, Isla is one of them. But no one ever sets out to be a single parent, taking on all those decisions and that huge responsibility on their own. I know children don't always come as planned, and if I was to get pregnant now I would absolutely do my best to raise it. But in an ideal world, children would come when I was happily married to a wonderful man, who would share the load with me.'

'I think choosing the right person to have children with is very important, someone who shares your beliefs and attitudes,' Jamie said.

She nodded.

They were silent for a while and then she propped her head back up to look at him. 'I think you'd make a fantastic dad. I see how you are with Marigold and Elliot and you have such a lovely way with them. And you have this endless patience; you don't seem to get fazed by anything. That is a wonderful quality to have.'

He smiled. He suddenly felt like they were on the same page. Obviously not now, and probably not for another year or two, but it felt like they both wanted the same thing.

'I've always wanted a big family,' Jamie said. 'Being one of four children was a great thing, there was always someone to talk to or play with. Meal times were noisy and chaotic and I wouldn't change it for the world.'

'I kind of thought that I'd have a few children too. I was one of three and I loved having a brother and sister to share my childhood with.'

He rolled on top of her and she let out a little squeal of protest at this sudden movement.

'So it seems we have ourselves a plan. When I propose to you, it needs to be somewhere private so we can have lots of celebratory sex after. We'll probably get married on the beach as we both love it so much, we can have amazing sandcastles as our wedding decorations.'

She giggled at this.

'And then we'll have fifteen children and live happily ever after.'

She grinned as she stroked his face. 'That sounds pretty perfect to me.'

Melody left her house later that evening just as the sun was leaving damson and candyfloss trails across the sky. It was a beautiful night and she couldn't help the huge smile that was spread across her face.

Her eyes went down the beach, following the line of golden sand as it met the turquoise waves. The sandcastles had been razed to the ground hours before and temporary flooring was being laid in the sand to give a firmer ground for the sculptures. Some sculptures, wrapped and covered to prevent prying eyes from seeing them, had already arrived on the beach and Melody knew more would appear overnight, although the bulk of them would be placed on the beach the following day before the big reveal tomorrow evening. She was going to place hers on the beach tomorrow lunch time and she couldn't wait to see Jamie's.

She walked up the hill towards Jamie's house, looking forward to a lovely evening. She was wearing a Cadbury's purple dress that Jamie had once said how much he loved, and she'd even had time to plait and curl her hair. It was going to be a perfect night.

After spending the afternoon in bed with Jamie, he had gone back to the studio to finish his sculpture for the Sculptures in the Sand Festival the following day and she had gone home to check in on Rocky and get ready for that evening. Jamie was taking her to her favourite restaurant and she was optimistic that, in someone else's hands, they might even have a disaster-free night.

She knocked on his door and when he opened it, she saw he looked happy and relaxed in just a shirt and jeans. She was glad he didn't feel like he had to wear a suit for her any more, she wanted him to be comfortable. His shirt was rolled up at the sleeves, showing tanned, muscular forearms. It was an odd part of his body to focus on, but she loved his arms, so strong and safe.

She looked up and could see his whole face had lit up at seeing her.

'God, I love that dress,' Jamie said.

'I wore it because you said you liked it. You said the colour really suited me,' Melody said as he stepped back to let her in.

He laughed and closed the door behind her. 'Now that we're sort of dating, I have a confession to make.'

She cringed a little at the words 'sort of' but decided to ignore it. 'You do?'

He kissed her on the cheek as a greeting. 'It was never the colour that I liked about this dress.'

'You don't like purple?'

'The colour is fine, but what I loved about this dress was that it's a halter neck. It always looks like the only thing that's holding it up is this little button at the back of your neck. Whenever you would wear it, I would often fantasise about undoing that single button and then your whole dress just sliding off.'

Melody stared at him and then burst out laughing. 'Jamie Jackson, Sandcastle Bay's most notorious gentleman, has a secret pervy side.'

He shrugged. 'I can't even deny it.'

'And what would happen, in your fantasies, when the dress came off?'

Jamie's smile slid off his face, a sudden darkness in his eyes. 'You wouldn't be wearing a bra.'

She smiled and bit her lip. Quite often, when she wore strapless dresses, she didn't bother with a bra. Her breasts were small enough that she could get away with it. Tonight she wasn't wearing one either.

'And when the dress slithered to the floor, you'd be left standing in just a tiny lacy pair of pants and high heels.'

They both looked down at her gold flip-flops she was wearing.

'Or bare feet,' Jamie quickly rectified. 'Sometimes in my fantasies, you'd be barefoot.'

She slipped out of her flip-flops so she was standing barefoot in his hallway. He swallowed.

'Then what?'

He didn't say anything for a few moments as he caught on to what was going to happen next.

'Then we'd have sex on the nearest hard surface.'

She laughed. 'Simple but effective.'

'My fantasies had multiple choice when it came to the positions, so it wasn't always the same fantasy.'

'And which one was your favourite?'

'I don't think I have a favourite position when it comes to you. Any way that we get to make love is fine by me.'

She smiled. 'Good answer. So why don't you undo this pesky button and let's see how this fantasy unfolds.'

He stared at her and then took a greedy step towards her before he stopped himself. 'How hungry are you?'

'Not enough that I can't wait.'

He smiled and kissed her, his hands spanning her bare back, his fingers gently trailing up her spine until they reached the button at the back of her neck. He teased his fingers around the collar, slipping his fingers under the material, tracing the edge round her collar bone before sliding them back up to undo the button.

She felt the material loosen and she stepped back away from him so he could watch. The dress didn't slither to the floor, her hips were a bit too wide for that. But she gave a little wiggle and the dress fell over her hips and onto the floor. By the look in his eyes, he didn't seem to mind.

He was suddenly on her, kissing her hard, his greedy hands exploring everywhere, touching, caressing, holding.

She wrestled his shirt from him, sliding her hands over warm, strong shoulders. She moved her hands to his trousers, but he picked her up, making her squeal a little against his mouth. She wrapped her legs around him and all he did was kiss her. One scorching hot kiss, followed by another.

She was vaguely aware that he was carrying her into the kitchen. He stopped and sat her on the edge of the dining table.

'Is this your flat surface of choice?' Melody asked.

'It works just as well as any,' Jamie said.

She shuffled back a little. 'Then come up here and join me.'

He caught her hips and slid them back to the edge of the table, his fingers playing with the waistband of her knickers. He gave the material a little tug and she leaned back on her hands and lifted her bum and thighs slightly so he could pull them off. He flung them across the room so she was completely naked.

Melody leaned forward to kiss him again and he shifted her legs apart and moved between them. He slid his hand up the inside of her thigh and with the lightest of touches he brought her to the very edge of her sanity before he stopped and that wonderful feeling started to slip away.

'Jamie,' she breathed against his lips.

But he was already grabbing a condom from his jeans pocket and wrestling himself out of the rest of his clothes.

He stepped back between her legs and with his hands on her hips and his eyes locked on hers, he slid inside her.

She leaned back on her elbows for a moment to adjust to the weight of him inside her. As he moved inside her again, he leaned over her and kissed her breast, slipping her nipple inside his mouth.

She let out a noise that was half grunt, half moan, cupping the back of his head as she stroked his hair. She wrapped her legs around him, holding him close.

He pulled back slightly, then settled himself on his forearms, kissing her hard. Her breath hitched as that delicious feeling started tingling through her and he pulled back again to watch her. His breath was heavy as he looked down at her.

'You're so beautiful, Melody Rosewood,' he whispered. 'So bloody lovely. What did I do to get so lucky to have you in my life?'

She stroked his face.

'It's me that got lucky. I've wanted to be with you for so long and now you're here, looking at me as if you...' she trailed off. She wouldn't put words in his mouth.

He frowned slightly then kissed her with so much urgency, she could feel this desperation for her emanate from him, like he couldn't take enough. That wonderful feeling escalated through her, and it was his need for her that sent her shouting out his name. He groaned against her lips and collapsed on top of her, his face buried against her neck.

She wasn't sure because her heart was racing, blood pounding through her ears and Jamie was breathing so heavily, but as he placed a kiss on her neck, just below her ear, she thought she heard him whisper, 'I do.'

CHAPTER 21

Holding hands, they walked towards Sea Breeze, the best seafood restaurant in the area. It had the most amazing views of Sunshine Beach and served the most incredible Dover sole Melody had ever tasted.

Jamie held the door open for her and she stepped inside.

'Table for two for Jamie Jackson. We're a bit late, I'm afraid,' he said.

Melody suppressed a smirk.

'Not a problem, we're not too busy tonight, we still have your table for you,' the hostess said, gesturing for them to follow her up the stairs.

They sat down in the window and looked out over the sea. The colours of the setting sun scattering like a mosaic over the waves looked magnificent.

Melody turned to Jamie, reaching across the table to take his hand, and realised his attention wasn't on her at all, but something behind her.

She turned in her seat but there was nothing out the ordinary and no one she knew. She looked back at Jamie and then followed his line of sight to a very pretty brunette sitting at the table across the aisle behind her. She had these wonderful, long curls that came down almost to her bum. She was wearing a gold dress, which showed every flawless curve and very very long legs.

Melody had never once thought that Jamie would be the sort to check out other women when he was with her. She didn't expect him to be a saint – even if she was happily married to someone, she would still recognise when a man was good-looking. Leo and Aidan were very handsome men, but it didn't mean she was attracted to them. Of course Jamie would admire other women, but she hadn't expected him to be so blatant about it, especially when he was on a date with her.

'You OK?' Melody asked, snagging his attention back on her.

'Yes… sorry,' he said, visibly distracted.

She waited for him to take her outstretched hand but he didn't. He stared at the menu in front of him, but she guessed that he wasn't actually reading it. She placed her hand back in her lap.

'So, are you going to give me any hints as to what your sculpture is for the competition tomorrow?' Melody asked.

He looked up at her and then his eyes slid to the brunette again, just briefly before he suddenly looked fearful. He swallowed.

'No, in fact, I'm probably not going to enter at all.'

'What? Why? You've been busy finishing it off all week.'

'It's not appropriate. It was silly of me to make this sculpture; I should have stuck with something much simpler like a seal or a dolphin, not this. I don't know what I was thinking.'

'I… don't understand. What's so bad about the sculpture you've made?'

'It was a stupid idea. I'll have a look to see if there is anything else in my studio more appropriate. If not, then I just won't enter. It won't matter. There'll be hundreds of entries tomorrow. No one will notice if mine is there or not.'

The waitress came over at that point.

'Hello, my name is Jenny, I'll be your waitress this evening. Can I get you two a drink while you are looking at the menu?'

Melody glanced down at the menu, thrown by this sudden about-turn from Jamie. She looked at the cocktails and chose something that had strawberries and prosecco in it. Jamie ordered a beer.

The waitress left a bread basket on the table and walked off to get their drinks.

Melody looked at Jamie.

'Are you OK, you seem…' She couldn't put her finger on how he seemed, but something was definitely up. She thought back over the last hour with him and the time they had spent together that day. Had she said something or done something to upset him?

'I'm fine. I'm sorry, just a bit… distracted.'

'With what?'

'It doesn't matter.'

She reached across the table to stroke his face and sent the bread basket flying onto the floor.

'Oh crap, sorry,' Melody said, leaning over to grab the bread and the basket. Jamie leaned over to help her too.

One of the waiters came hurrying over and took the bread basket off them. 'Let me get you a fresh one.'

'Sorry,' Melody said again.

'It's not a problem,' the waiter said, easily, before moving off to get them another basket of bread.

She turned her attention back to Jamie.

'Look, shall we go?' he said.

She stared at him. When he'd offered to take her to a restaurant of her choosing and she'd suggested Sea Breeze, there had definitely been hesitation on his part before he had agreed. It was a bit more upper class than she would normally choose, but the food was amazing and so were the views. Was he not comfortable here; was it too posh for him?

'Why? I'm starving and I really fancy the Dover sole. Why do you want to leave?'

'It doesn't matter.'

'You keep saying that, but something is bothering you.'

'It was a mistake coming here, that's all.'

The waiter came back with a basket of bread and placed it on the table before moving away. She watched as Jamie deliberately moved the basket away from the edge of the table to the other side near the window, clearly so she couldn't knock it off again.

'Why, because you're embarrassed by me?' Melody muttered.

His head snapped up. 'What? Why would you say that?'

'You're being weird.'

Jenny returned at that point with their drinks order. 'Strawberry Passion for you and a beer for you. Are you guys ready to order?'

'Sorry, we need a few more minutes,' Jamie said.

'No problem.' Jenny wandered off.

Jamie returned his attention to the menu as if desperately trying to find some food that he liked. It was all pretty basic stuff, various different fish served with chips or potatoes. It might be slightly overpriced because of the location but it wasn't fancy food.

She watched Jamie carefully, wondering what was upsetting him so much. Keeping her eyes on him, she snatched up her cocktail and took a sip, not realising that there was a small fruit kebab sticking out the top. It stabbed her in the cheek and as she yanked back away from the pain she managed to tip the whole drink over herself.

'Crap!' Melody said as she shook the drink and ice off her. She looked up and saw that Jamie had a look of anger and frustration on his face. She felt like she had been slapped. It was that same look her dad had whenever she spilt something down her and later, after her dad had left, the impatience that her mum had shown her. 'I'm sorry.'

His eyes slid to the brunette again. Maybe he was wishing he was with her instead.

'Let's go home,' Jamie said, standing up and throwing some money on the table to cover the drinks.

Melody grabbed some napkins and attempted to dry herself before she stood up too. Any appetite that she'd had was suddenly gone.

Jamie put his arm around her and ushered her out the restaurant, breathing a huge sigh of relief as soon as they stepped outside.

She stepped out of his embrace as they walked back along the beach and they fell silent as Melody felt her heart breaking inside.

Bloody Polly Lucas, after all this time.

Jamie stared out at the sea as he walked with Melody back towards her house. He hadn't seen Polly since that day they had broken up. Since the day she had laughed at him when he'd told her he loved her. She'd said she wasn't interested in any kind of serious relationship but after they'd split up she was rumoured to be dating a doctor who lived in the next town. Within a month of breaking Jamie's heart, she had moved in with this doctor and married him six months later. So when she'd said she wasn't looking for anything serious, what she actually meant was that she wasn't looking for anything serious from him.

He'd known it was a mistake going to Sea Breeze that night. Not only was it Polly's favourite restaurant, but her brother owned it, so the likelihood of her being there was quite high.

And sure enough, there she was, sitting on the table just behind Melody. He'd stared at her wondering what he ever saw in her. She was pretty, there was no denying that, but as he watched her toss her hair back as her husband came back to the table, he found it impossible to remember any of her redeeming qualities. She wasn't kind or gentle or generous, she wasn't funny or loyal or brave. In fact, the only thing he could think of was that she had been pretty good in bed.

Was that all he had fallen in love with? Surely not. But his feelings for Melody went way beyond what he'd felt for Polly so maybe he'd never been in love with Polly at all. Maybe it was lust, pure and simple.

His cheeks burned at the memory of the humiliation of when he'd declared his love for her. How she had laughed so much. And because of it, the thought of telling Melody that he loved her filled him with so much fear. That was why he had thought about pulling the sculpture from the competition the following day. He couldn't do it again. Melody was so different to Polly, in every way, but still he couldn't bring himself to utter the words.

God, Polly really was a nasty cow. He knew that, of course he did, who laughed at someone when they confessed their love for them?

But when Melody had dropped the bread basket on the floor, Polly had looked over at them and giggled. And then when Melody had poured her drink over herself, Polly had literally burst out laughing.

Jamie had been consumed with so much anger at that. He wanted to protect Melody from her and ushered her out the restaurant before he decided to let rip at Polly. Though what good that would do, he didn't know. It was clear Polly didn't have a remorseful bone in her body.

'I'm sorry I embarrassed you,' Melody said, quietly.

'What? Christ, why would you think that?'

'Gee, I don't know, maybe because of the speed we exited the restaurant at after I threw my drink over myself. Maybe the look of complete irritation and anger that crossed your face as soon as I'd done it,' Melody said, sarcastically.

His heart dropped into his stomach. He stopped and snagged her arm. 'Wait, I wasn't pissed off with you.'

'Just something completely unrelated that had nothing to do with me throwing my drink everywhere.'

He paused too long, trying to find a reasonable explanation, and Melody walked off again, up her garden path and into her house.

Jamie hurried after her and managed to catch the door before it slammed in his face.

'My ex was in that restaurant. The brunette in the gold dress. I'm sure you didn't notice her but—'

'I noticed her. Well, I noticed the way you were staring at her. Wishing you were with her instead, were you?'

He stared at her in shock. 'What the hell is wrong with you tonight?'

'What's wrong with me?' Melody asked, incredulously. 'I wasn't the one who was staring at another woman the whole time we were there. And when I threw my drink all over myself, I have never seen anyone look so pissed off before. No, that's a lie, that was the exact same look my parents used to give me every time I spilled something as a child. I just never expected to see that from you.'

He winced. The very last thing he wanted was to hurt her or make her feel like her parents had made her feel. But he couldn't tell her that Polly had laughed at her, she was so sensitive about her clumsy side. Just as she was becoming more accepting of being accident-prone, laughing at herself when things went wrong, all of that would go straight out of the window if she knew other people were laughing at her because of it. She would be mortified.

'I was pissed off with her, not you,' Jamie said. 'I was angry with myself for falling in love with her, when she has such an ugly heart. I was angry for letting myself hold back from every relationship I've ever had since her because I was scared of getting hurt again. She's a cow and she didn't deserve to have my love. I should never have let someone like that have such power over me. She ruined my life and I let her. It's the first time I've seen her since we broke up and all those emotions I felt after she dumped me came flooding back.'

None of that was a lie, even though he had omitted the part about why he'd suddenly realised she was so horrible.

Melody stared at him, clearly not sure whether to believe him. It probably was too much of a coincidence that he would be angry with Polly at the exact time that Melody threw her drink over herself. He was still holding back from telling her the truth, not just about Polly laughing at her but also what had happened the day he had told Polly he loved her. The fact that she had burst out laughing was so humiliating, he couldn't bear to share that with Melody. Though from her sceptical face, it was clear she knew he was holding something back from her.

'So you weren't the least bit annoyed with me?'

'No, of course not.'

'You moved the bread basket.'

Had he? He remembered now that he had. 'So?'

'Because you didn't want me to embarrass you by knocking it off the table again,' Melody said.

'No!' Christ, this was getting worse.

'This is my life, Jamie, disaster follows me everywhere. You really want to put up with that shit?'

'I'm not putting up with anything. Why can't you see what I see?'

She started pacing around the room. 'Everything has gone wrong since we started dating.'

He couldn't believe how this conversation was unfolding. 'How can you say that? It's been the best week of my life.'

'I've poisoned you, we got caught kissing on the beach by the police and then the whole town heard we were having outdoor sex. We got trapped in a cave, I spilt beans on toast on you, I set fire to you, I've fallen face down in a sandcastle, I've spilt an entire drink over me.'

'And we've held hands and kissed and made love. We've laughed and talked and made plans for the future,' Jamie said.

'Maybe we are better off just being friends, it would probably be safer for you,' Melody said as if she hadn't heard any of that, as if none of that mattered to her. 'That's what you wanted anyway. You told Klaus that we had a friends with benefits arrangement.'

'No, wait, I never said that.'

'Just friends with sex. Was that all it was to you?'

'Of course it wasn't!' he exploded. 'How could you even think that?'

'You kept referring to it as a "sort-of" relationship, or that we were "sort-of" dating.'

'That was… You were the one that said you wanted to be friends that date. I didn't really know what label you wanted to attach to what we had after that. I didn't want to get the wrong one.'

Christ, he really was rubbish with women. For once, why couldn't he say the right thing?

'You were never looking for a relationship and I forced you into that.'

'You never forced me into anything. Why are you being like this?'

Her voice broke when she spoke. 'I can't be with someone who is disappointed in me.'

'I've never been disappointed in you. Your little calamities and accidents have never pissed me off. You're putting all that on me and that isn't the case at all. You're just trying to protect yourself and I get that, I really do, but you don't need to protect yourself from me.'

'You'll get tired of it; everyone's patience wears thin eventually. You know why my last relationship ended? I dropped his laptop. That was it, the final straw. Admittedly, this was after weeks of accidents and clumsiness that he'd had to put up with, but the laptop was obviously worth more to him than I was. When I left home, I spent years telling myself that I didn't need people's approval. This was me and I was happy with who I was, but just like that my worth was reduced to nothing.'

'But you haven't resolved those issues at all. You just avoid talking to your mum who makes you feel bad about yourself every time you see her. Avoidance is not dealing with it. Until you talk to your mum and face it head on, it's never going to go away.'

'Says the person who has avoided any kind of relationship for years because you're scared of getting hurt,' Melody said.

He pushed his hand through his hair. She had him there.

Anger suddenly bubbled over in him. He was losing her and there was nothing he could do to stop it.

'You're looking for perfection and I can never give you that,' Jamie said. 'I will always say the wrong thing or do the wrong thing and I can't change that. You've read so many of these romance stories and now you expect the fairy tale. This week has been incredible but if you insist on only seeing the negative then there's nothing I can do.'

'I don't want you to change, I don't want perfection.'

'You want the perfect date, the perfect relationship. You picked the wrong guy for that,' Jamie said.

'I don't want that.' Melody was close to tears. 'I'm scared I'll drive you away. Your face in the restaurant—'

'You want to know what got me so angry? Bloody Polly Lucas laughed at you when you spilt your drink. My anger was at her, not at you. But if you think so little of me, if you think I could possibly walk away from you because of a little clumsiness, then maybe we should call it a day now.'

He stormed out of the house and slammed the door behind him. He moved quickly onto the beach and stared at the sea, the waves rolling in and crashing on the shore.

What the hell had he just done?

Melody stared at the closed door in horror. She moved to the sofa, sat down and let her head fall in her hands. Rocky immediately came over to her, obviously sensing that she was upset. He pushed his nose into her hands and wagged his tail. She sank to the floor, put her arms round his shoulders and cried into his fur. Rocky just stood there and let her do it.

What was wrong with her?

It all seemed so hopeless all of a sudden. How the hell were they supposed to get past this?

She thought back over the evening. Had she overreacted? She still felt angry with Jamie, angry with bloody Polly Lucas. She had every right to be upset. He had spent the whole time in the restaurant staring at another woman. Who would be OK with that? Why hadn't he explained why he was so distracted? Although, to be fair to him, he had said he wanted to leave and she'd said no. Was he still hung up over his ex? There must be some underlying feelings for him to get so upset about seeing her again. Had he been looking at Melody and thinking that he would never feel for her what he'd felt for Polly Lucas?

She groaned, because in reality she was more angry at herself. This fear that she wasn't good enough had ruined everything.

It had all been going so well between them. Granted, every date so far had been a bit of a disaster but none of that seemed to matter to Jamie. He enjoyed being with her despite all of that. But that hadn't helped to push away her fears. He was right, those worries that she wasn't enough, brought about by her dad leaving and exacerbated by years of living with her mum's negativity, were never going to go away. Not unless she faced up to them. Right from the very first date she had been fearful of losing him, of driving him away, and in the end that fear had pushed him away anyway.

Why would he want to put up with that crap?

Maybe he didn't.

He'd said before that if he loved someone he would never walk away from them. But tonight he had walked away from her, so was that really it between them? Was it really over?

She stood up. She had vowed she was never letting him go. It might be over but she was going to at least try to fight for him.

She had no idea what she could say to him to make this right, but she was going to give it a go.

She grabbed her keys and quickly left the house.

Jamie sat down on the beach, propping himself up against an upturned boat that had been dragged up onto the sand. The argument was still ringing in his ears.

He was an ass, he knew that. Melody had every right to be mad at him. He had been on a date with her and he had spent the night staring at another woman. What was she supposed to think? Shit, he shouldn't have told her Polly was laughing at her. She'd be hurt by that. He'd rather she stayed angry at him than hurt her like that. Bloody Polly Lucas. He'd let her ruin his life for too many years to count and now he'd let her ruin what he had with the woman he loved too.

But he was angry at Melody too. She had pushed him away. He had let fear enter their relationship, letting it stop him from telling Melody how he felt for her, but she had let fear break them completely. Maybe she didn't love him at all if she could push him away so easily. How could she doubt what they had after the week they had spent together? When they had made love, did she not feel what he felt; had she not experienced that connection between them?

He stood and threw a stone in the water, causing silvery ripples to dance across the waves.

He wasn't sure there was any way past this now.

He looked back towards Melody's house, then turned and walked away.

Melody banged on Jamie's door and heard the dogs going mad inside. The lights were on so she knew he was in. She could even hear music playing – it sounded like a radio was on, playing some cheesy love music.

She heard a noise behind her and turned to see that Dobby had come from the back garden to find out who was at the door. He didn't seem too perturbed to see her as, after an idle glance her way, he carried on pecking at the garden.

There was no answer from inside so she banged on the door again. She had no idea what she was going to say to Jamie but she knew she had to say something. She had to try.

She saw the curtain twitch in the lounge window. It was pulled back a few inches and then let go. Jamie had clearly seen who was at the door. She waited but to her surprise he still didn't come to answer it.

He didn't want to speak to her.

She stared at the closed door in shock, emotion clawing at her throat.

Anger suddenly filled her and she banged on the door again. 'Jamie Jackson, you open this door right now, do you hear me. We need to talk about this. This is not over. I'm not letting you go.'

There was still no response.

The lump in her throat got bigger, the pain in her chest hurting even more than it had when he'd left her house. Tears filled her eyes. She pressed her head against the door and cried.

'Please, open the door. I'm so sorry, for everything. I love you. Please.'

She heard shuffling behind the door but it still didn't open. And then the light went off.

Tears falling down her cheeks, she turned and walked away.

CHAPTER 22

Melody knocked on Isla's door the next day after having spent most of the night in tears. She knew she needed to fix this thing with Jamie, but she didn't know how. If he wouldn't speak to her, there was no way to make this better.

Leo opened the door holding a laughing Elliot on his hip. They were both topless and soaking wet and, judging by the water pistols they both held, they were apparently in the middle of a water fight.

She smiled weakly, for Elliot's benefit, but clearly it wasn't enough for Leo, whose face fell as soon as he saw her.

'What's wrong?' Leo said.

'Nothing.' Melody waved it away.

'You look like you've been crying,' Elliot said, insightfully. 'You need to have a hug from Leo.'

Melody smirked despite everything.

'My hugging services are freely available,' Leo said, opening one arm.

'Thanks, but I'd rather have a hug from my favourite nephew,' Melody said, and Elliot immediately held out his arms so she could hold him.

She scooped him into her arms and held him tight as Leo stepped back to let her in. Elliot was soaking wet but a hug from him always made her feel better, albeit temporarily.

'Isla's in the bath,' Leo said, awkwardly, obviously out of his depth in dealing with an emotional woman.

Melody plonked Elliot down on the kitchen top and he ruffled Melody's hair affectionately, which was obviously something that Isla and Leo did to him. She couldn't say anything to Leo while Elliot was there but maybe just being around her nephew for a little while would be enough to ease the pain.

'Elliot, why don't you go and get your magic show ready? Choose your top ten favourite tricks and then you can show Melody how brilliant you are,' Leo said.

'Yes!' Elliot said, hopping down from the counter, excitedly. 'You are going to be amazed.'

He ran off, his feet thundering on the stairs as he went up to his bedroom.

'Coffee, tea, something stronger?' Leo said, indicating she should follow him into the kitchen.

'Tea is fine, thank you,' Melody said.

Leo started making three cups of tea, probably hoping Isla would be down shortly to help him out.

'Want to tell me what happened?' he said.

And although she hadn't planned on talking about this with Leo, she couldn't stop the tears forming in her eyes again as she thought about what a mess she'd made of everything.

Leo turned round and saw her crying and immediately stepped forward and hugged her.

'Come on, whatever it is, I'm sure it's fixable,' Leo said, holding her tight. 'Have you and Jamie had a row?'

'We broke up,' Melody sniffled.

'No, I don't believe that for one second. He is crazy about you. This is a blip, nothing more.'

'I pushed him away,' Melody said against his chest.

'So that's it? I don't think so. Jamie is not going to walk away from this because of a silly row.'

Melody pulled back from him and saw Isla had come down. She was watching them with a look of complete love for Leo on her face. Isla moved over to hug Melody, and then pulled her down to sit at the dining table with her as Leo continued making the teas.

'What happened?' Isla said gently.

'I don't know. Everything was going great. I mean, our dates weren't exactly smooth running, I bloody poisoned him on our first one and I set fire to him a few days ago, but he didn't seem to care about any of our little disasters. Then last night we went out to a restaurant and he saw his ex, Polly, and—'

Leo groaned as he carried three mugs over to the table. 'She's a nasty piece of work, that one. She broke him.'

To her surprise, Leo sat down to join them instead of escaping the drama.

'Because she dumped him?' Melody asked.

'Because he told her he loved her and she burst out laughing, right in his face.'

Melody had no words at all. She suddenly remembered what Agatha had said, that Polly had told everyone that he was only good for sex. No wonder Jamie had held back from relationships for so long, that kind of experience would be enough to put anyone off love for life. How could you ever risk your heart again after it had been damaged so badly? It must have been so humiliating for him.

'Oh god, poor Jamie,' Melody said quietly.

'I imagine he wasn't too thrilled to see her again,' Leo said.

'No, he kept staring over at her. I could tell how unhappy he was, but I didn't know why. He never told me who she was until we were back at my house. I started to think he was unhappy with me. I spilt a drink over myself and apparently she laughed at me,' Melody said, sadly. 'He was so angry and I thought...'

'That he was angry at you,' Isla finished for her.

She nodded.

'Oh honey, of course you would think that. Years of being exposed to Mum's negativity and Dad didn't really have the patience for your clumsiness either. Seeing Jamie react in seemingly the same way, that has to hurt.'

'But he was angry at her, not me. I put my fears on him, that wasn't fair.'

'And he should have explained what was going through his head too, not left you in the dark,' Leo said. 'We all have baggage, we get scared and we push the people we love away before we can get hurt. But you're only scared because this means so much to you. Jamie will be back, because you mean as much to him as he does to you.'

Melody shook her head. 'I went round to see him last night after we had argued and he refused to answer the door. The lights were on, and the radio was playing, and I saw the curtain move when he looked to see who was at the door. But when I banged on the door and shouted at him to answer it, he simply switched off the lights and went off upstairs to bed.'

'That doesn't sound like him,' Leo said.

There was a knock on the door, just as Elliot came rushing back in, wearing his top hat and carrying a box.

Leo got up to answer it as Elliot laid out his things on the table.

Tori and Aidan came into the kitchen and Tori rushed over to Melody as soon as she saw her.

'Oh, I'm so glad you're here. We went to your house and you weren't there and so we thought we'd try here. Are you OK? Did you and Jamie have a row?'

'Yes, why? Have you seen him?'

'Yes, on Sunshine Beach, outside your house. He's waiting for you. He asked us to find you and to tell you to meet him on the beach. He's tried calling you but you're not picking up.'

Melody grabbed her bag, but it was quite clear her phone wasn't in there. She must have left it at home.

'What does he want, did he say?' Melody asked, nervously.

'He looks awful, he hasn't slept all night, he's been down at the studio finishing off his sculpture for the competition,' Aidan said.

Melody thought about this. He was down at the studio all night, not at home?

'Melody, he has placed his sculpture for the competition on the beach,' Tori said.

'But he said he wasn't going to submit one this year.'

'Well obviously he changed his mind. You need to see it.'

'You've seen it?'

'It's not covered,' Tori said.

'But all the sculptures are supposed to be covered until tonight.' Why was she focussing on that? 'What is it?'

Tori shook her head. 'It's incredible, but you need to see it yourself.'

Melody stood up and saw Elliot look up at her. Immediately she sat back down again.

'I need to see Elliot's magic show first, I've really been looking forward to seeing it.'

As much as she loved her nephew, she hoped to god that this magic show was quick.

To her surprise, Elliot shook his head. 'It's OK, Melody, you need to go and find Jamie. If he's as upset as you are, he probably needs a hug from Leo too. But I bet he would prefer a hug from you more.'

'I think you're probably right,' Leo said. 'Go and get him and then bring him back here and we can all watch the marvellous magic show together.'

'Are you sure you don't mind?' she asked Elliot.

He shook his head. 'Jamie makes you happy; I want you to be happy again.'

She smiled with love for her nephew and gave him a big hug. Then she scrambled up, grabbed her bag and, with a quick wave at the others, she ran out of the house.

CHAPTER 23

It was easier and quicker to run along the sea front, passing the other sculptures that had appeared that morning, all of them currently under wraps. Her eyes cast along the beach, searching for Jamie. Up ahead, near to her house, she could see a sculpture that was nearly as tall as she was. Was that it? But there was no sign of Jamie. She drew closer to her house and realised the sculpture was a figure, a woman who looked like she was dancing. Her heart skipped a beat.

The sculpture was of her.

She stumbled as she took the last few steps and then she was standing right in front of it. It was incredible; it was so lifelike, so detailed. She reached up to stroke the statue's cheek – it was silky soft. The mystic topaz stones that she had sold Jamie a few days before shone out of the statue's face as eyes. She looked so happy.

Suddenly the significance of this hit her with the force of a double-decker bus. The sculptures were supposed to show the thing that people loved the most about Sandcastle Bay. The thing that Jamie loved the most was her.

Tears fell down her cheeks, her chest heaving with suppressed sobs.

He loved her.

Oh god. This was such a big risk for him, putting out his heart and expressing his feelings in such a public way. Especially after he had been crushed in such a humiliating way before. This was why he had suddenly been scared about submitting this statue to the competition the night before. After seeing Polly, all those feelings of betrayal and embarrassment over what happened when he'd told her he loved her had come flooding back. Yet despite that, the sculpture was here, for all to see. He really did love her.

She wiped her tears away and took a step back to look at the statue properly. The statue was sculpted to look like she was wearing a dress and there were beads around the statue's neck that made it look like she was wearing a necklace. She moved closer to get a better look at the beads. They weren't beads at all, they were gemstones. In fact, these were the gemstones that she had sold to Emily a few days before, when she had asked for gemstones for different meanings. All forty-two of them. She spotted bravery, kindness and loyalty. Her heart thundered in her chest. Jamie kept saying that he wished she could see all her qualities and here they were.

She ran her fingers over each of the different gemstones. Creativity, imagination, warmth…

'It's beautiful, isn't it?'

Melody whirled around and saw her mum standing a few feet away.

'Jamie is a wonderful man; I think he's perfect for you.'

Melody smiled. 'He really is.'

Her mum stepped closer. 'He showed me this a few days ago. You can see how much care and attention has gone into this sculpture, the love he has for you just shines from it.'

'He showed you? He never shows anyone his sculptures until they're finished.'

'He wanted my help with suggestions for the necklace. He already had a list of thirty qualities he saw in you and he asked me if I could think of any more.'

Melody resisted saying that she thought her mum would have found that hard. Then her heart filled with love for Jamie at what he had done with that gesture. She hadn't heard one positive thing from her mum in nearly twenty years and Jamie had directly asked her mum for compliments about her. Even if she never heard the words from her mum, the evidence that her mum did think positively of her would be there, preserved in the statue forever.

Her mum smiled sadly. 'As I was rattling off all these wonderful things about you, it occurred to me that I've never told you any of these things.'

Melody stared at her. 'I can't honestly remember the last positive thing you've said to me. I suppose it must have happened once, I have very happy memories of playing with you when I was a child, but those memories seem so far away now.'

Her mum winced. 'I know. After your dad left, I was angry at everyone, including my own children.'

'I know, I was there. No matter how hard I worked at school, no matter what I did, nothing seemed to please you.'

'I didn't see any of that. I was so wrapped up in my own grief and anger, I wasn't aware of anything or anybody else. I know how much that must have hurt.' She sighed. 'I had this whole life planned. Right from seventeen years old, I knew who I was going to marry, where I was going to live, what job I would have, how many children. And I ticked every box. I wanted this perfect life and I lost sight of what was most important, my husband and my children. Without them, I had nothing. I pushed your dad away with my constant need for perfection and, when he left, my whole world fell apart. My carefully laid plan was reduced to dust.'

'But you still had us, me, Matthew and Isla, and you pushed us away too with your anger and negativity,' Melody said.

'I know. I didn't realise it at the time, but I saw it later and by then the gap was so big between us I didn't know how to bridge it.'

'An apology would have been a good start,' Melody said, then regretted it because her mum was clearly trying.

'You have no idea how sorry I am. When you spend so many years being angry at the world, it becomes so hard to break out of that default setting. I don't want to be that angry person any more. Being with Trevor is helping me; it's wonderful to feel loved again.'

Melody felt a little guilty at that. She had probably not shown her mum any love for many years, and neither, she suspected, had Isla or Matthew. There had been no affectionate hugs or words. That had been because her mum had pushed them all away but it must have been very lonely for her mum nonetheless.

'Looking after Elliot helps too.' Her mum's face lit up at the mention of her grandson.

'Don't push him away,' Melody said, protectively. 'He loves you and he doesn't deserve that.'

'I won't, I promise. He makes me laugh and it's been a long time since I've laughed at anything.'

Melody looked back at the statue. She wasn't sure if their relationship would ever go back to how it had been before her dad left, whether they would ever have a loving, affectionate one, but this was a start. They both needed to make an effort and it seemed her mum was willing to try so she could too.

'Want to know which qualities I picked? Jamie showed me the relevant gemstones; let me see if I can remember which ones meant which. Oh yes, this black snowflake one—'

'Snowflake obsidian,' Melody said.

'That's for persistence and determination. I'm so proud of you for setting up your own business and making a success of it. Not many people can do that, especially alone, and not only did you make a success of it in London, but you've adapted and made it work down here in Sandcastle Bay too.'

That had been hard work. No one was interested in buying diamond necklaces or sapphire rings in Sandcastle Bay. So she'd spent many months sourcing new jewellery, researching unusual styles and being a lot more creative when she was making her own. She'd never really considered that to be a quality before.

'This moonstone is for patience. I see how you are with Elliot and you are wonderful with him. And this green peridot one is for positivity. You've had some setbacks in your life, your dad leaving, your mum being a cow and your brother dying. But you never seem to let it get you down. You always seem so happy. Especially of late, though I think your young man has something to do with putting that big smile on your face. Speaking of which, maybe I should let him talk through the rest of the gemstones.'

She nodded down the beach and Melody looked around and saw Jamie walking towards them. Her heart leapt in her chest.

'Why don't we have lunch tomorrow? I'll ask Isla and Elliot too,' her mum said.

Melody turned her attention back to her. 'I'd like that.'

Her mum gave her a little wave – it was too soon for hugs and kisses goodbye – and walked off the beach.

Melody turned back to Jamie who was approaching slowly. He ran his hand through his hair, nervously.

'I've been looking for you,' he said.

How could she find the words to describe how this statue had made her feel, to say she was sorry, to explain?

'I wanted to say—' he started.

Maybe she didn't need words. She launched herself at him, throwing her arms round his neck and kissing him hard. She felt the sigh of relief against her lips as he held her tight. Tears soaked her cheeks and she didn't even care.

'I love you,' she said. 'I love you so much. I know you're scared to say those words to me and I understand why now and I don't need to hear them. This…' she gestured to the statue and her voice broke as she looked at her again '… is everything to me.'

He grinned. 'I didn't bring you down here to show you a statue to represent how I feel for you. I want you to know, so there is no doubt. I love you, with everything I have. Not *despite* all your clumsy quirks, but because of them. I love you because of every single one of these wonderful qualities. Patience, compassion, wisdom. I love how brave you've been giving up your life in London and coming down here to help your sister raise Elliot. I love your wonderful imagination that helps create such beautiful and unique jewellery pieces. I love your kindness and patience when it comes to Elliot, the loyalty you show your friends. I love your passion, especially in the bedroom.' He winked at her.

'Oh god, I've been such an idiot. I never wanted the perfect relationship or the perfect date, I just wanted you to think it was perfect. And you did. You saw in me all these wonderful qualities that I never saw myself. Last night you said you'd had the best week of your life being with me and that didn't even register until you walked out. I was so scared of losing you, of pushing you away. But you were right, I was putting my fears on you.'

'I did the same. I held back from telling you how I feel because I was fearful of your reaction after what happened with Polly. I held back from letting anything happen between us for months because I was too scared. But no more hiding our feelings. If we are going to work, we have to be honest with each other. I really do love you.'

'I love you too.'

He leaned down to kiss her again.

God, they really were going to be OK.

She pulled back. 'I came to see you last night, after you'd walked out. But you didn't answer the door. I thought we were over.'

'I was in the studio all night finishing off my sculpture.'

'Yes, Aidan said that's where you were.'

'I wanted you to see it as soon as you walked out of your house this morning but you'd already left.'

She frowned in confusion. 'But I saw the curtains move.'

'Probably Sirius, nosy little bugger. He's always at the window when people are walking past or come to the door.'

'And the radio was playing.'

'I always leave it on for the dogs,' Jamie explained.

Melody smiled as realisation dawned on her. 'And I'm guessing that the light going off was a lamp on a timer.'

He cringed. 'Yeah, it was. I always have the lamp come on at certain times so if I'm not there the dogs aren't left in the darkness. I'm so sorry, I can only imagine how you must have felt, thinking I wasn't answering the door.'

She waved it away. 'God, none of that matters now. I'm here where I belong.'

He kissed her and then pulled back slightly. 'Why don't we take your imagination and passion up to your bedroom and put that silly argument behind us once and for all?'

She smiled and kissed him briefly. 'I would love nothing more than to do just that, but I have a marvellous magic show to go and watch and I'm under strict instructions to bring you back with me.'

He laughed. 'I can definitely think of better ways to spend my afternoon but I can wait until tonight.'

As he slipped his hand into hers and they walked off the beach, she couldn't help the huge smile from spreading on her face. Tonight couldn't come soon enough.

The sky was a beautiful flamingo pink with trails of lavender as Melody walked hand in hand with Jamie down Sunshine Beach, enjoying the Great Sculptures in the Sand Festival. There were food tents and craft stores all the way along the beach and many people were making their way around those before the evening's entertainment started.

She and Jamie wandered around the sculptures and Tori, Aidan, Isla, Leo and Elliot walked with them, admiring the different statues and models. Melody liked the eclectic mix, some made from wood, some made from recycled bits of plastic bottles and pots, some made from old shoes. It really was a wonderful display of the best bits of Sandcastle Bay. There were lots of seaside-themed sculptures, sandcastles, boats, ice creams, fish, dolphins and seals, but like Jamie, some of the people of the village had interpreted the theme much more personally.

'So this is mine,' Melody said, nervously. She looked up at Jamie but he was smiling as he looked at it.

'So the thing you love most about Sandcastle Bay is…?'

'Walking to work with you every morning, when the beaches are almost empty and it's just us and the sun rising over the golden sands. That's my favourite thing about Sandcastle Bay.'

His smile grew. 'This is us?'

'It's supposed to be. I'm not as crafty as you.'

'I love it. I have to say, it's my favourite part of the day too: me, you, two crazy puppies.'

She grinned.

'That's wonderful,' Isla said.

'That's so sweet,' Tori said and then turned to Aidan who was walking next to her with his arm round her shoulders. 'I kind of feel we should have done something more personal to us now.'

They'd already seen Tori and Aidan's heartberry model, Max, and he was a big hit with the villagers.

'Max is personal to us. We met because you were here picking heartberries. Besides, our next animated advert is going to reflect us and our life,' Aidan said.

'It is?' Melody asked.

'Max and his heartberry girlfriend Jenny are going to get married and there's going to be a little heartberry baby,' Tori explained, exchanging a look of love with Aidan.

Melody's heart filled with happiness for them. 'Are you guys thinking of getting married soon?'

'I think it will be this year,' Tori said. 'I think I'd quite like to get married before I start showing too much. I don't want to be waddling down the aisle or having the baby on our honeymoon.'

'I'm happy to get married sooner rather than later,' Aidan agreed.

'We thought we'd get married up on the farm, maybe September or October when the main fruit season is over. We might get a marquee.'

'Sounds lovely,' Melody said.

Up ahead, Elliot was dragging Leo through the sculptures, laughing and pointing at the different ones.

'Elliot can't wait to see the horse that Leo has made for the festival, it's all he's talked about for days,' Isla said.

'You've not seen it yet?' Jamie asked.

'Bits of it – the bit that moves and churns with the water and the bit that seemingly has lightning inside and we've seen the head – but we've not seen it all put together. Elliot has been helping him, well I say helping, he's been watching Leo make some bits of it. I have no doubt it will be something incredible, if I know Leo,' Isla said.

'He really does have a talent for stuff like this,' Melody said.

'I keep saying he should expand his business and make installations and sculptures like this. I bet lots of companies would be interested and he could do stuff like this around zoos and theme parks too. He is so good at getting things to light up and move, he's so clever at things like that. Anything with pyrotechnics, animatronics, pneumatics or hydraulics is right up Leo's street.'

Elliot came running back to them, Leo following close behind.

'Isla, our horse is just ahead, you need to come and see it.'

'I can't wait,' Isla said.

Leo took her hand. 'You need to stand in the right place to appreciate it at its best.'

Melody followed behind as Leo placed Isla and Elliot in the right place. He told Elliot to stay with Isla for a moment as he slipped off to start the mechanics of his sculpture. She saw a large glass horse modelled to look like it was running through the sand. It was made out of several chambers and one chamber had waves crashing against rocks inside, another had real forks of lightning going off inside. Melody had no idea how Leo had done that. The neck, shoulders and part of the head were made from mirrored panels, making the horse look very sci-fi, as if it belonged in another time. It was marvellous.

She looked over at her sister and nephew. Elliot was jumping up and down with joy and excitement but Melody was confused by how quiet Isla was as she stared at the horse. Leo hadn't seemed to notice as he moved round the horse checking the mechanics were all working properly. Melody followed her line of sight to see what she was staring at and realised that Leo had placed them in the exact place that Isla and Elliot could very clearly see their own reflection in the mirrored neck of the horse. Melody's heart leapt. Was this Leo's way of telling Isla that the thing he loved most about Sandcastle Bay was her and Elliot? She looked over at Isla's reaction again. It was quite clear that her sister was thinking the same. Why else had he chosen that exact position for Isla and Elliot to stand when you could see the wonder of the horse from pretty much anywhere around it?

'What do you think?' Leo turned round and, for the briefest of moments, she saw him check Isla's reaction before he moved his gaze to Elliot.

'I love it!' Elliot yelled, clapping his hands together with excitement.

Isla didn't say anything.

Melody decided to step in. 'So, the thing you love most about Sandcastle Bay is?'

Leo hesitated for a second and then placed his hand on the neck of the horse, where Isla and Elliot's reflections were.

'Storms over the sea, clouds rolling across the sky, when the view is theatrical and dramatic, when the waves are crashing on the shores and the sea looks like wild horses.'

He looked at Isla again for a moment.

Isla cleared her throat. 'It's lovely.'

Aidan stepped up, awkwardly. 'Well, we're going to go and get some ice creams, who wants one? Elliot, want to come and choose which one you want?'

Elliot immediately left Isla's side and took Aidan's hand. They walked off towards the food huts.

'We're going to carry on looking at the other sculptures,' Melody said, though she didn't think Isla heard her.

She walked off with Jamie and gave a last glance to Isla, who was still staring at Leo and the horse.

'Did you see what I saw?' Melody said, quietly.

'I think everyone did, well apart from Elliot.'

'Christ, that's a big step for Leo.'

'Huge,' Jamie said.

'I hope they can sort themselves out, they both deserve to be happy,' Melody said.

'Something tells me they're going to be OK.'

She looked back over at Isla who had now moved to admire the horse more closely. She was talking to Leo and, though Melody couldn't hear what was being said, she hoped Jamie was right. Surely it wouldn't be long before they worked this out between them.

They had arrived back at Jamie's sculpture by then. She couldn't help but stare at it again, it was so incredible.

'I'm surprised you never noticed where the third mystic topaz stone I bought from you is,' Jamie said.

She frowned and looked at the necklace where all the other gemstones were, but she couldn't see it.

Jamie pointed to the statue's left hand and Melody saw the statue was wearing the mystic topaz as a ring on her wedding ring finger. Her heart leapt.

Jamie slipped it off the statue and offered it out to Melody. 'It's a promise ring, my promise of my commitment to you and to our future. It feels too early for us to get engaged and I'm still determined to get this right, but what we have, this is forever for me.'

'Me too,' Melody said. She looked at the ring, the mystic topaz gleaming blue set into a ring of silver clay. 'Did you make this?'

He smiled and nodded. 'I learned from the best.'

She grinned and slipped it on. It was beautiful. She leaned up to kiss him.

Jamie had said she was looking for the fairy tale as if it was an impossible dream, but she had found it with him. He was her happily ever after.

The End

A LETTER FROM HOLLY

Thank you so much for reading *The Cottage on Sunshine Beach*, I had so much fun creating this story and I hope you enjoyed reading it as much as I enjoyed writing it.

To keep up to date with the latest news on my new releases, just click on the link below to sign up for a newsletter. I promise to only contact you when I have a new book out and I'll never share your email with anyone else.

www.bookouture.com/holly-martin

One of the best parts of writing comes from seeing the reaction from readers. Did it make you smile or laugh, did it make you cry, hopefully happy tears? Did you fall in love with Melody and Jamie as much as I did? Did you like the beautiful Sandcastle Bay? If you enjoyed the story, I would absolutely love it if you could leave a short review. Getting feedback from readers is amazing and it also helps to persuade other readers to pick up one of my books for the first time.

If you loved the other characters in this story, Tori and Aidan's story can be found in *The Holiday Cottage by the Sea*. Leo and Isla's story, *Coming Home to Maple Cottage*, is out in September.

Thank you for reading and I hope you all have a wonderful, sparkly summer.

Love Holly x

HollyMartinAuthor

@HollyMAuthor

hollymartinwriter.wordpress.com

ACKNOWLEDGEMENTS

To my family, my mom, my biggest fan, who reads every word I've written a hundred times over and loves it every single time, my dad, my brother Lee and my sister-in-law Julie, for your support, love, encouragement and endless excitement for my stories.

For my twinnie, the gorgeous Aven Ellis for just being my wonderful friend, for your endless support, for cheering me on, for reading my stories and telling me what works and what doesn't and for keeping me entertained with wonderful stories and pictures of hot men. I love you dearly.

To my friends Gareth, Mandie, Angie, Jac, Verity and Jodie who listen to me talk about my books endlessly and get excited about it every single time.

For Sharon Sant for just being there always and your wonderful friendship.

To my wonderful agents Hayley Steed and Madeleine Milburn for just been amazing and fighting my corner and for your unending patience with my constant questions.

To my lovely editor Natasha Harding for being so supportive and being a pleasure to work with. My structural editor Celine Kelly for helping to make this book so much better, my copy editor Rhian for doing such a good job at spotting any issues or typos and Loma for giving it a final read through. Thank you to Kim Nash for the tireless promoting, tweeting and general cheerleading. Thank you to all the other wonderful people at Bookouture; Oliver Rhodes, Ellen, Lauren, Alex, the editing team and the wonderful designer who created this absolutely gorgeous cover.

To the CASG, the best writing group in the world, you wonderful talented supportive bunch of authors, I feel very blessed to know you all, you guys are the very best.

To the wonderful Bookouture authors for all your encouragement and support.

To all the wonderful bloggers for your tweets, retweets, Facebook posts, tireless promotions, support, encouragement and endless enthusiasm. You guys are amazing and I couldn't do this journey without you.

To *The Greatest Showman*, thanks for the music, which has pretty much been blasted out while writing every word of this book.

To anyone who has read my book and taken the time to tell me you've enjoyed it or wrote a review, thank you so much.

Thank you, I love you all.